NELDA SEES
RED

Helen F. Sheffield

NELDA SEES RED

A murder mystery

Helen F. Sheffield

To order additional copies of this book, contact:
Xlibris Corporation
1-888-7-XLIBRIS
www.Xlibris.com
Orders@Xlibris.com

CONTENTS

I dedicate this book to my husband, Bill. Without his patience and love this book would not have been possible.
I would also like to thank Marge Haislet and members of my critique group:
Wendell Horne, Jo Mason, Ruth Smelser and Mark Troy. Their critiques and genuine support were invaluable.

PROLOGUE

The nude man in room 102 smiled in the darkness. He sat on his own examination table. "Where are you Pussy Cat?" he whispered.

A warm hand reached out to explore his body. He sighed as he breathed in a sweet fragrance. A few moments passed and the hand was replaced with a cold, hard object pressing into the left side of his chest.

"What the hell!" he cried, attempting to push the offender away.

"*Pro bono publico,*" came the laughing retort.

A muffled sound reached his ears as he faded into oblivion. His limp body fell backwards from the force of the Colt 45, and brown eyes stared into space.

Suddenly, a chilling breeze filled the room as the AC kicked on. The perpetrator turned on the overhead lights and looked around. She carefully slipped on latex gloves, wiped his body with alcohol and taped a message to his chest. Reaching down, she pushed on the corners of his mouth with her fingers until his lips became a smile.

With a satisfied nod, she walked out the back door whistling "One Bad Apple."

CHAPTER ONE

For The Public Good

On the corner of Chestnut and Fourth Street, Nelda Simmons' large ancestral home glowed softly in the first rays of sunlight. The covered porches surrounding the house were still in dark shadows, even though a couple of Carolina wrens flew quietly out of a hanging basket into the cool spring morning. Suddenly, a noisy truck delivering the Stearn, Texas newspaper broke the morning silence. A periodic plop could be heard as the carrier delivered his printed cargo.

Inside her high-ceilinged bedroom, Nelda woke up at 5:30 a.m. with a feeling of impending doom. Her body ached from playing tennis the day before. She hoped some strong coffee would ease her pain. Flipping on a light, she crawled out of bed, pulled on an old terry cloth robe and padded barefooted into the kitchen. After pouring a cup of hot coffee and picking up the newspaper, she retreated to the back porch with hopes that her day would soon be brighter. It wasn't.

She sat in her favorite rocker and opened the weekly *Stearn Gazette*. Nelda read with sadness about the death of four-month old Carlos Sanchez. Theresa, the mother of the baby, was Nelda's former student and a high school dropout. Nelda sighed and ran her fingers through her graying hair. I wish, thought Nelda, that Theresa's hormones hadn't kicked in until she finished high school. But maybe I can still do something for her. I'll find out "what" from Theresa's mother. I'm sure she still works at the Farmer's Market.

Satisfied with her plans for the day, Nelda hurried into the house to get dressed. Just as she stepped inside, the phone started ringing. "I'm not going to answer it," she muttered. "Early morning calls are just bad news." After hesitating for a few seconds, she worriedly picked up the receiver on the fifth ring.

It was her niece, Sue Grimes. "Aunt Nelda, I know I probably woke you up but I need your help. Dr. Coldsby wants me at the clinic early and I can't get my car started."

"I'll pick you up in twenty minutes."

"Thanks, Aunt Nelda. I can always depend on you."

Nelda smiled and knew she shouldn't be doing this favor for her niece. Sue needed to learn how important it was to take care of her car. But it wouldn't happen today.

She hurriedly dressed, backed her old Ford wagon out of the drive, and drove to Sue's apartment. Sue's Pacer was parked in the driveway. When Nelda walked over and opened the door, the dome light didn't come on. She shook her head in disgust. The battery was down again.

Several minutes later Sue, a tall slender blonde in a partially buttoned uniform, came running out of the apartment. "Thanks a million, Aunt Nelda. I can't imagine what's wrong with my car."

"The battery died," Nelda said. "Did you leave the dome light on again when you combed your hair?"

"No, I didn't!" Sue exclaimed through clenched teeth. "Steve borrowed my car because his is in the shop."

Steve was Sue's fiancé, a hot tempered featherhead in Nelda's opinion. But she kept her mouth shut and concentrated on her driving.

The morning sun was barely peeking over the horizon when they arrived at the clinic. Nelda couldn't imagine an uglier building. It looked like a big, white, sterile box with gray shingles. Dr. Albert Coldsby, who owned the clinic, had built it as cheaply as possible. It made Nelda ill just looking at it.

"The lights are all on," Sue said. That stingy Coldsby will have a fit if he finds out."

"I'll agree with him on that one," responded Nelda. "What a waste of energy."

When Sue opened the back door of the clinic, Nelda shuddered. She hated the antiseptic smell that filled every nook and cranny of the place. It reminded her of a killer who almost took her life. Nelda's snooping helped nab him, but it cost her a long stay in the hospital.

"Come on, Aunt Nelda, I know you can't stand to be here, but as a favor, please help me get things ready before the doctors get here."

"Why didn't you call the other nurse to help you?" asked Nelda, following Sue into a small room equipped with sterilizing equipment.

"Violet is taking the morning off. We've got a substitute coming in at 8:00 a.m."

"All right, what goes where? Just tell me and I'll do it. It's still a mystery to me why you work for that despicable doctor." Nelda was thinking of what Sue had told her earlier. She said Dr. Coldsby had pushed her up against a wall, kissed her and told her not to tell. If only Sue had let me set him straight, mused Nelda. But no, she just had to handle it herself.

"Don't worry. I'm trying to find another job. In the meantime, let's get everything ready before the old creep shows up. Take this tray of instruments to room 102." Sue was unloading the autoclave as she spoke.

Nelda grabbed the covered tray and walked down the hall. She breathed through her mouth trying to keep the clinic odor out of her nostrils. When she arrived at the room, she cautiously balanced the tray on one hand while she pushed the door open. The room was dark; she groped for the switch and blinked as the light flooded the room. She gasped. There on his own examination table lay Dr. Albert Coldsby naked as a jay bird. For a few seconds she stared in disbelief and then in horror. Coldsby's skinny arms were dangling from the sides of the table. Edging closer, she could see he'd been shot. That wasn't all! He had a note written in Latin with red ink taped to his chest. Nelda couldn't believe it. *"Pro bono publico,"* she read out loud. She shook her head in amazement. An educated killer!

His body reminded Nelda of an unclothed mannequin except, of course, a mannequin would not have a small hole in its chest with congealed blood around it.

"Sue, come in here!" Nelda shouted.

"What's the problem, Aunt Nelda?" Sue said as she stood in the doorway. "Oh my God! He's dead, isn't he? Someone killed the doctor."

"He's been shot. Go call Sheriff John Moore, and don't let anyone in this room."

Nelda was no stranger to a crime scene. She knew from working with her late husband, who was sheriff for thirty years, that evidence could be destroyed if people got excited and started milling around in the area. That was one reason she sent her niece to call the sheriff.

While Sue made the call, Nelda looked closely around the examination room for more evidence. The doctor's clothes were neatly folded and placed on a stool behind a screen. It looked as if he'd taken them off for a physical. Everything else in the room seemed to be where it belonged.

Returning to her Aunt, Sue grabbed Nelda's arm and pleaded for her to move to the office. "Come on, Aunt Nelda, let's get out of here; this room is giving me the willies. He was a wicked man, but he didn't deserve this."

"Of course not! Nobody does. You've got to pull yourself together because the Sheriff is going to ask a lot of questions. What you need to do is go to the secretary's desk and cancel both doctors' appointments for today and notify Violet's substitute not to come in."

"What will I say?"

"Just tell them there is an emergency. They'll find out what's wrong soon enough. It'll be on the evening news."

A few minutes later Nelda heard a knock on the back door of the clinic. She opened the door and there was John Moore: broad shoulders, dark hair and sky blue eyes. Nelda thought he looked like Dudley Doright, a famous cartoon character that depicted a Canadian Mounted Policeman. She hadn't seen John since she helped him solve the murder of the assistant principal at Stearn high school. Nelda taught Science and Latin there before retiring.

"Is it really you, Nelda?" John asked, acknowledging her presence with a hug. "It's good to see you, but what in the world are you doing here?"

Nelda grimaced and shook her head. "I'm just helping my niece, Sue; she was Dr. Coldsby's nurse and needed a ride to work."

"Well, what's this all about? Someone called and said Dr. Coldsby was murdered. Where's the body?"

"Down the hall in room 102. Certainly a strange situation."

"What do you mean?" John raised a quizzical eyebrow.

"His clothes are neatly folded on a stool, and he's on the table naked with a hole in his heart. He also has a note written in Latin taped to his chest. "

"A what?" asked John in amazement.

John stepped quickly into the room, looked at the note on the body and then stared at the neat opening in the doctor's chest. Powder burns were fairly obvious on the skin surrounding the wound. He turned away and searched the room for other clues, possibly a gun. There were none.

"You were the Latin teacher, Nelda. What's the meaning?" He pointed to the note.

"For the public good," Nelda said. "Somebody is trying to justify his death."

"That's the weirdest thing I've ever seen, a Latin note written in red. Crazy!"

Nelda watched John from the doorway and could tell by his pursed lips that he was upset because she beat him to the crime scene. It wasn't her fault. She sure didn't ask to be here.

John had been her late husband's deputy for five years and learned the duties of a sheriff from him. There was a close bond between John and Nelda because of that association. Besides, Nelda knew everyone in town and most of their business; at least in her mind John ought to find her an indispensable ally.

"Did you discover anything else?" questioned John.

"No, I left everything undisturbed. It's no suicide."

"I agree," John said. "He didn't shoot himself and then hide the gun. We'll close off this area and I'll get a fingerprint expert from Smitherton to go over the place. I've got a call in to the Justice of the Peace to come over and declare him dead. Can't remove the body until that happens, but I sure don't want the public to know about that note. Please remind Sue not to talk about it."

"Sue didn't see it and you can depend on me." Nelda said, hoping she could help with the interviews. It would be curious to see the employees' reactions to Coldsby's death.

"I know I can," he said smiling. Do you know the clinic employees?"

"Yes, two are my former students, but I don't know the others very well. Sue will be able to tell you about them."

"Good, where is she now?"

"Calling patients to cancel their appointments for today."

"Let's go find her. I need a list of the staff, so I can get statements from them as they come in."

Nelda led the way to the secretary's office. Sue was just hanging up the phone.

"You remember John don't you?" asked Nelda. "He was about four years ahead of you in high school."

Sue got up, shook hands and managed a weak smile. "I remember John. He used to be my football idol when I was in middle school. How are you?"

The sheriff turned red. It seemed to Nelda that everyone remembered him as a boy. Nelda wondered how old he'd have to be before folks realized he was grown.

"I'm fine, Sue, but could you tell me who works for the clinic and what they do?"

"Sure, let's see," she answered nervously, twisting on a strand of long blonde hair. "Well, there's Marcie Gibbons, the secretary; she comes in at 8:00 a.m. Then, the lab technician, Carol Scrubbs, arrives about 8:30 a.m., so does Dr. Walter Goodman and his nurse, Violet Rosin. That makes up the staff with the exception of myself, and ordinarily I come in at 8:30 a.m. too. Sometimes we have temporary help, but the ones I named are our regular people."

"Why did you come in before 8:00 a.m. this morning?" John asked, tapping his pencil on a pad.

"Violet and I take turns coming in early to put the sterilized instruments in the examination rooms."

"Okay," said John as he finished jotting down the names and occupations on a note pad. "You continue calling the patients who are supposed to come in today, and we'll wait in Coldsby's office to talk to the employees. Ask them to come to the office as soon as they arrive."

Sue sat down heavily. "Are we all suspects in this murder, John?"

"Yes," John declared.

For some reason that Nelda couldn't explain, she began to worry about her niece's involvement in the murder.

CHAPTER TWO

They all have motives

Nelda was glad John had asked her to be there when he interviewed the clinic personnel. After all, she knew most of them and could help him solve the case. This one was special because of Sue. But surely, she reasoned, there was no connection between the doctor's death and her niece.

Walter Goodman entered the clinic a little after 8:00 with a look of disbelief on his face. He looked from Nelda to John for an explanation of what had happened. Nelda thought he hadn't changed much in appearance from his high school days. His shaggy brown hair needed styling and his brown eyes were still too intense. Walter had been one of Nelda's brightest students, but she used to worry about his never having any fun. The fact that his boss had just been murdered hadn't lightened him up. She acknowledged his presence by introducing him to John.

"Walter, this is John Moore. I suppose Sue told you about Coldsby."

Walter nodded at Nelda and turned to John. "I can't understand why this happened. When was he shot?"

"I don't know when he died or why. I'm sure his death is a shock to you, but I need to know where you were between the hours of 5:00 p.m. last night and 6:00 a.m. this morning." John opened up his pad to take notes.

"I realize you have to question me, but it sounds like you believe one of the clinic employees killed him."

"We don't know. We've just started the investigation."

"Walter frowned, then sat down on the leather couch that occupied one wall. "I left here at 5:30 p.m. after my last appointment, and went directly to Smitherton to check on my two patients in the Methodist Hospital. After that, I went home and probably got there about 7:00 p.m."

"Can you verify the times you got to the hospital, left the hospital and arrived back home?"

"Yes, a hospital nurse, Nancy Winget, accompanied me on my rounds at the hospital, and Violet Rosin, my nurse, can tell you when I got back to Stearn. She cooked steaks for us at my place."

"How long have you had a partnership with Dr. Coldsby?"

Walter's voice was strained. "It wasn't a partnership. This was my third year to work for him."

"How was your working relationship with him?"

"I don't mind telling you that I wasn't satisfied. I should have been a partner," Walter said shaking his head.

"Did you argue over this?"

"Yes," Walter said loudly, "I tried to convince him that I deserved a partnership; he wouldn't budge. But, I wouldn't have killed him over it."

"Okay, Doctor, we'll get the phone numbers of the hospital and your home number from Sue. Let me know if you plan any trips out of town."

"I'll close the clinic for today," Walter said. "Do you want me to call Mrs. Coldsby?"

"No, we're trying to locate her now." John stood up.

Walter got up and walked out of the office deep in thought. Nelda wondered if he was thinking about how this death would affect his future.

"You seem to know him pretty well, Nelda. What do you think of his story?"

"I knew him well when he was my student. I don't know about

now. It won't be difficult to check his hospital story, but I hardly know Violet Rosin. Sue told me she moved here from Tulsa and is in love with Walter."

There was a loud knock on the office door. Nelda opened it to admit the lab tech, Carol Scrubbs. Carol bristled with hostility as she entered the room. Her plump body was tightly garbed in a white pantsuit. Green eyes set in a round, angry face gave both of them an accusing stare. "Why, may I ask, are we being treated like criminals? Just because we worked for Coldsby doesn't mean we shot him. It seems to me you'd be looking for some dope peddler who wanted to steal drugs from the clinic."

"Hold on, Carol." Nelda said. "No one is accusing you of anything. You know good and well the Sheriff has to find out where everyone was when the Doctor was murdered."

"Well, it seems like a waste of time to me, but I'll cooperate if I have to." Carol put a hand to her head as if it was hurting and sank to the couch.

"I'm sorry to upset you Ms. Scrubbs," John said, "but we hope you'll help us get a lead on this crime. Describe your activities after you left the clinic yesterday."

"I left the clinic at 4:00 p.m. and went to visit my husband, Shelby. He's terminally ill and lives at the hospice on Washington Avenue. After I left there, I went straight home to my apartment on Carson Street. I live alone so you can't check my story. I was totally wiped out when I got home. It's always so depressing to visit Shelby because he's dying and I can't do anything to help him get better." Carol cradled her head in her arms and cried.

Nelda put her arm around the younger woman. "I'm so sorry, Carol. No one told me about this."

"I really don't want to add to your stress, Ms. Scrubbs," said John, pacing up and down. "I just need the answers to a few more questions. Are you happy with your job here? And did you have a good working relationship with Coldsby?"

Carol spoke angrily, while dabbing at her eyes with a tissue. "Dr. Coldsby was difficult to work for. He expected you to work overtime without pay and never praised you for doing a good job. Most of us are looking for other positions."

"Do you know who'd want to harm him?"

"No, believe it or not, we're pretty civilized in this clinic."

There was a pause while John waited for Carol to speak again. Instead, she bit her lip and looked down at the floor. No words came out.

John opened the door for her. As she walked out, he handed her his card and said, "If you think of anything else, call me."

After she left, Nelda spoke up. "She talked about drugs, but Sue said the cabinet where the drugs are stored is still locked up."

"Yes," I know. "What do you think about Carol? Is she hiding something?"

"I believe so. I don't know what."

John consulted his list. "Now let's see, Nelda, who do we have left to talk to?"

"Violet Rosin is taking the morning off and Marcie is probably in her office. I'll check on Marcie for you." Nelda got up to leave.

"Thanks, I'll call the JP while you're gone and see if he's on his way."

Nelda walked down the hall toward the secretary's office. Through an open door, she could see several people in the waiting room. Walter seemed to be explaining to them why the clinic was closing. John's young deputy, Cari Hanks, was escorting a couple to the front door and they were leaving reluctantly.

Nelda knocked and pushed the secretary's office door open. Marcie, a good-looking brunette in her late thirties, had her head down on her desk. When she heard Nelda enter, she wiped her tear-stained face and looked up. There was a definite sadness in her big, green eyes. Nelda's heart went out to the grieving secretary who had been Coldsby's employee for many years.

"Marcie, the Sheriff needs to ask you some questions. Do you feel like you could answer them?"

"Oh, Nelda, I feel so terrible. Nobody cares that the Doctor is dead. I know he pinched pennies and was short-tempered, but he didn't deserve to die."

"I guess someone thought he did, that's why the Sheriff needs to talk to you. Maybe you could shed some light on why this happened."

Marcie stood up by her desk. "I don't think I can help, but I'll try."

They were entering the doctor's office when Violet came rushing in from outside, with her long, blonde hair trailing behind her. Nelda thought Violet looked stylish in her green jumpsuit and sandals to match, however her face was overdone. All the thick mascara, rouge and lipstick made her look coarse.

"Ms. Simmons," Violet asked, "is the sheriff accusing Walter? I got over here as soon as Sue called. I've got to talk to the sheriff and tell him I know who killed Dr. Coldsby."

Both women looked at Violet in disbelief. Would the murder be solved so quickly?

Nelda held the door open for Violet and Marcie.

"John," Nelda said, this is Walter's nurse, Violet Rosin, and Coldsby's secretary, Marcie Gibbons. Violet came in as soon as Sue called her because she thinks she knows who the killer is."

"Sit down, ladies. Now, what do you have to tell me, Ms. Rosin?"

"I'll tell you exactly what happened. Last week a young Spanish girl brought a sick baby in for Coldsby to treat, and he wouldn't do it because she didn't have any money. He told her to go to the free clinic. And then we heard the baby died the next day. Sue was a witness to the whole thing."

"Did the mother take the baby to the free clinic?" asked John.

"No, she didn't want to walk that far, so she went back home. I don't think she knew how sick her baby was. Anyway, the baby's grandfather, Berto Sanchez, told everyone in a local bar he was going to kill the Doctor."

"Who heard him say that?"

"Marcell White, he's the janitor for the clinic. He was right in

the bar when the old man made the threat. Marcell
was so drunk somebody had to take him home." Violet's fa
animated as she told the story.

"Do you know the name of the bar and what night this happened?"

"I'm sure it happened last Saturday night, and I can't remember the name of the bar. You'll need to ask Marcell."

"Marcell works here after the clinic closes?"

"Yes, usually from five to seven. He has other places he cleans
too."

Nelda became upset when she heard the story, even though
she thought of herself as a calm person. She knew exactly whom
that baby belonged to; it was her former student, Theresa Sanchez.
What a sad experience for the young girl, and now her father,
Berto, was accused of Coldsby's murder.

Marcie stood up. "I have the phone numbers and addresses of
everyone who works here."

"Good," said John, "If you'll get that list together I'd appreciate it." He opened the door and watched her leave, then turned
back to Violet. Now Ms. Rosin, what time did you leave the clinic
and what did you do when you left?"

Violet didn't hesitate with her answer. "I usually leave work at
5:30 p.m., but I was taking this morning off and needed to write
a note to my replacement. It was 6:00 p.m. before I got away.
Then I picked up some steaks at Apple Tree, and went over to
Walter's place to fix dinner. He came home around 7:00 p.m.
looking pretty beat. We ate, cleaned up the kitchen and I left at
8:00 p.m. I was in bed by 10:00 p.m."

"Thanks, Violet, I appreciate you telling me about the baby.
We'll be in touch."

Violet rushed up the hall, while Nelda pondered Sanchez's
role in the death.

CHAPTER THREE

Berto Flees

Marcie was leaning against the wall out in the hall when John told Violet good-bye. He invited her into the office and motioned for her to be seated. "Thanks for waiting, I'll take that statement from you now."

Nelda was happy to see that Marcie had her feelings under control. You could still see the paths of tears in her makeup from her emotional outburst, but her face had lost the pained look. The secretary avoided sitting on the leather couch. Instead, she chose an overstuffed chair covered in burgundy linen.

"Can you add anything to the story of the young Spanish girl and her baby?" John asked Marcie.

"I really can't. In fact, I wasn't in the outer office when she asked to see Coldsby. I heard about it through Sue. But it's not unusual for doctors to refer a patient to the free clinic. They can't afford to treat people for nothing. You have no idea the costs the doctors have. The insurance alone is enough to break them."

"So the doctor didn't know the baby was critically ill?"

"Heaven's no," she said, shaking her head for emphasis.

"How many years have you worked for the doctor?"

"Fifteen," she answered with a sad smile. " I was his first employee when he opened the clinic."

"Was your job going well?"

"I've never had any complaints until recently. Dr. Goodman

has more than doubled our patient load since he joined the clinic. Now, I'm always behind in my work. Dr. Coldsby complained about me being so slow. I was at my wit's end and looking for another job."

"Now tell me how you spent your evening," continued John, turning the page of his notebook.

"I locked up and left right after Violet at 6:00 p.m. We were the last ones to leave."

"Do you always lock up?"

"I usually do unless someone works late. All of us have keys to the back door, and we can set the alarm and turn it off. The janitor makes sure everything is secure before he leaves around seven."

"When you left, did you go straight home?"

"Yes I did. Mother and I have lived together for the last fifteen years. I fixed the evening meal and we watched an old movie on TV, 'The Man in the Gray Flannel Suit.' Mother loves Gregory Peck," Marcie said, smiling at Nelda.

"You didn't go out at all last night?"

"No," she said, shaking her head.

"One other thing, Ms. Gibbons, do you know of anyone who would have a strong enough motive to kill Dr. Coldsby?"

"No, not really. I know he was having trouble at home, but I don't know the details."

"Thanks, I appreciate your cooperation. Give the addresses and phone numbers of all the employees to my deputy, and we'll be in touch."

Marcie had just disappeared out the door when the JP knocked. He was a big, bald headed man with a red face. "Well, Bob, it's time you showed up," John said. "Nelda, do you know Bob Alder?"

"Course I do. You remember me don't you Bob?"

Bob grinned. "How could I forget! Always bugging me about a death."

"I'll be interested in the report on this one too. Will the autopsy be in Smitherton?"

"Yes, and soon, I hope. As for the time of death, I'd have to guess about 10:00 p.m. because rigor mortis wasn't complete."

"Thanks," said John, walking Bob to the door. "Send the report soon."

John saw Bob out, and then he and Nelda sat in silence gathering their thoughts.

"There sure are a lot of suspects, Nelda. I hardly know where to start."

"You have three more to interview."

"I know: your niece Sue, Joan Coldsby and Berto Sanchez."

"At least you don't have to worry about a grieving widow if the gossip is true."

"What have you heard?" John leaned back in a chair and stretched his long legs out.

"Sue said Joan wanted a divorce, but Coldsby wouldn't give her one. It had to do with splitting up the estate. He didn't want to let go of any money."

"All the employees seem to agree with that," John said, "but I haven't been able to get in touch with Mrs. Coldsby. The only thing I hear when I call is the message on the answering machine. I'll try to find out where she is when I get back to the office."

Nelda realized she needed a break. The morning was almost gone, and she had several things she needed to do. "John, I'm going as soon as I find Sue."

"Okay, I'll contact you later, but I need to talk to Sue before you leave."

Nelda found Sue talking to Marcie. "John wants a statement from you Sue."

They walked back to John. He opened up his notebook, while Sue sat rigidly in a chair waiting for instructions.

"Sue, just tell me when you left the clinic and what you did after that."

"I left at 5:15 p.m. Dr. Coldsby had already left. I went to my apartment and Steve Evans, my fiancé, came over at 7:00 p.m. His brother dropped him off; Steve's car is on the blink. Then we went to The Catfish House for a bite to eat. As you know, that place is always crowded. We had to wait to be served. I'm sure it was 8:30 p.m. before we got home. Steve borrowed my car and I went to bed."

"Nelda said your car wasn't working."

"That's right. I believe Steve left the lights on inside the car when he brought it back."

"Were things going all right at work?"

"No, Coldsby kept making passes at me. I was looking for another job."

"Who do you suppose killed him?" John inquired.

"I have no idea. I've never heard anyone threaten him."

"Thanks, Sue, you go ahead with Nelda. If you think of anything I need to know, call me."

Nelda and Sue walked out to the parking lot and climbed into Nelda's old Ford wagon. They couldn't believe it was almost noon.

"Aunt Nelda, just let me out at Farr's garage. I'll get someone to drive me home and look at the car."

When they arrived at the garage, Sue got out of the car and had a final word for her aunt. "Thanks, Aunt Nelda, I'm sorry I got you into this mess."

"Forget it. If it had to happen, I'm glad I was with you this morning."

Nelda was famished. She found herself conjuring up a mouth-watering Caesar salad, with anchovies and Parmesan cheese. The Farmer's Market made the best one in town. She decided to go there instead of home.

As she approached the market, brilliant colors filled her vision. There were barrels of geraniums with showy colors: coral, strawberry pink, rose-red, bright red and white blossoms. Nelda marveled at the countless variations of red and yellow hibiscus in the woven baskets that hung on every conceivable part of the verandah. With considerable control, she pulled herself away from the flowers and turned her attention to finding Mary Sanchez. She soon spotted her arranging strawberry plants on a long wooden table.

"Mrs. Sanchez," Nelda called across the verandah, "it's good to see you."

"It's good to see you too," Mary said with a sad little smile. Many things have happened to us since I saw you last."

"Have you had your lunch break yet?"

"No, I have a break in ten minutes."

"Please let me treat you to lunch. We have so much to talk about."

"Thank you but no. I brought my lunch. I'll bring it to your table and eat with you if it's all right."

"Good, it's all settled. I'll see you inside in a few minutes."

Nelda made her way into the dining section of the market. It was a large screened-in area lined with wooden tables covered with checkered oilcloths. Big ceiling fans hummed quietly while waiters moved among the customers carrying large pitchers of herbal iced tea. The aroma of fresh bread permeated the area. The thought of eating some of it made Nelda walk faster to an empty table for two. Having eaten here before, she didn't have to pore over the menu before making a decision. When the waitress came, she ordered.

"I'll have Caesar salad without the croutons, fish court-bouillon with rice and fresh peach-glazed cake. Don't forget to include some of that fresh bread and bring some herbal tea now, please."

Nelda had just received her tea when Mary appeared. "I'm going to feel guilty eating this lunch while you eat a sandwich. Would you have something else?"

"Thanks, I'm going to be fine. I'm trying to take off a little weight. I'll just have coffee with my sandwich."

"How have you been, Mary? I hope it's all right to use your first name."

"Of course, you are a good friend. You worked so hard to keep Theresa in school. I know it never worked out, but you really tried." Mary's eyes became teary. "Did you hear about poor little Carlos? Theresa's baby."

"Why don't you tell me about it Mary?"

"The baby was sick, so I told Theresa to walk over to the clinic."

"She couldn't find anyone to take her in a car?"

"My husband, Berto, was picking fruit in the valley and needed the car. It was a little walk to the clinic, but the Doctor wouldn't see the baby. He told her to go to the free clinic on Ashford Street about eight blocks away. She was tired from staying awake all night with Carlos so she wouldn't go. Theresa came home and that's when he really got bad. When I realized how sick he was, I called an ambulance, but it was too late. They said he had viral pneumonia."

"Is Theresa blaming herself?"

"Yes, I couldn't console her. The priest tried to help her by praying with her, but she screamed at him and I had to ask him to leave. My husband, Berto, didn't help either. He was so mad at Dr. Coldsby, he wanted to kill him."

"He really wouldn't do that would he?"

" No, he knows it would be a great sin."

"Where is Theresa now?"

"She went to stay with her grandmother. She needed someone to stay with her."

Nelda was about to tell Mary that Berto needed to talk to the sheriff when the waiter interrupted her. He set aromatic dishes in front of her. The food didn't seem nearly as appealing now because Nelda's mind was on other things. How was Mary going to react to the news that Berto was a murder suspect? She didn't have to wait long for Mary's reaction. An employee brought a message to Mary, who rushed from the table with an anguished cry. Nelda ran after her and found her crying under the hanging baskets.

"What's wrong? Could I help?"

"It's Berto, he received a phone call telling him the doctor is dead and the police think he killed him. Berto is going away and he may not ever come back."

"Did the Sheriff call Berto?" Nelda knew this wasn't John's style. He usually went to talk with a suspect or had his deputy bring the suspect in for questioning.

"Oh no! It was a woman who said they were going to put him in jail, so he better go now."

"You've got to stop him. They only want to question him about the threats he made in a night club."

"It is too late. Berto is leaving the country and will never come back."

Nelda consoled Mary while trying to imagine the identity of the informant. Someone was trying awfully hard to make Berto seem guilty.

CHAPTER FOUR

Sally Comes to Visit

Nelda called John from a pay telephone. "I've got to report what happened at the Farmer's Market. I've been visiting with Mary Sanchez, the wife of Berto Sanchez. It seems a woman called Berto and told him the authorities thought he killed Dr. Coldsby. When he heard that, he ran. His wife said he's leaving the country."

"I know! I sent Carl over to pick him up for questioning and he couldn't find him anywhere, so I put an alert out on his car. If I only knew who called, I'd be way ahead," John said nervously, drumming his fingers on his desk.

"When the autopsy report comes back, you'll find out what kind of gun was used. Then, if we're lucky it'll be found and registered to someone we know," Nelda answered, covering one ear to hear John's response. The phone booth was surrounded by noise.

"I'm not going to get my hopes up about the gun, but finding out what time he died will help. I'm trying to check out his movements after he left the clinic. No luck so far," John sighed.

"I'm calling it a day, John. I've got a busy day tomorrow with lots of sick folks to visit." Nelda stared back at a teenager waiting to use the phone.

"One other thing," John said. "I finally located Joan Coldsby. She's on a Caribbean cruise, due back tomorrow."

"She picked the right time to be gone," Nelda said and hung up.

Nelda climbed back into her old station wagon and headed

home. A nice cup of coffee on her shady porch was what she needed. Plans had to be made for the next day.

There was a faded blue, 88 Volvo in her driveway when she got home. "There's Sally," she muttered to herself. "So much has been going on, I forgot I invited her for the weekend."

Nelda and Sally went way back. Sally Feddington had been the senior English teacher at the school where Nelda taught, but now recently retired to the country. She still maintained a close relationship with Nelda.

Sally knew where Nelda hid the house key and had made herself at home. Nelda could smell coffee brewing when she opened the side door to the kitchen.

She looked at her old friend with affection as Sally sat at the kitchen table reading the newspaper with half-lens spectacles perched on the end of her pudgy nose. Her curly graying hair made a halo around her head, giving her the appearance of a kindly grandmother. She looked up and smiled at Nelda with dimpled cheeks.

"I knew you were hiding from me," Sally said. "Your comic books were still here, so you had to show up sooner or later."

"You old hussy, since when do I hide from my best friend? You won't believe what's happened today!"

"Too late, Sue called while you were out and told me about Dr. Coldsby. I guess the boredom is over; you're off on another adventure."

"Jim's death has slowed down my mystery solving, so I have to latch on to a mystery when I find one. Do you know how long Jim was sheriff first and my husband second? Thirty years. I always tried to help him with his cases even though teaching school took up most of my time. At first it was because the county couldn't afford a deputy. Then I was hooked. I've loved solving mysteries ever since, just can't stop myself."

"What does the new sheriff, John Moore, think about you helping him solve his cases?"

"He's a good sport about it. I think he gets a little put out with the way I go about getting my information. Still, he never turns it down."

"Okay, what's on the agenda for tomorrow? I know you'll be doing something related to this crime. Let's grab a cup of coffee," Sally said holding up the coffee pot, "and go out on the porch and discuss it. I'll try not to spill any coffee in your clean kitchen."

Nelda caught herself cleaning up after Sally's coffee making, and even managed to smile as she sponged up water on the floor in front of the sink.

"You're going to love this Colombian coffee," Nelda said. "I know all that caffeine isn't good for us, who cares? Maybe it will help the old gray matter start to perk. I think I'll need all the help I can get on this case."

She poured the hot, dark fluid in some cups Sally had out. "Fix your coffee," Nelda ordered, "and let's go out on the porch. I'll tell you what I've planned for tomorrow and if you don't like it, we can come up with something else."

"No, whatever is planned is fine. Just tell me what to expect."

Nelda made her way to the porch, then pulled out chairs from around a small redwood table. But before sitting down, she inspected her flowerbeds. The blue hydrangeas and pink geraniums in the back yard were beautiful. She felt sure the blossoms could win a prize.

"Tomorrow," Nelda said, sipping her coffee, "we're going to the hospice. There are two people we can try cheering up. You know, ever since Uncle George died I've regretted not visiting my terminally ill friends. I was under the impression that they didn't want to be visited by anyone but close family members. I was wrong! Uncle George told my aunt he felt terribly alone, because hardly anyone came to see him when they found out he was dying."

"I think it's because we don't want to think about death. It's always happening to someone else," said Sally, looking over her glasses at Nelda.

"Of course you're right, but it doesn't have to be an unhappy visit," Nelda emphasized, feeling Sally wasn't in agreement with her plan.

"Who do you plan for us to visit?"

"You remember Fly Catcher, that old baseball coach who retired a few years back? He's terminally ill with lung cancer." Nelda's eyes filled with tears.

"I sure do remember Will Campbell. I thought he smoked too much even before we knew how bad smoking is for you. I'll be happy to see him, even though he brought the disease on himself."

Nelda was taken aback at Sally's attitude about Will, but continued with her conversation. "And do you remember Carol Burns?"

"Don't tell me that young girl is dying. Why she couldn't be over twenty-five, wonderful English student too." Sally took her glasses off and rubbed her eyes.

"No, no she's not dying; she's a lab technician at the clinic. Her husband is the one who's terminally ill. His name is Shelby Scrubbs and Carol said he doesn't have any family or friends that visit him. I think it's time for him to have two new friends. How about it?" Nelda hoped Sally would give her a straight answer.

Sally looked away thoughtfully. "That name, Shelby Scrubbs, sounds awfully familiar to me, but I can't place it."

Nelda stood up and pulled some dry leaves from a small barrel of strawberry plants. "I don't remember him from Stearn High School," Nelda said. "Perhaps he's from some other place. Carol did go off to Blair State, which is located in Goalsby. There's a chance she met him there."

"Good heavens, that's the place that tried to legalize marijuana in the seventies." Sally gave Nelda a horrified stare.

"Yes, I'm afraid it's not just liberal arts anymore, it's liberal everything. But getting back to Carol, when John interviewed her she wasn't telling all she knew. Maybe, Shelby could shed some light on that," Nelda said while watching a large blue jay sip water from a birdbath.

"So, you really have two reasons for visiting Carol's husband tomorrow," Sally said, walking to the edge of the porch.

"Yes I do. It's not that terrible is it?" Nelda yanked on a dead stem in aggravation.

"Now, don't get in a dither, Nelda. I know you have good intentions. Why don't you tell me about the other suspects. Have you found out anything that might help you?" Sally sat back down.

"Not much, I'm afraid. There are too many people who disliked Coldsby. Even Sue is considered a suspect." Nelda picked up a half-filled watering can and watered the strawberry plants.

Sally slipped off her shoes and wiggled her toes. "You wrote me she was looking for another job, but didn't say why."

"I didn't say why because I was too upset with Coldsby. The rotten man thought it was his right to make passes at her just because she worked for him. Still makes my blood boil when I think about it." She sat the can down with a bang.

"Who else works for him?" Sally inquired. She swatted at a mosquito that lit on her arm.

"Marcie Gibbons was his secretary and she's such a good looking woman. I'm afraid she's let life pass her by. She never married."

"Just because she's single doesn't mean she's not leading a full life," Sally said sharply.

Nelda realized she had offended Sally, who never married. "I know," Nelda said soothingly, "but this woman wanted a husband and children. She confided in Sue that she did. Too bad she couldn't find a man who suited her."

"Did she have a complaint about the doctor?"

"All of them did," Nelda answered. "In Marcie's case, she said she was overworked. What's really odd though, she's the only one that grieved for him. I'm beginning to wonder if they were lovers."

"Wouldn't Sue know that?" Sally asked, watching a brown wren take his turn at the birdbath.

"Sue said she never saw any indication of it. However, Sue has only worked for Coldsby five years and Marcie has been his secretary for fifteen. I'm sure he tried to have an affair with her," Nelda answered as she refilled the watering can from an outdoor faucet.

"Is Walter Goodman under suspicion too, Nelda? He was one of my favorite students, smart too and such wonderful manners."

"All the employees are suspects. Walter wanted a partnership and Coldsby wouldn't give him one. Everybody said he deserved it; he had more patients than Coldsby." She turned the faucet off and watered some pansies near by.

Sally sipped the last of her coffee and wondered out loud. "Why in the world didn't he go off on his own? His patients would have followed him, wouldn't they?"

"Oh, I'm sure of it," Nelda replied, but it takes money to set up a practice, and it's not easy to get a loan anymore. You know the trouble the banks and loan companies have had. They're really cautious with their loans now. He would need thousands of dollars for office space and equipment, and his family is too poor to back him."

"I understand Walter has some backing from his nurse," Sally said grinning. Sun and shadow flickered across her face.

"I can tell Sue has really been filling you in. Nurse Violet is something else. She dresses like a streetwalker and sometimes speaks like one too. However, Walter is her love and she'll do anything for him. I'm sure that would include giving him an alibi if she had to." Nelda put the watering can up on a shelf.

"Are there other suspects?" Sally asked, slipping her shoes back on.

Nelda gathered up the cups. "At least two. Coldsby's wife wanted out of the marriage, but he didn't want to give her a divorce for financial reasons. She has an alibi by being out of the country when he died."

"That wouldn't keep her from hiring someone to do the job," Sally said, wiping the table off with her napkin.

"That's true. If she wanted him dead, I'm sure there would be someone to oblige her." She waited for Sally to get up.

Sally stood up and opened the door for Nelda. "Okay, who's the other one?"

"Do you remember Theresa Sanchez?" Nelda asked, as she and Sally walked to the kitchen.

Nelda paused to give Sally a chance to think back. She knew how hard it was to remember students. The good ones and the ones that misbehave seem to stick in your memory bank, but the others get jumbled. She and Sally must have taught thousands of students over the last thirty years.

"Say, I do remember her. She was bright, but rebellious. Her father was hard on her, never wanted her out after dark. Then, I heard she quit school and had a baby with no sign of a husband around."

"That's the one," Nelda said, rinsing the cups and placing them in the dishwasher. Coldsby refused to treat her baby and it died. Theresa's father, Berto, got drunk and threatened to kill Coldsby. Now he's skipped the country. Theresa's mother thinks he's gone back to Mexico."

"Do you think he's the murderer?" Sally asked, studying a spoon collection on the kitchen wall.

Nelda answered while fixing the coffeepot for the next morning. "No, it's one thing to get drunk and threaten to kill, but another to carry it out."

"Sounds like you have a real puzzle here. I'm sure a clue will turn up soon."

Nelda checked her watch. "Come on, Sally, let's catch the five o'clock news. This is the biggest thing that's happened in Stearn since that drug ring was broken up four years ago." They moved inside and turned on Nelda's nineteen inch TV.

"One of these days I'm going to treat myself to a big screen TV, Nelda. I saw one at Foleys' the other day. It's almost like you're in a movie theater."

"This one is big enough. If you can't see well enough, just move your chair closer. Shhh, look they're interviewing John."

The interview was taking place outside the sheriff's office. Channel Four had sent Evelyn Chasing, their roving reporter, to be the interviewer. Evelyn's short blonde hair bounced spasmodically as her head oscillated between the camera and sheriff. There was a smug expression on her face as she began the interview.

"Sheriff Moore, do you have anything new to tell us about the death of Dr. Albert Coldsby?"

John spoke with a cold stare at the reporter. "There's nothing new to report."

"Come now, we've received word that you have the murder weapon." She held the microphone closer to him.

"We'll have that information after the laboratory has examined the gun," he spoke through clenched teeth.

"Our caller was certain it was the murder weapon she sent to you," badgered Ms. Chasing.

John's lips were taut and there was a wary look in his eyes as he responded. "I have nothing more to say." He abruptly turned and walked away.

Nelda had new fuel for speculation.

CHAPTER FIVE

Shelby Confesses

Nelda and Sally approached the hospice with some timidity, an unusual feeling for Nelda. Even though the two sick men knew they were coming to visit, Nelda wasn't sure how welcome their visit would be. Then, it was always worrisome about what to say. How do you make conversation with a person who has only a few months to live?

The hospice was an elegant old home with large columns and a grand front porch. Nelda pushed the heavy front door open and stepped into a large foyer. The interior of the home had been completely renovated to accommodate a dozen patients and attending personnel. The nurses' station was located on the right side of the foyer.

Stepping up to the desk, Nelda came face to face with a large black nurse in a spotless white uniform. She wore her hair braided around her head and had no jewelry on or makeup on her shiny face. Her attitude was one of caution.

"How can I help you?" she asked.

"My name is Nelda Simmons and this is Sally Feddington. I called earlier about visiting Will Campbell and Shelby Scrubbs."

"Yes, We were expecting you; I'm Nurse Washington. Which one would you like to visit first?"

Sally spoke out quickly. "Let's visit Will and find out how that old Romeo is feeling. I'd sure feel better talking to someone we know."

Washington led the way down a long hall that divided the house into two equal parts. There were patients' rooms on either side of the hall. The names of the occupants were printed on nameplates attached to the centers of the doors. Nelda and Sally heard the sound of a television in one or two rooms and soft moaning in another. They finally came to Will's door. There was no sound from within. Washington knocked briskly.

"Come in, I'm decent," a voice called out. This was followed by several seconds of coughing within the room.

The nurse pushed the door open. Nelda hoped her face didn't convey what she felt when she saw Will's wasted body propped up in bed. The few strands of hair he had left on his head were as gray as his face, and faded blue eyes looked out from the shell of a dying man.

Nelda and Sally stood beside Will's bed smiling down at him. For once Nelda couldn't think of anything to say. Antiseptic odors made her want to run out of the room.

Sally seemed to sense Nelda's predicament and came to the rescue. "It's so good to see you Will. We sure missed you after you left school. No one else can tell stories like you can." A big smile appeared on her face.

Will looked at Nelda and then at Sally. There was an expression of pain in his eyes, not just physical pain, Nelda thought, but pain for an era that he had enjoyed so much, and would never experience again.

Nelda grabbed his hand. "Will, you old rascal. I know the nurses have a hard time keeping you in line." She squeezed his hand gently.

"Sit down, girls. You must really be hard up for men if you've got to visit me." He laughed between spasmodic coughing spells. "I remember when I had to give a speech on Parents' Night and you stole my notes. I sure was doing a lot of stuttering before you returned them." He dabbed at his mouth with a tissue.

Will knew just how to break down the barriers that separated him from his former colleagues. Just pretend he was not going to die.

The jam session started with Nelda giving Will a rundown of all the old teachers they knew. She sat on the edge of a straight-back chair and willed herself to block out all the sickroom odors.

"It's great to hear about those old flakes." He grinned broadly and then closed his eyes and gasped for breath. Fine beads of sweat broke out on his forehead.

Nelda knew it was time to go because his face had turned ashen. "Will," Sally said softly, "we've got to be going."

He opened his eyes and held a hand out in their direction. Nelda held it and gently kissed him on his forehead. She knew it might be for the last time.

"Good-bye, Will, think about us sometime. We're going to visit someone else here, Shelby Scrubbs. Maybe you remember his wife? Her maiden name was Carol Burns."

"Oh no," Will sighed. "What a terrible thing to happen, and she's so young."

"What on earth are you talking about?" Nelda quizzed.

"That young man she's married to is dying of AIDS."

Nelda and Sally were speechless. Poor Carol, Nelda thought, no wonder she was mad at the world. The dread of seeing someone you love have such a disease and being exposed to it yourself must be a heart breaking experience.

"We weren't aware of that. Do you think our visit will do him any good?"

"Couldn't hurt. I've visited with him and he seemed to appreciate the company. He said his folks won't visit him and he has no friends."

Nelda and Sally waved good-bye just as nurse Washington came hurriedly down the hall with a tray of medication.

"Did you wear Romeo out?" she inquired, arranging the bottles on the tray.

"I think we did stay long enough," Nelda said.

"Good, now let me escort you to Mr. Scrubbs' room. I think he's ready for your visit. Just stay for a few minutes because his condition is subject to change at any time."

"We sure wouldn't want to tire him," responded Sally, lagging behind.

Nelda sensed Sally didn't want to visit a dying man she didn't know. "Sally, maybe you could wait for me in the car. I'll only be a few minutes."

"Thanks Nelda, I sure wouldn't do him any good. I'll meet you back at the car."

Nelda knocked lightly on Shelby's door. There was a faint whirring sound within. In a few seconds, Shelby opened the door. He was a good looking man with a shock of long, black hair and dark eyes that looked out from under heavy eyebrows. He grasped the arms of the wheelchair and breathed heavily. The effort to push the wheelchair had used up the little energy he had.

"Come in. I'm glad you're here to visit me." He waved Washington out of the room, then motioned for Nelda to be seated. There were two armchairs arranged by the window.

"I'm sorry my friend, Sally, couldn't visit you too, but she's not feeling well and thought she'd better not expose you to anything," Nelda said sitting down in one of the chairs.

Shelby, dressed in a red plaid robe, stared at Nelda with sad eyes. His wasted body sat limply in the chair, chin touching his chest.

He threw his head back and laughed harshly. "There's nothing more that anyone could do to me. I'm sure Carol told you I have AIDS. It's just a matter of time before I die, the faster the better. I'm so tired of it all."

"I'm sorry for all your suffering. Are they treating you well here?"

"Yes, but there's really not much they can do. It's Carol I'm worried about," he said sighing heavily.

"I don't think you should worry about her. Carol certainly seems capable of taking care of herself. She loves you very much."

"I know," Shelby wrung his hands. "What a horrible thing I've done to her. It was my foolish college days when I just had to experiment with drugs. And now she'll probably pay for my sins too."

The truth of what he was saying finally dawned on Nelda. "She hasn't tested HIV positive has she?" Nelda found herself standing up.

"Not yet. Please God, I hope it doesn't happen."

"Let's not borrow trouble, Shelby. I'm sure they're close to a cure. Besides that, she'd probably already have the disease if she was going to get it." Nelda was praying that what she was saying was true.

"I hope so! I've already experienced several bouts with this stuff that are as bad as dying. I don't want this to happen to her too."

"Has Carol's family been able to help? I remember them from her high school days. They seemed a close family."

"No, they're not speaking to us. They tried to keep her from marrying me. They knew I fooled around with the wrong crowd, but Carol set out to reform me. She did, but too late."

"What can I do to help you and Carol?"

"This wretched business with Dr. Coldsby... is my wife a suspect?" he asked in a loud voice, straining to sit up straight.

"Yes, all the employees at the clinic are suspects. No one has been cleared. Carol said she visited you that night and then went home. I'm sure they'll try to check her movements that night."

Shelby gripped the arms of the wheelchair and his head fell forward.

"I've stayed too long. I hope you'll allow me to visit another time." Nelda edged toward the door.

"Come back when you can," Shelby said weakly. "I'm going to need the nurse to get back into bed." He pushed a button by his side.

"I'll get one for you. You just rest and try not to worry about Carol. We'll help her all we can."

Nelda went down the hall to find one of the nurses. She saw Washington coming out of a patient's room.

"Mr. Scrubbs needs to get back into bed," Nelda said.

"I'm on my way. Thanks for visiting him and come back." The nurse hurried down the hall with heels clicking on the tile floor.

Nelda made her way to the parked car and found Sally snoozing on the front seat. She woke her up getting into the car.

"Well, how did your visit go? Did he seem glad to see you?" asked Sally stifling a yawn.

"I think he did appreciate my visit, but there was something I said that really upset him," Nelda said, starting the car.

"What did you say?" Sally asked, as they buckled up.

"I told him the Sheriff would be checking Carol's alibi. She said she was visiting him that night."

"Don't you think she was?" questioned Sally.

"I don't know," Nelda exclaimed, driving out on the street. "I've never heard of a case like this one. Almost everyone Coldsby knew had a motive for killing him. Let's go home and forget the whole thing for awhile."

Nelda drove home after a brief stop at the grocery store. She and Sally carried the grocery bags in and had just started unpacking them when the phone rang.

She answered and responded to John's greeting on the other end. "How's everything going? We saw you on television yesterday."

"Everyone did unfortunately. I won't comment on that interview now," John responded. "Nelda, something else has come up and I need to talk to you."

"Do you have anything new on the case?" Nelda inquired, motioning for Sally to put the ice cream in the freezer.

"I'd rather not discuss it over the phone. Come to the office about 2:00 p.m. and we'll talk."

"My friend Sally is here for the weekend, so I can't stay long."

"That's okay," John said and hung up.

Nelda wondered what John had on his mind. At any rate, this would give her an opportunity to find out about the gun he received and other pertinent facts he'd accumulated in the last few hours.

* * *

John and his deputy, Carl, gave his office a good cleaning. "You know why I'm doing this don't you Carl?" John asked, grinning.

"Because it needs it," Carl answered with a broom in his hands.

"That too, but mainly the reason is Ms. Simmons. She impressed upon me the need for cleanliness and order when she had me redo my dirty, disorganized Latin notebook in high school."

Carl laughed. "I remember her working our butts off."

Nelda was in the Sheriff's outer office at exactly 2:00 p.m. Martha, the Sheriff's secretary, looked up at the clock and noted the time.

"Nice to see you again, Ms. Simmons. The Sheriff is waiting for you in his office."

Nelda walked down the hall and knocked on John's door. He came out and ushered her in.

"Nelda, you go ahead and sit down." John walked over to a coffeepot sitting on a small table in the corner of the room. He poured out two cups of strong coffee and handed Nelda a cup.

She frowned at the thick black liquid in the cup. "Must be something pretty important, John. I guess this coffee is supposed to be my bracer."

"Did you visit Carol's husband, Shelby Scrubbs, this morning?"

"Yes," answered Nelda and I'm sorry to hear the reason for his illness. He has AIDS and apparently doesn't have much time left. We had just returned from our visit when you called." She tasted the coffee and grimaced.

"What did you and Scrubbs talk about?"

"Mostly about his illness. He did ask if Carol was a suspect and I told him all the employees were suspects. Now, what's this all about? Has something happened to him?"

"Shelby Scrubbs has confessed to the murder of Albert Coldsby."

CHAPTER
SIX

Sue's in Trouble

Nelda stared at John in disbelief before she spoke. "There is absolutely no way that Shelby could kill anyone. The disease has made him an invalid." She noticed that John had a few gray hairs at his temples, and no wonder with the way this case was going.

John agreed. "His doctor said it would be physically impossible for him to leave the hospice on his own." He looked out the window as though he wanted to escape.

"What I don't understand," said Nelda, glancing appreciatively at the neat stacks of paper on John's desk, "is why he thinks Carol needs protecting."

"I'll tell you why. Coldsby found out that Shelby had AIDS. He figured it would just be a matter of time before Carol came down with it. He didn't want her working for him when that happened. If people found out that he had a lab technician with AIDS, they would shun his clinic." He tapped on his desk waiting for Nelda's reaction.

"Is that what Carol said? Did you question her about this?" Nelda couldn't believe Coldsby could be so cruel.

"Yes, Coldsby told her she had to find another job. If she didn't leave right away, he wouldn't give her a good recommendation." John bit on his lower lip.

"Poor Carol," Nelda said, shaking her head sadly. "She certainly was pushed to the limit. But would her conscience let her commit murder?"

"I don't know. The maddening part is how many of his own employees are glad he's dead." John couldn't hide the disgust in his voice.

"What about the gun, John? Was the one sent to you the murder weapon?"

"Yes, a Colt 45." He shoved a photograph of it across the desk.

"And," Nelda said expectantly as she looked at the picture.

"He was killed with his own gun," John sighed.

"Did he keep it in his office?" Nelda asked, scratching a few notes on a pad.

"That's what his staff said." John stretched and grimaced as though his back hurt.

"Meaning everyone at the office had access to it," Nelda said, wishing John would be still for a minute.

John nodded while looking through his notes. "We're checking everybody's alibi, and I'm trying to find out where Coldsby had his last meal. The coroner said he'd eaten right before he was killed. We didn't find any trace of food at the clinic, so I'm sure he ate out. When we find the restaurant, we'll be able to establish the time of death."

"I'm going to have lunch with Sue today. I wish she wasn't involved in any of this. If she remembers anything you should know, I'll call you." Nelda rose to leave, but John motioned for her to stay seated.

"Nelda, Sue's car was seen parked on a side street near the clinic at 9:00 p.m. the night of the murder." He glanced over at her to see her reaction.

Nelda had an uneasy feeling. Her voice trembled as she spoke. "Sue said Steve borrowed her car. Have you spoken to him about it?" She started twisting on the pen in her hand.

"No, but I'll try to do that after my interview with Joan Coldsby. She's back and I'll visit her this afternoon." John opened up the file cabinet and jammed his notes in a folder.

Why in the world would Steve be near the clinic, Nelda wondered. Out loud she said, "I'm going to ask Sue about that and see if there's some reasonable explanation for her car being there." This was sounding more and more serious to Nelda.

"I'm sure there is. We'll get to the bottom of it," John declared, pacing back and forth.

Nelda told John good-bye and drove home to pick up Sally. She was determined to enjoy the rest of the day, because Sally was leaving the next day.

She and Sally drove to Sing Lees' restaurant on Olive Street. Sue's car was already in the parking lot. The parking lot was small and already filling up. They parked and made their way through the gravel lot.

Nelda chatted as they walked toward the entrance. "The food here is awfully good, Sally, but I really wanted to take you to the Green Shallot in Smitherton."

"Well, why didn't you?" Sally led the way around a family with small children.

"Sue insisted we come here. We'll go to the Green Shallot tonight." Nelda hoped Sue had a table for them. She hated to waste time standing in line.

The doors to the restaurant were dark green with embossed dragons on them. When they entered, Nelda saw a large display of oriental fans on the wall. She pointed to one simple fan with a wooden handle. "Do you remember when we used a fan like that, Sally?"

"I sure do, but I bet that fan is not advertising Green's mortuary on the back like the fans we used."

Both were still grinning when a pretty Oriental girl greeted them. Nelda described Sue to her and she led them to Sue's table by the window.

Sue rose and gave Sally a big hug. "It's so good to see you, Sally. Sorry that we're in the middle of a big mess. I'm sure Aunt Nelda has filled you in."

"I think I've got the picture. I just hope it's all resolved soon."

"I'd really like to forget it for awhile, just relax." She'd already ordered herself a glass of white wine.

After Nelda heard Sue's comment, she decided not to bring up the question about the car until after they'd eaten.

"What do you suggest Nelda?" asked Sally. The spicy aroma of oriental dishes filled the air.

"Why don't we eat from the buffet? The Shrimp and Chicken Ding and Moo Goo Gai Pan are two of my favorites, but we have a lot of other dishes to choose from, too."

They walked around the buffet loading their plates with food. Nelda took small portions, because she had noticed in the last few weeks that her slacks were getting a little snug. She dreaded the thought of aerobics. It might come to that if she wasn't careful. Right now she had more pressing things on her mind.

"Well," Sue said after they were all seated with food and large glasses of iced tea, "I suppose the two of you will be going to the antique show at the Smitherton Center tomorrow. I've seen it advertised and it promises to be a really big one." She looked expectantly from one to another.

"You know we wouldn't miss it. You're staying for that aren't you Sally?" Nelda asked. She hoped Sally would, because the trip to the hospice had not been a fun trip for either one of them.

"I really hadn't planned on it. I will if you think I might find some of my discontinued china."

The clatter of knives and forks along with good conversation eased the tension that Nelda felt when she entered the restaurant.

"Sure you can," Nelda said with a smile. "We'll plan a big outing tomorrow and then you can go home."

Soon after, they paid their checks and were out in the parking lot. Nelda felt she had to find out about Sue's car. She took a deep breath to find the courage to ask.

NELDA SEES RED   51

"Sue, the sheriff said your car was parked on a side street near the clinic at 9:00 p.m. on the night of the murder. He's got to know what Steve was doing there." Nelda didn't anticipate Sue's reaction to her statement.

"Oh my God!" Sue cried, "I can't believe he actually went to the clinic." She covered her eyes and wept.

"What are you saying?" Nelda said in a hushed tone. "Did he kill Coldsby?"

"Oh no! Aunt Nelda. He wouldn't do anything like that. He told me he was going to warn Coldsby to keep his hands off me or he'd punch him in the nose." Sue leaned against a car for support.

"I'm sorry Sue, but I'm afraid Steve may be in trouble. Did Steve talk to Coldsby?"

"He said he didn't; Coldsby wasn't at the clinic." Opening her purse, Sue fumbled for a tissue.

"Why did he think the doctor would be there?" Nelda wondered why Sue hadn't told her about this earlier.

"Because Steve had called him and Coldsby said he was coming back to the clinic to do some work." Sue shredded the tissue as she talked.

"Does he ever work late?" Nelda knew she had to find out the whole story.

"No, he would hardly work during office hours." Sue cried softly. "I'm so afraid for Steve."

Nelda put her arms around Sue. "Go home and don't worry; I'm sure everything can be explained."

Sally and Nelda drove home in silence. Nelda knew establishing the time of

Coldsby's death was more critical than ever. She would try to hide her fears from Sally.

Once they were home, Nelda entertained Sally with pictures taken since the last time they were together. She showed Sally snapshots of her mini vacations and some taken at Christmas parties. One of the Christmas pictures caught Sally's eye.

"Nelda, is this a picture of all the employees at Coldsby's clinic?"

"It sure is. They had to throw their own party, and then the old skinflint stuck his head in the picture."

"I'm surprised he gave them the time to have it."

"He didn't; it was after hours. All he did was furnish the clinic."

Nelda was putting the albums up when she had a sudden inspiration. She pulled the Christmas picture of the employees' party out of the album and put it in her handbag.

The rest of the day was spent out on the deck talking gardening. They also made a list of things they would look for at the antique show.

"One thing I really want to find is a 1977 Copenhagen porcelain Mother's Day plate. It's the only one I'm lacking in that series," Nelda said.

"And I'll be looking for the Rose pattern dinner plates in my Haviland china."

Nelda couldn't get her mind off the murder case. "You know, Sally, I feel guilty thinking about frivolous things when this murder case is waiting to be solved. Look at all the lives it's affecting."

"Realistically, Nelda, what else could you be doing?"

"I'm going to find out where that man ate before he died. I'll start asking questions at the Green Shallot."

"That's in Smitherton thirty minutes away; he died here in Stearn."

"He left early and could easily have driven to Smitherton for a meal. There are only a handful of places to eat in Stearn. John can investigate those, but in Smitherton I counted over one hundred restaurants."

"John didn't give you the authority to do that did he?"

"I don't need his authority to ask questions. If they won't answer I'll just report it to him," Nelda said, looking down at her wrinkled dress.

"Some of the staff might know where he ate," Sally said, leading the way back inside.

"If that's true, I hope they'll come forward with that information." Nelda looked at herself in the hall mirror. She was a mess; her hair needed curling and her skin was dry.

They both headed for a shower. Sally changed into a blue jean skirt and a blue denim shirt with an Indian design painted on it. The blue shirt contrasted nicely with her white hair. It was a little something she had picked up in New Mexico while on vacation. Nelda wore her favorite navy blue skirt with a red cotton blouse. She looked fresh after applying a good face cream and curling her hair. Both were looking forward to their evening meal.

After they were in Nelda's old station wagon, she carefully wrote down the mileage that showed on her speedometer. She was not surprised that it registered 123,000 miles.

They made the thirty-mile trip in twenty-six minutes driving within the speed limit.

The Green Shallot was located on the north end of town and consisted mostly of glass windows and long wooden decks. Tables on the decks overlooked a large herb garden. There were fresh flowers and sweet-smelling herbs on every table. Sally was delighted with Nelda's choice.

They were seated on the deck and took plenty of time studying the menu.

"I do feel guilty, Nelda, eating out twice in the same day." Sally placed her napkin in her lap.

"Now really, Sally, how often do you do that?"

"Never."

"So enjoy it!" ordered Nelda, inhaling the smell of fresh baked bread.

Nelda looked up expectantly when the waiter came to take their order. She was disappointed that it wasn't her ex-student, Wanda Baker, because she needed Wanda's help. Instead, it was a red-headed guy with blue eyes and a shaggy mustache.

Sally ordered first. "I would like the grilled salmon steak, steamed pea pods, new potatoes, tossed salad and poached pears with raspberry sauce. Doesn't that sound wonderful, Nelda?"

"Great selection, Sally. I want Lobster Newburg, asparagus, Caesar salad and no dessert." She'd worry later about the weight gain.

After finishing their meal, Nelda looked around trying to locate Wanda.

"Who are you looking for?" Sally inquired.

"Wanda Baker."

"Not that nosy student. I didn't think you approved of the way she gossiped."

"Well I don't, but maybe she worked Friday night and could tell us if Coldsby was here."

As they paid their bill, Wanda came out of the kitchen with a tray of food.

"Wanda," Nelda called. "Could we speak to you for a minute?"

"Just a minute, Ms. Simmons, let me deliver this food. I'll be right back."

Nelda and Sally waited for her in the foyer. Nelda pulled the Christmas picture out of her purse. After several minutes, Wanda returned breathlessly in a blue uniform buttoned tightly over her curvaceous figure.

Wanda greeted them with a smile. "Good to see both of you. Did you enjoy your meal?"

"It was wonderful," Nelda said, "but I've got a favor to ask. Would you try to identify the man on the left in this picture and tell me if he ate here Thursday night?"

"I know him real well. That's Doctor Coldsby, the man that was killed the other night. He wasn't here Thursday night, but he used to come in all the time with that girl," she said pointing to the picture.

"What girl are you talking about?" Nelda asked.

Wanda put her finger on Sue's face. Nelda's legs turned to rubber.

CHAPTER SEVEN

Nelda Visits Joan

Sally broke the silence that covered them like a blanket on the way home. "I think you're worrying needlessly. You know Sue wouldn't have an affair with a married man." She looked anxiously at her friend.

"I hope you're right! But there are too many coincidences involving Sue and the doctor." Nelda couldn't bear to have Sue hurt.

"Will you call her immediately when you get home?"

"No, she and Steve have gone to the horse races in Lafayette, Louisiana. They won't be back until tomorrow night." She gripped the steering wheel wishing it was Steve's throat.

When Nelda arrived home, she decided Sue's situation needed to be on the back burner. Why worry? No need to ruin Sally's visit. She'd try to act happy.

"Sally," she said cheerfully. "Have a good nights' sleep. We'll have a big day antiquing tomorrow."

"You too, Nelda. See you in the morning." Sally saw the comfortable-looking four poster bed in Nelda's guest bedroom and gave a happy sigh as she sank down on it.

The next day Nelda and Sally puttered around the house until the antique show opened at 1:00. They bought the first two tickets sold. The show was taking place in the City Center, a huge covered area with booths set up in rows. Shoppers could walk down long aisles to view the wares on either side. The merchants were still putting merchandise out and arranging it when they started their shopping.

"Look at this J.R. Sheffield dessert basket, Sally." Nelda pointed to an ornate, sterling silver piece. "But goodness! The price they're asking." Nelda shook her head.

"Now, Nelda, if you take that stingy attitude you'll walk away empty handed."

"Well, I know my limits and who will want these antiques when I'm gone?" Secretly, she hoped to whet Sue's interest in antiques.

"I'm living for today," Sally said. "If it pleases me, I'm going to get it, within reason of course." She gave Nelda a brisk nod for emphasis.

Nelda was distracted from a detailed inspection of a baluster wineglass by voices coming from a group that had just entered the center. She glanced around and found Marcie Gibbons, Violet Rosin and Carol Scrubbs headed toward her.

"I guess I can have a heart attack now," she whispered to Sally, "most of the clinic workers have arrived."

When they stopped to say hello, she introduced Sally to Marcie and Violet. Carol remembered Sally from high school and gave her a big hug.

"We're on our way to look at the antique jewelry," Carol said, looking at her small gold watch.

Nelda realized that Shelby hadn't told Carol about their visit to see him, or of his false confession concerning Coldsby's death. She wasn't going to tell her, eiher.

"And I want something with plenty of glitter," interposed Violet. As she talked, long crystal drops swayed from her ear lobes.

Nelda and Sally watched them walk away. Carol was dressed in a shapeless, blue tent dress, but the other two looked very much in vogue with colorful long fitted skirts and silk blouses to match.

"I must say Albert Coldsby knew how to choose a good look-ing staff," Sally said.

"Yes, I'm sure that was a prerequisite, except for poor Carol. He probably didn't have a choice there. Good laboratory technicians are hard to come by."

"It's strange to think that one of them might have killed Coldsby," commented Sally.

"They look so carefree."

"Carol doesn't. It might be sometime before she can forget her troubles." Nelda couldn't erase the memory of Shelby's face.

"Nelda, let's split up and I'll see if I can find my Haviland China. Meet me back here in two hours." Sally walked off in the direction of the china booths located in the back of the building.

"Good idea," said Nelda. "The furniture on display over there is calling me back. That fern stand with spool legs would be perfect in my den."

Nelda made a beeline for the furniture. She noticed the girls from the clinic had stopped to talk with a slender woman dressed in a smart blue suit. The woman's back was turned, so Nelda couldn't identify her. As Nelda inspected the fern stand, someone tapped her shoulder. She thought at first it was the owner of the furniture, but turning she discovered it was Joan Coldsby in a blue suit. Classy is the term that came to mind when Nelda looked at her. Her short black hair was styled to perfection. It made a nice frame for Joan's attractive, yet haughty face. Her brown eyes smiled at Nelda.

"Joan, how are you getting along?" Nelda asked.

The two women respected each other. They became friends after serving together on several charity committees. Nelda felt sympathy for Joan, because the town's people thought she might have instigated her husband's death.

"Nelda, I was hoping I'd get to talk to you. We had a private graveyard service for Albert yesterday. You know I'm not missing him very much, but I loathe his murderer."

"Yes, and now everyone at the clinic is under a cloud of suspicion, including my niece, Sue. It has me worried sick."

"All of us would benefit if the Sheriff found the killer quickly. Are you trying to help, Nelda? I remember you working with your husband."

"In a small way I think I'm helping, but we need some more information." She hoped Joan would take the hint.

"I can't talk anymore, now. Why don't you visit me at home about six? Bring your swimsuit, we'll have dinner by the pool."

Nelda perked up right away. This might be the break they needed. Joan was going to give her information about the killer; she just knew it.

"That will work out fine. My friend Sally is visiting me and will be gone by then.

Thanks for the invitation." She smiled to herself as Joan hurried down the aisle.

There was a rustle behind a large oak chifforobe. Nelda wondered if someone she knew might be standing there. She hurried to look behind the antique piece, but there was no one there. Nelda laughed and scolded herself for being so melodramatic. She certainly hadn't learned enough to be a threat to the murderer.

Two hours passed quickly. Nelda stood waiting for Sally with a fern stand and several old comic books to add to her collection. She was especially pleased with her purchase of a first edition *Catwoman* comic book that featured a fight between Lois Lane, Superman's girlfriend, and the Catwomen.

When Sally showed up several minutes later, she had nothing in her hand except her handbag.

"I can't believe you're empty handed," Nelda said in a scolding tone, "not after the lecture you gave me about being stingy."

Sally only smiled and motioned to a man standing behind her. He was pulling a small wagon piled high with packages.

"I didn't waste my time. I even found the Mother's Day plate you're missing."

"Good heavens," Nelda commented, "I just hope we can get it all in the station wagon. Was that plate expensive?"

"Not to worry, you old skinflint. It's my birthday present to you."

Nelda didn't like the idea of Sally spending money on her, but tried to make a joke of it. "I'll send you candy money when you're in the poor house," she responded.

They piled everything in Nelda's old Ford station wagon and headed home.

"After you left, Sally, I had a visit with Joan Coldsby. She invited me to visit her at 6:00 this evening. I'm not sure what she has on her mind."

"Did the sheriff get any information from her?" Sally asked, looking at Nelda over the bundles in her lap.

"Not that I know of. He was supposed to interview her yesterday." Nelda said. They arrived at Nelda's home and loaded up Sally's car for her trip back. As Nelda waved good-bye, her heart was heavy. Who would she have to confide in now?

At 5:45 p.m., Nelda headed out to visit Joan, who lived in the Great Oaks Estates, the most fashionable residential section in town. Albert Coldsby hadn't pinched pennies when he was spending them on himself. Nelda noticed all the lots in the subdivision were at least an acre; most of them were more. His house was of modern architecture with lots of glass windows and doors. It was certainly not the design Nelda would have chosen for this beautiful spot with all the splendid old oak trees. She knew a colonial home would have been perfect.

After stopping in the circular drive, she saw no movement of any kind. The home was dark and quiet. Nelda had an uneasy feeling, as though something was amiss; the shadows of the big oak trees did nothing to allay her fears. Cautiously, Nelda got out of the car and moved toward the front door. She rang the doorbell, and waited for a response. There was none.

Nelda glanced toward the driveway leading to the triple-car garage. There were no cars parked outside. She knew Joan had a housekeeper, but her car was gone. Anxiety started building in

Nelda's mind. It was not like Joan to miss an appointment. If something came up to change her plans, Joan would have called.

Following a curved path around the house, Nelda discovered a terraced brick patio leading to a large oval shaped swimming pool. Each tier of the deck was furnished with chairs and round tables. Some of the tables sported brightly colored umbrellas. One table near the edge of the pool held a portable telephone, a stack of telephone bills, napkins and a glass partially filled with liquid and ice.

Branches of the great oaks cast shadows across the water in the swimming pool. Nelda glanced out over the dark blue water. She thought she saw something move.

"Joan," she called, "Is that you?"

Moving in for a closer look, Nelda grew faint with fear. There was a limp figure in a red bathing suit bobbing up and down in the water. Nelda ran to the side of the pool and recognized it as Joan's.

Her first impulse was to run away as fast as she could, but suppose Joan could be saved? She hurriedly called 911, then tried to find something that would help her steer the body close to the side of the pool. On the far side of the pool she found a net with a long handle. She grabbed the net and waded out in the shallow end of the pool.

Struggling with both hands she hooked the net around one of Joan's arms. She had successfully guided Joan to the edge of the pool when she heard sirens leading up to the house. Holding the limp body steady, Nelda waited for the paramedics to make their appearance.

When the medics took over, Nelda phoned the Sheriff's office. "John, this is Nelda.

I'm over at Joan Coldsby's home. When I arrived a few minutes ago, I found Joan floating in the swimming pool. You'd better come right away; I think she's dead."

Nelda was completely overcome by her emotions. She hadn't been a close friend to Joan, but felt she understood the woman more than most people. Crying silently, she reached for a napkin on the table, then remembered it could be a crime scene. Nelda saw the drink sitting on the tray by the telephone. She viewed the liquid suspiciously, wondering if the drink were poisoned.

The medics' efforts on Joan's body were fruitless. They had given up by the time John and Deputy Hanks found their way to Nelda's side.

"What happened here?" John asked Nelda.

"Joan invited me here at 6:00 p.m., but as I explained on the phone, she was in the pool dead when I arrived.

"Was it just a social visit, Nelda, or did she have some information for you?"

"She hinted that she did have some information for me." Nelda was feeling faint and sat down in a chair.

"When did she call with the invitation?" John asked, looking at the things on the table.

"She didn't call; I saw her at the antique show in Smitherton. It was about 1:30 p.m.

"Was she still there when you left the show?" he asked, making notes in a notebook.

"I don't know. Sally and I left a little after 3:00 p.m.." Nelda wished she hadn't gone to the antique show. Maybe then, Joan would still be alive.

"Of course it may not have been foul play. Something else may have happened to her," John said, looking over at the body on a stretcher.

"Did she tell you anything yesterday?" asked Nelda, trying to compose herself.

"No, she said she didn't have a clue as to who shot her husband." He tapped his pen on the side of his cheek.

Nelda glanced toward the tray where the drink was sitting. "There were two drinks sitting on that tray."

"How do you know that? Those two wet rings may have been made by the same glass," he said, moving in for a closer look.

"If you'll notice, John, one ring is smaller than the other."

"We'll photograph the tray and then take the drink to be analyzed."

"Have you made any progress at all with the case?" Nelda questioned, averting her eyes from the body.

Before John could answer, Hanks interrupted them. "Look what I found in the bottom of the pool." He held up a pool leaf screen containing a fluted wineglass.

"The bottom of that wine glass probably fits the ring on this tray," Nelda said. "I wonder what happened to the bottle of wine."

"And which glass contained Joan's drink," John said.

"We'll have to wait for those answers, but you haven't given me a progress report."

Nelda got up to leave.

"I was trying to delay the news, Nelda, because it's not what you want to hear."

"What is it?" Nelda clenched her fist and waited.

"The fingerprints of Sue's fiancé, Steve Morris, were found on the door casing of the examination room where Coldsby was killed." The words rushed out of his mouth like a bad taste.

Nelda was shocked and her face must have shown it. She wanted to reach for a chair, but instead sat on the ground.

"Steve was in Sue's car when he went to the clinic. I have a witness who saw the car there," John said.

"What are you going to do?" whispered Nelda. How was Sue going to react to this? she wondered.

"I'm sorry, but I've had to bring Steve in for questioning." John's eyes looked troubled.

"That's not possible; he's not even here. He won't be back until tonight."

"You're wrong, Nelda. We found him within a few blocks of here only thirty minutes ago."

CHAPTER EIGHT

Walter Buys Clinic

When Nelda arrived home, Sue was waiting for her. She didn't have time to open the door before Sue was standing next to her, sobbing. Of course she knew what that was all about.

"Slow down, Sue. I know why you're upset, but Steve's only at the sheriff's office for questioning."

"He didn't do it," she said wiping her eyes. "And I just heard on the radio about Joan's death. That must have been terrible for you to find her."

"Joan's death is a real tragedy, but we've got to solve one problem at a time. We're going to the Sheriff's office right this minute. I want you and Steve to tell the sheriff everything you know, and be truthful about it," Nelda declared.

"I've been truthful the whole time. I've never lied about anything," Sue said, wiping the tears from her face.

"The sheriff doesn't say the same about Steve. His fingerprints were found in the same room Coldsby was killed."

"I didn't know, but he had a good reason for being there," declared Sue, shedding new tears.

"There is never a good reason to lie. All that gets you is more trouble." Nelda didn't realize until this moment how upset she was with Sue and Steve. "Get in the car, Sue. I promised the sheriff I'd bring you in to talk to him. We've got to get this business straightened out."

After they buckled their seat belts, Nelda drove down the street. The gloomy silence that hung like a curtain between them in the car was finally broken by Sue. "Why are you mad at me, Aunt Nelda?"

"You didn't tell me you went out to eat with Coldsby. I had to find out the hard way by showing the Christmas office picture to Wanda Baker at the Green Shallot."

"So that's what you're upset about?"

"It certainly is. I'm sure the sheriff will be interested too."

"Those were not dates. When I first started to work for Coldsby, he would ask me to drive to Smitherton with him to check on some patients in the hospital. On the way back, he would invite me to eat with him. That's all there was to it."

"Why did you stop going with him to make the rounds?"

"He started pushing me to have an affair. I also found out I didn't need to go with him on hospital rounds, because there were nurses at the hospital for that purpose."

"I suppose Steve was aware that all this was going on?"

"Yes, and I shouldn't have told him. I could have handled Coldsby myself."

Nelda quit talking, parked at the Sheriff's office, got out, slammed the car door and stalked in. Sue, teary-eyed, was right behind her.

Deputy Hanks saw them come in and knocked on the door to John's office. As John opened the door, Nelda saw Steve Morris sitting in a chair opposite the sheriff's desk. John didn't smile at Nelda or Sue.

"Take a chair out here, Sue," John said, motioning to some straight back chairs in the small waiting room. "Nelda, you come in here with me."

Nelda entered the office, closed the door and acknowledged Steve's presence with a nod. "Steve was just telling me what really happened on the night Coldsby died. Why don't you repeat what you said for Ms. Simmons, Steve?"

"I've been a fool, Nelda. I should have told the truth right off, but I was scared to death no one would believe me." His face was ashen and wet with perspiration.

"What is the truth, Steve?"

"When Sue told me Coldsby wouldn't leave her alone, I made an appointment to come and see him the night he was murdered."

"Did you call him at the clinic?"

"Yes."

"Who answered the phone?"

"Marcie answered and put me on hold. She said the doctor was with a patient, and would be with me in a minute. He picked up the phone a minute or two later. I made an appointment with him to talk about Sue and hung up."

"What time was the appointment?" Nelda asked.

"At nine, he said he'd be working late and to come on over."

"Go on," Nelda said.

"As you know, my car was out of commission, so I borrowed Sue's car. I drove to the clinic after leaving Sue's apartment. She didn't know I was going to see the Doc. That's why she didn't tell you about it."

"What time did you get there?" John asked.

"About five minutes to nine, if Sue's car clock is right."

"Did you see any cars?" Nelda inquired.

"The doctor's BMW was parked in the front."

"Then what?" Nelda asked. She knew it was important for Steve to remember everything about that night.

"He told me on the phone to come to the back of the clinic, and ring the bell. I did that and no one answered, so I opened the door and went in. Most of the lights were on in the clinic. I called several times, and then started looking in the rooms; that's when I found him. The doctor was just lying on the table buck naked. I knew he was dead and it scared the hell out of me. He looked like a wax figure in one of those horror museums. After staring at him for a few seconds, I grabbed the door casing, turned myself around and ran like 'Man O' War'. That's the truth, I swear it. That's why you found my fingerprints."

"How did you know he was dead?" Nelda asked.

"Okay, so I didn't know for sure, but he looked dead."

For several reasons Nelda hadn't formulated yet, she realized Steve was not good husband material for Sue, but at the same time she believed he was telling the truth.

John continued the questioning. "What was your reason for coming back from the horse races early?"

"Sue acted like she had a burr in her underwear. She kept hammering at me about where I was after I left her the night of the murder. I finally told her to get off my back, and that's when she said she wanted to come home."

"Where were you from twelve to five today?" John asked

"We were on our way back from Lafayette. Deputy Hanks picked me up just as Sue and I drove into town."

"Sue was with you the whole time?" Nelda asked.

"Of course, we were on our way back." Steve looked exhausted; his handsome face was furrowed with worry lines.

Nelda gave a sigh of relief. She felt certain Joan Coldsby had been murdered, and Steve couldn't have been involved in this crime.

"Steve, the secretary will write up your statement for your signature. I don't have enough evidence to arrest you, but I'm still looking. For your sake, I hope you've told me the truth."

Sue ran to Steve as he walked out of John's office and put her arms around him. Nelda could feel the tension between them as Sue walked him to the front door. This was a romance in distress.

While the two were saying goodbye, Nelda explained to John why Sue was seen eating out with Coldsby.

John called Sue into the office and closed the door. "Nelda has already told me about your meals with Coldsby, Sue. Were there others that went with him on his hospital rounds?"

"Yes, all but Carol and Walter."

"Even Marcie the secretary?" Walter gave Sue a quizzical look.

"Yes, when I first came to work for the clinic, Marcie went with him all the time. I think Marcie and Coldsby had something going a while back."

"Are you sure Violet went with him?" asked Nelda, wondering how Coldsby had the energy to expend on all those women.

"She couldn't stand to be around him very much, but Violet did her tour of duty when she first started working for him."

"When was this?" questioned Nelda.

"Four years ago. You see, when I came to work for the clinic, Violet became Walter's nurse."

"Why didn't Coldsby keep Violet on as his nurse?" John asked, standing up to stretch his long legs.

"Walter and I were both new at our jobs, and he wanted Walter to have the more experienced nurse. At least that's what he told us."

"Thanks for coming in Sue," John said, if you'll wait outside, I have just a few more things to take up with your aunt."

"All right, but I tell you Steve had nothing to do with Coldsby's death."

"I'm becoming more convinced of it too," he said opening the door for her.

Nelda got up; her back was hurting from John's hard little office chair. "Do you mean what you said?" asked Nelda as soon as Sue was gone.

"I sure do. Do you know what was in that glass and pitcher of liquid sitting on the tray by Ms. Coldsby's pool?"

"Poison," shot back Nelda without hesitation.

"No, it was the muscle relaxant, Baclofen. The drink probably caused Joan's muscles to become so relaxed she couldn't breathe."

"You sure found that out in a hurry. How did you do that?" Nelda asked in a surprised tone.

"One of the hospitals in Smitherton has a new lab that can identify chemicals right away. I had Carl take it to them as soon as we left the Coldsby residence." John had a smile of satisfaction on his face.

"But the autopsy hasn't been performed yet, has it?"

"No, not until tomorrow," he answered rubbing the back of his neck.

"What about the autopsy on Coldsby? Did you establish the time of his death?"

"I haven't had a chance to tell you what Coldsby had to eat the night he died and where the food came from."

"I'm listening," Nelda said getting a little anxious about Sue in the waiting room.

"He went to the Dairy Queen on Second Street at five o'clock, picked up a hamburger, chocolate malt and fries. He took the meal home to eat."

"How did you find that out?"

"He ordered it to go. The girl at Dairy Queen remembered him picking it up. Then, Ms. Coldsby found the remains of his hamburger on the kitchen table when she came home from her trip. She called me to come over and see for myself."

"At least now we have a time frame for his death," Nelda said.

"The coroner thinks he died between seven-thirty and nine p.m.," John responded.

"Marcie and Sue are the only ones with alibis," Nelda remarked.

"One other thing," John continued, "all those telephone calls from Aspen, Colorado were circled on Ms. Coldsby's telephone bills."

"I wonder what it all means. Do you suppose she wanted to show those to me?" Nelda asked beginning to edge toward the door.

"I don't know, but I'm certainly going to find out about those calls. There might be a direct link to the killer."

"How long ago were those first calls made from Aspen?"

"Eight years ago," John said, sitting on the edge of his desk. "The last ones were last summer."

Nelda leaned against the wall looking pensive. "Too bad I didn't get to talk to Joan. I believe there was someone who wanted to make sure of that."

"Nelda, if you're in any danger, I want you to stop digging for clues right now. I appreciate your help, but not at the expense of you getting hurt, or worse." His worried look made Nelda respond quickly.

"There's no need to worry. Whoever did this thinks I don't know anything; the sad part is I haven't a clue."

"I'm sure Steve will be off the hook after we get the autopsy report back on Joan Coldsby's body," John said. "Those two deaths are connected."

"I'm going to take Sue home now. At least I can breathe easier about her involvement with the doctor."

"Call me if you hear or see anything," John said, opening the door to his office. "It's going to be pure hell around here when the media find out about the murder of Ms. Coldsby. People will begin to wonder if I can handle this job."

"The murderer will be caught, it's just a matter of time," Nelda assured John. She hoped, for everyone's sake, she told the truth.

She joined Sue in the outer office, and they made the short trip back to her house. Stopping in the driveway, she looked at Sue bathed in the glow of the street light, and realized how bone weary her niece was. Sue looked like a disheveled orphan with her long blonde hair tangled, and dark shadows under her eyes. Nelda had the urge to tuck her in bed like she did when she was a little girl."

"Sue I want you to go home and right to bed."

"I'm too wound up, Aunt Nelda. A new doctor is supposed to come in tomorrow. She's taking Coldsby's place. I don't know how the death of Joan is going to affect the clinic."

"Who's running the clinic now?"

"Walter. Joan had a financial agreement with him. She signed the papers for him to buy the clinic before she was killed. He said the payment terms were some he could handle."

"Good news for Walter. He's getting the whole business instead of a partnership. Are all the employees staying on?"

"Yes, with a small raise, and more vacation days. Even Carol has something to smile about," Sue said, leaning her head back on the car seat.

"How did you go about taking vacations when Coldsby was alive?" Did you take turns?" Nelda knew she should let Sue go, but felt like she was on to something.

"No! Coldsby shut the place down. He used this time to make repairs to the clinic. If any of our patients had an emergency, a doctor across town would handle it."

"When Coldsby was the only doctor in the clinic, did he close it until he got back from vacation?"

"That's the way I understand it, I wasn't there then," Sue said.

"Do you know where Coldsby went on his vacations?"

"Sometimes he'd mention a trip, but mostly he didn't talk about them. Why are you asking all these questions, Aunt Nelda?"

"It might be important to the case."

"Probably the only one that can answer that now is Marcie. She made all his vacation plans including picking up the plane tickets."

Suddenly, the events of the day got the better of Nelda. She felt sad and tired. "I've got to go in and get some rest, Sue. I'm sorry I got mad at you, but it's just because I was so worried about you. Would you like to spend the night with me?"

"No, Aunt Nelda. I love you too, but I'd better get home so I can get going early tomorrow. I'm sorry Steve got into all this trouble over me."

"It's certainly not your fault. He'll be fine if he's telling the truth."

Sue trudged wearily to her car. Nelda went into her house by a side door. She listened for sounds within the house before walking to her bedroom. For the first time in many years, she slept with a night light on in the hall.

CHAPTER NINE

Let The Reader Beware

The sun was shining brightly when Nelda finally woke up the next morning. She sniffed the air for the aroma of coffee, but realized she forgot to set the timer on the coffeepot. After slipping on her robe, she made for the kitchen and remedied that.

While the coffee was brewing, Nelda retrieved the newspaper from the front lawn. She gave a gasp as she unfolded the paper. On the front page was a large picture of her in Joan Coldsby's swimming pool holding Joan's body. The phone rang before she could read the caption under the picture. It was Sue.

"Hello," she said still staring at the picture.

"Aunt Nelda! Have you seen the morning paper?"

"I just opened it. I don't even remember anyone taking that picture. This is terrible. How could the *Gazette* print a thing like that."

"Come on; a corpse on the front page sells big time."

"I'll call you back later, Sue. I haven't read it yet."

Nelda read through the whole article, but it didn't mention one word about murder or the drug in the drink. When the autopsy report came back to John, the Gazette would have another front page sensation to print. Nelda knew Joan was murdered.

She scanned the rest of the paper while drinking her coffee. Joan's death wasn't listed in the obituary column...not enough time, Nelda thought. Her brother George, and two nieces were

Joan's survivors. Nelda wondered when they would have the funeral.

She hurriedly fixed a bowl of oatmeal, ate it, and dressed. The best part of the day was slipping by. Her flowers needed attention. While watering her pink and white caladiums an old blue Chevrolet truck drove up. Attached to the truck was a trailer loaded with mowing and trimming equipment. Dennis Toliver stepped out of the truck.

"Hi, Ms. Simmons," Dennis said. Looks like you made the newspaper again. How do you manage to come up with all those dead bodies?"

Nelda turned off the hose and looked at Dennis. He was a clean-cut young man with brown hair streaked blonde from the sun. He'd been her student several years back, and went on to the university to receive a BS degree in archaeology. Of course he couldn't get a job in that field with just a BS, so here he was mowing yards and saving money for another degree.

"Seems to be a habit, Dennis. Weren't you her gardener?"

"Yardman. In fact I mowed her lawn a couple of hours before you found her in the pool."

"You did! Well, did you tell the sheriff about it?"

"There was nothing for me to report. However, she did have a visitor while I was there. Dr. Goodman left in a big hurry about 4:00 p.m. She walked him out to his car."

"It would be a good idea to tell the sheriff. Let him decide if it's unimportant."

Nelda was happy Walter bought the clinic before Joan died. Joan's brother, George, was a tough old business man.

"Come on in Dennis," said Nelda changing the subject. "I've got something to show you. I bought it at the antique show." Nelda was grinning with pleasure as they entered the house. She and Dennis had a common interest, comic book collecting.

Nelda hadn't unpacked her purchases. She retrieved her newly acquired *Catwoman* comic book from the dining room table, and showed it to Dennis. He thumbed through the book in reverence.

"How many *Catwoman* comic books do you have now?"

"Only three counting this one. Would you like to see them?"

"Yes, I sure would. I'm sorry I couldn't go to the antique show, but I was behind with my mowing, because of the rain last week. I'd like to add to my *Batman* series."

Nelda went to the hall closet and pulled out the box of comic books. She had them filed by name and year. The box had a top, but even so the books were full of dust.

Some of the dust from the top of the box filled the air as she set the books on the dining room table. Lying on top was a comic book she had never seen before.

"Oh God!" she said as she stared at the book.

"What?" asked Dennis with concern.

"That!" she said pointing to the comic book on top of the box.

It was a horror reprint titled "Deadmen Don't Talk" with its cover showing a man with a rag stuck in his mouth and a bullet hole in his forehead. Blood filled his eyes in living color. Stuck on the edge of the cover was a note with a Latin phrase, *Caveat lector,* written in block-red colors.

"What in the heck does that mean?" Dennis asked peering at the note.

"Let the reader beware," answered Nelda in quivering tones.

"Gruesome," said Dennis. "I wouldn't have thought this comic was your style."

"It's not, I don't know how this got into the box," said Nelda, wondering if this was one of Sally's attempts at a practical joke. If not.....maybe Sue put it there. But of course, neither one of them knew about the Latin note found on Coldsby's body.

She hurriedly found the other two issues of *Catwoman.* The dust sent her into a sneezing frenzy, while Dennis flipped through them oblivious to the cause of her stress.

"Dennis," she said, in between sneezes, "The next time we have a rainy spell, and you can't work outside, could I hire you to take these comic books to the garage and clean them?"

"You bet, I would enjoy that. I guess I'd better get busy mowing your lawn. Thanks again for sharing *Catwoman* with me."

Nelda had Dennis put the comic books back into the closet except for the horror one and the note in Latin. She intended to call Sally about it.

Her sneezing didn't abate. She tried an over-the-counter nose spray to no avail.

Finally, she decided to get professional help, and called Dr. Goodman. Marcie answered the phone.

"Marcie, this is Nelda. I'm having a terrible time with my allergies. Do you suppose Walter could squeeze me in between his appointments?"

"Sure, Nelda. Come in about one and he'll be able to see you then."

"Thanks, Marcie." Nelda hated that she even had to go in. A few years back her doctor would just call a prescription to the drug store, and she could pick it up without seeing him. But the danger of lawsuits had changed all that.

Nelda sniffled through the rest of the morning. She called Sally before she left for the clinic. There was no answer.

The parking lot was full of cars when Nelda arrived at the clinic. The new doctor was getting a good reception. She could imagine patients stuck in every little examining room on the premises. Parking her old station wagon under a tree, she hurried inside.

Her watch showed one 1:00 p.m.

In between sneezes, Nelda chatted with Marcie, who wanted to know all about Joan's death. Nelda deliberately changed the subject. "Marcie what's the new doctor's name?"

"Elizabeth Gomez, and we really like her. She's smart and fun to be around."

"I'm glad to hear it. Looks like Walter is the head rooster with a lot of hens around him."

"He's certainly in the minority, but I don't think he minds."

At last, Violet came to the reception room door and guided

Nelda to one of those little examining rooms. "Something got your allergies going, Nelda?" asked Violet.

"It was some dust from those old comic books."

"Oh, do your collect them?"

"Yes, we talked about it last year, remember?"

"Sure, I had forgotten. Listen, Walter will be here in a minute. We're really swamped today." She left the small room, closing the door as she walked out.

Nelda noticed Violet looked especially pretty. She had toned down her makeup and her hair wasn't teased to resemble a haystack. Had she talked Walter into making the big leap? she wondered. Nelda had plenty of time to think about it. Twenty minutes passed before Walter came into the examining room. She had used all her tissues and was now working on a box that belonged to the clinic. Nelda was just about to walk out, allergies or no allergies, when Walter walked in.

"Good afternoon, Nelda. I never expected to see you here today. I can see by your red nose there is something in the air."

"This time it's dust, Walter. You didn't have to go to medical school to figure out what's wrong with me today did you?" Nelda said while wiping her nose.

"No, but I'll fix you up. I have some sample tablets you can take right now, and I'll write out a prescription for later."

"Thank you Walter. I appreciate your help."

"Nelda, I know how upset you must have been to find Joan's body in the pool. The odd part was that I did some business with her only two hours earlier."

"I tell you Walter, it was a real shock. I've always liked and admired Joan."

"Me too, I just hope it wasn't foul play."

"Why, do you think it might be murder?"

"I wasn't her doctor, Nelda, but Albert always said she was as healthy as Arnold Schwarzenegger."

"The Sheriff doesn't know why she died, or at least he didn't know when I talked to him last."

"When will this business ever end?" Walter said shaking his head.

"Let's talk about something we can be happy about," Nelda said. "Congratulations on becoming the new owner of the clinic, Walter. You deserve the break."

Walter beamed. "I should have known Sue would keep you informed of events here.

Thanks Nelda. My dream was to own a clinic and have a virtuous wife, and now I'll have both of those. Violet and I are going to get married."

Fifty percent of a dream is not bad, Nelda thought. Out loud she said "I'm happy for you."

As soon as Nelda settled her account for the visit, she made a beeline for Sue's side of the clinic. She waited out in the hall for Sue to come by. Finally Sue walked briskly toward the reception area.

"Sue," Nelda called.

She whirled around and faced Nelda. "What's wrong, Aunt Nelda. They didn't pick up Steve again did they?

"No, nothing like that. It's about me this time. My allergies were acting up and I needed to see Walter."

"Good....I mean."

"I know what you mean," Nelda said. "Let me ask you a question, Sue. Have you every bought me a comic book?"

"No, you always told me you wanted to pick them out yourself. Besides that, I couldn't afford to. Why?"

"I found an strange one in my box of comic books; I don't know how it got there."

"It wasn't me... maybe Sally. I've got to get back to work." Over her shoulder she said "See you later." Sue whisked off, leaving Nelda alone in the hall.

Still deep in thought, Nelda stopped at the drugstore to fill her prescription and made her way back home. She dialed Sally's number as soon as she got home. The phone rang several times before Sally picked it up.

"Hello."

"Sally, it's me. How was your trip home?"

"Fine, just fine. What's wrong, Nelda? Has anything happened since I left?"

"I'm okay, but things have been happening. Steve was picked up for questioning in the murder of Albert Coldsby, and now Albert's wife, Joan, is dead."

"My God! did he kill them both?"

"He didn't kill either one."

"Well, why was he brought in?"

"Steve went to talk to Albert and left his fingerprints in the room where the murder took place. John didn't have enough evidence to hold him."

"What happened to Joan? Weren't you supposed to visit her late yesterday?"

"I did visit her, and found her floating in the swimming pool."

"Oh, Nelda, how horrible. You think it's murder don't you?"

"Yes."

"I'm coming back to stay with you until this is over. I think you're in danger."

Nelda noted Sally's genuine concern, but wouldn't comment until she asked the question she had called to ask.

"Sally did you buy a comic book for me, and put it with the others in the hall closet?"

"Good heavens no. That birthday plate I gave you cost an arm and a leg. I had to save some money for myself."

She decided not to tell Sally about the Latin note or what kind of comic it was.

"Well, somebody did and it worries me that neither you nor Sue put it there. You are the only two that are supposed to have access to this house."

"You're joking. That front door key is hidden under a flower pot, and half the people in town know where it is. You're about as safe in that house as Central Park. I'm coming back tomorrow and bringing Sugar."

"Why do you want to bring that old dog?"

"You know you love him, and he's a good watchdog. He's perfectly trained."

"My allergies are acting up and Sugar would make them worse. You stay home and I'll be fine."

"You're not allergic to Sugar. You've been in my house many times, and it didn't bother you at all."

"Okay," said Nelda giving up the fight. She did like that old chocolate Labrador Retriever, and having Sally around would be a comfort.

She told Sally good-bye, and immediately went to look under the flower pot where she hid her front door key. It wasn't there. She looked under all the flower pots, but the key had vanished.

CHAPTER
TEN

Lunch With Mary

Nelda had a terrible time falling asleep. She heard sounds from every part of the house. Settling, she reasoned, and nothing more. The business with the comic book was another matter. Someone came into her home to intimidate her with that book, and just thinking about it made her furious. She'd get the locks changed tomorrow to prevent a return visit. Finally, after an hour of rolling and twisting she turned on the bedside lamp and read three chapters of *The Inner Game Of Tennis* by W. Timothy Gallaway, before falling asleep.

When she woke up, the sun was streaming through the bedroom window. She scolded herself for sleeping so late. Glancing out the window, she realized it was going to be a gorgeous day. Maybe, she could put some of that psychological reasoning she read about in the tennis book to use. The phone rang as she slipped on her Adidas tennis shoes. It was Janet Gibbons reminding her of their tennis match this morning.

Nelda tried to play tennis at least three times a week in good weather. She loved the sport, but found her sense of concentration was lacking in most of her matches. Her mind invariably left the match and started working on some problem she needed to solve. She hoped by reading Gallaway's book she could learn to focus on her game.

She retrieved the morning paper, spread it out on the kitchen table, and read it as she ate her usual breakfast of oatmeal, orange juice, toast and coffee. For some reason the food tasted better than ever today. Maybe her breakfast would be more enjoyable if she waited until this time of day to eat instead of the crack of dawn.

The obituary column about Joan Coldsby was quite lengthy. Nelda was not surprised to learn that Joan had been involved with every charity in town. It's a good thing Joan had inherited money, she thought, because being married to that skinflint, Albert, would have been a detriment to her generous nature. The funeral was set for tomorrow afternoon. Nelda intended to be there.

Finishing up her bathroom routine by brushing her teeth, Nelda grabbed her tennis bag, racquet and water bottle, before heading to the courts. It was five minutes to nine when Nelda got to the club, early as usual. An aerobics class was in process. People should exercise sensibly, thought Nelda, and sensible exercise didn't include gyrating on the floor.

Inside the clubhouse, she signed in while chatting with several younger members. Most of them were drinking their breakfast out of a can. Nelda wished she could remember the health article she had read about the dangers of drinking from aluminum cans, or maybe that was cooking with aluminum. Oh well, next they would probably find something wrong with glass containers too.

Janet Gibbons finally arrived ten minutes late. Nelda didn't think she looked anything like her Aunt Marcie, Coldsby's secretary at the clinic. She was short, stout, had a pug nose and wore her long black hair in a pony tail. Certainly not the physique of a tennis player, but it didn't stop her from playing a good game. The only time Nelda could beat her was when Janet was having a bad day.

"Sorry I'm late. I had to go to Aunt Marcie's to borrow a racket; mine is in the shop. Then, wouldn't you know, Grandma Gibbons forgot where she put it."

"Grandma's memory is pretty bad?"

"Yes, bless her heart. The doctor says she has Alzheimer's disease."

"I'm sorry to hear that. I suppose Marcie must have a hard time communicating with her."

"No, but she doesn't try very hard. She just leaves her with someone to play movies for her. Grandma Gibbons will watch them all day."

"Well, let's get going. I feel pretty lucky today."

Betsy's response was to laugh, which didn't build Nelda's confidence. They walked out to court four. Both sported white tennis skirts and shirts; there the resemblance ended. Nelda's skirt was almost to her knees, while Janet's barely covered her buttocks. The older woman was glad there were no men around to view this spectacle. She felt sure Janet's bottom had grown some since she purchased the skirt, because her skimpy panties were in full view each time Janet reached down for a ball.

The match didn't go well for Nelda. Instead of quieting the mind and stroking the ball, she was stroking the ball first. It seemed she was getting chapter four of Gallaway's book mixed up with chapter three. Then there was something Janet said about Marcie's mother that kept nagging at her. The mother couldn't remember things, and yet she was supposed to be Marcie's alibi at the time of Coldsby's murder. There was certainly no alibi there, if this were true.

When the slaughter was over, Nelda thanked Janet for the exercise, and realized a few lessons along with Gallwey's book might be in order. Returning home, Nelda showered, dressed and then called a locksmith she knew, Don Barnes. She wanted the locks changed before Sally arrived. The earliest he could come out was the next day. That would have to do, she reasoned. Whoever it was that left the threatening comic book would know she was on guard now. Still, Nelda worried that they would return before the locks were changed.

Picking up her handbag, Nelda crawled into her station wagon and headed for Sam's Club. Sugar would be needing something to sleep on. She knew if he didn't have a bed, he'd lay with his back touching one of her chairs or sofa. Those old brown hairs just wouldn't do all over the furniture.

Nelda parked her station wagon as close as she could to the front of the store. She recognized Dennis's pickup truck, because his lawn mowing equipment was secured in the back of it. If she saw him, she'd remind him of his promise to get rid of the dust on the old comic books.

The picture they had taken to identify her at Sam's was the worse thing she had ever seen. Nelda groaned every time she had to show it. It was worse than one of the tintypes of her early ancestors. While she was digging around in her purse trying to find it, she came across the Christmas picture Sue had given her of the employees at the clinic. There were three people in the back row that she hadn't bothered to identify. She would ask Sue who they were. Two of them looked of Mexican descent, but the third one's face was partially obscured by Walter's head. Nelda stuck it back in her purse and continued the search for the club card. She finally located it wrapped up in a tissue. After flashing her unsightly card to a worker, she gained entry into the store. Nelda hurried to the pet supplies in the back. She was examining some canvas covered dog beds when she heard someone call her name. It was Dennis, just the person she wanted to see.

"Hi, Ms. Simmons. Getting a dog?"

"No, my friend Sally is coming to visit with her Lab and I'm going to buy a bed for it. But I'm glad I ran into you, because I need those comic books cleaned. How about doing that in the next couple of days."

"No problem, the grounds are so wet from the last rain I can't work out in the yards anyway. I'm free late this afternoon."

"Good, see you then."

Nelda chose a dog bed with a dark brown cover. She put it on the floor and tested it for comfort by sitting on it. It felt like the bed was stuffed with little balls of Styrofoam. She decided she wouldn't trade it for her tension-ease inner spring mattress, but a dog might find it better than the hardwood floor.

With the bed loaded up, Nelda headed for the restaurant area in the Farmer's Market. After all the exercise, she found she was

famished. Of course, there was another reason for her destination
too. What had ever happened to Roberto Sanchez? The man who
fled the country because he was wanted for questioning in the
death of Dr. Coldsby. Was he still in Mexico or had he returned?
His wife, Mary, might still work at the market. If she did, maybe
some of Nelda's questions would be answered and she could eliminate a possible suspect in the Coldsby murders.

The restaurant in the Market was crowded with patrons, because of its good food and the scarcity of eating places. Nelda
stood in line for fifteen minutes before she was seated. Ordinarily
she wouldn't have tolerated such a wait, but she had this burning
desire to end this part of the investigation involving Roberto
Sanchez.

After she was seated, she placed her order for a green salad
with Arcadian dressing, fish court-bouillon with rice, and peach-
glazed cake. There was just a tinge of guilt for not waiting for Sally
to have this delectable meal, but it didn't last past the first course.
By coffee and cake time the "Sleuthhound," as Sheriff Moore re-
ferred to Nelda, spied Mary Sanchez coming out of the kitchen.
Leaving the table she waited by the kitchen doors so she could talk
to her when she returned to the kitchen. Mary sailed by in a few
minutes. Nelda grabbed her arm. The startled younger woman
almost dropped the tray of dirty dishes.

"I'm sorry, I didn't mean to startle you."

There was recognition in Mary's eyes, but no smile for Nelda.
"Why are you here? Are you going to say that Roberto is responsible for Mrs. Coldsby's death too?"

"What's wrong Mary? Have I ever accused your husband of
Dr. Coldsby's death?"

"No, but as long as the person who did it is out there, I will
not have a husband. He will not come back from Mexico. It is
hard to make a living for us without him, and I am lonesome."
Mary's face was thin and lined with worry. Tears filled her dark
eyes as she blinked hard to keep them back.

"I'm sure he can come back without being arrested," Nelda

said with compassion. "Would you like to go with me to talk to the sheriff?"

"Can you go with me Tuesday?" Mary asked.

"Yes I can. You meet me there at 2:00 p.m."

"I'm sorry I was not friendly with you. You were so good to my Theresa and I have not forgotten. I must go now, but I will see you next Tuesday."

Nelda watched Mary disappear beyond the swinging doors of the mammoth kitchen. She was determined to help this unfortunate family.

Paying the bill turned out to take almost as long as being seated. Stearn could do with another good restaurant, and soon!

It was almost three before she got home. Oh no! Sally was sitting in the driveway locked out. Nelda jumped out of the station wagon and walked to Sally's car. That's when she was hit from behind by eighty-five pounds of dark brown dog. Down she went into the yellow chrysanthemums with Sugar adding insult to injury by licking her face.

"Sally, get this horse off of me," she cried. "I must have been mad to let you bring him here."

"Come," shouted Sally to Sugar. The dog obeyed in an instant.

"Thank goodness for obedience school," Nelda said as she scrambled out of the flower bed. Straightening the plants, she realized there was no serious damage to the plants or to herself. "Didn't mean to be so gruff, but I must say Sugar gave me a start. I'm sorry you were locked out; should have gotten home sooner."

"We haven't been here long. I'm just glad you stopped hiding the key for the whole town to use."

Nelda helped Sally bring in her luggage and dog paraphernalia: dog biscuits, food, blanket and leash. Thank goodness Sally hadn't brought Sugar's bed. Returning things to stores was not high on Nelda's entertainment list.

"You want to swap places with the cars, so you can put yours in the garage?" Sally asked.

"No, this afternoon Dennis Toliver will clean my comic books in the garage. You can put yours in there when he gets through."

Sugar sniffed everything in the house. Nelda wondered if he'd had an opportunity to relieve himself outside. No need to worry she decided. Sally was used to taking care of details.

"I have something I bought for Sugar at Sam's. I hope he's going to like it so I can keep all his brown hair off the furniture."

"Don't tell me you bought him a coat." Sally laughed at her own joke.

"No, it's a comfortable bed. I tried it out by sitting on it."

"That's sweet, Nelda, but I intended for him to sleep on the back porch. It's not cold and he'll let us know if we have any unwanted guest."

"Well, he can use it when he's inside." Seeing the dog zonked out on the floor, Nelda had her doubts about Sugar turning into a vicious dog.

CHAPTER ELEVEN

Looking for Sugar

Before Sally unpacked, she started grilling Nelda about what had happened in her absence.

"Now let me get this straight. After I left, you went over to Joan Coldsby's house and found her dead in the pool. Both you and the Sheriff think she was murdered?"

"That's right," answered Nelda. "We think there was something in her drink. The autopsy report should be back by now. John will call me with the results."

"If she was murdered, that's going to rule out Sue's boyfriend and Berto Sanchez," Sally reasoned.

"We think both murders were committed by the same person. Neither Berto nor Steve were in town at the time," agreed Nelda.

Nelda was impressed by Sally's ability to remember the people and events in this case. She smiled indulgently when Sally pulled out a small notebook to jot down some comments. Had she created another sleuth, or did Sally intend to protect her from the unknown? Neither idea appealed to Nelda, who knew she could solve the case without involving Sally. Her old friend certainly couldn't protect her.

"Have any more of the original suspects been eliminated?" asked Sally.

"Let's just run through the list and see what we have. We can scratch off Sue and Steve. They were coming back from the horse races when Joan was killed."

Sally scratched Sugar's ear and listened attentively. Her pen was poised over the little notebook.

"We already know," Nelda continued, "that Roberto wasn't around when Joan died; he was in Mexico. And instead of poor Joan being a suspect, she has become a victim."

Nelda paused and watched with delight as the glass sun-catchers, hanging from the top of her window, caught the late evening rays of sunlight. They glowed in hues of orange, blue, green, purple and yellow. Reluctantly, she turned her attention back to the possible list of suspects.

"Marcie Gibbons used her mother as an alibi. After talking with her niece, I don't believe that alibi will hold up."

"Why?" questioned Sally.

"According to her niece, Marcie's mother has a terrible memory. If that's the case, she couldn't remember if Marcie was home at the time of the murders."

"Do you think Joan was a scorned woman?" Sally asked.

"I think so. However, she was one of the few people who had any regrets about Coldsby's death."

"What about Walter and Violet? They certainly stood to gain by Albert's death."

"You mean by being able to buy the business?"

"Yes."

"But did they know that for sure?" Nelda said, opening the refrigerator to get ground beef out for a meat loaf. She looked down to find Sugar peering into the lower part. Nelda laughed at his insatiable curiosity.

"It's hard to concentrate on the case," Sally said grinning, "with that dog's shenanigans."

"Getting back to Walter," Nelda continued, "he had no way of knowing Joan was going to sell him the business. I just don't think he would have committed murder to own a business. Violet doesn't seem to have a good reason for murder either."

Sally frowned at the last name on her list, Carol Scrubbs. "Coldsby threatened to fire Carol, because she was exposed to AIDS. She was feeling low, and sometimes depression can lead to strange behavior."

"That's true," agreed Nelda. "Also, no alibi."

They were interrupted by a knock on the door. Nelda opened it to find Dennis standing there with a wide grin. He looked like a high school kid in his faded blue jeans and "Save the Earth" tee shirt.

"Hi Ms. Simmons, I'm all ready to do the dirty work for you." He spied Sally sitting in the kitchen, and walked over to give her a hug.

Sugar growled as he approached. "Watch it Dennis," Sally cautioned. "He's been known to nip at a person that doesn't pay attention to his growl. Take a piece of this ground meat and see if that changes his attitude."

The dog sniffed the meat suspiciously before wolfing it down. Then he allowed Dennis to approach Sally.

Nelda didn't think much of Sally's approach to the dog problem, but didn't want to discuss it in front of Dennis. Instead, she directed him to the closet where the comic books were stored, and opened the back door so he could take them out to the garage for cleaning.

Sally watched Nelda out of the corner of her eye. She knew her friend was miffed about something. "All right, out with it Nelda. What are you upset about?"

"I don't think it's a good idea for you to have a stranger bribe your dog."

"You mean I should train him as you would a child, not to take candy from a stranger?"

"That's right. If you want him to be any kind of a watch dog, he shouldn't be friendly with everyone."

"I suppose you're right. I just have a hard time thinking of my ex-students as strangers."

Nelda was sorry she had flared up at Sally. They were such

opposites. Her friend was extravagant, flighty and always assumed the best about everyone, never looking beyond their facade.

"Come on Sally, let's have a little glass of wine while I fix us a good old meat loaf." Pulling out two of her prettiest wine glasses, she poured generous servings of blush into each glass.

Congeniality reigned supreme as both helped prepare the evening meal of meat loaf, tarragon potatoes, peas and onions, and fruit in cassis. Not to be forgotten, Sugar barked for his bowl of dinner. He was served dog chow out on the back porch.

A couple of hours later Dennis returned with the clean comic books. Nelda paid him for his time and he left with his new friend, Sugar, following him to the backyard gate. She watched as he gave the "now" friendly dog a pat on his head before leaving.

After dinner, Sally discussed Joan's upcoming funeral. "I'm not going with you, Nelda, unless you just want me to keep you company."

"No, that won't be necessary; Sue will pick me up. We'll probably sit with the employees from the clinic."

"Isn't that something?"

"What?"

"Probably the person who killed her will be sitting near you."

"Probably so."

"I'm going to turn in early, Nelda. I'll just put Sugar out in the back yard."

"Let's not let the dog bed go to waste," her practical friend replied. Nelda gathered up the canvas bed and put it down by Sugar on the back porch. He sniffed the brown canvas and gingerly sank down in the middle of it as she watched with satisfaction.

The night sounds Nelda heard, as she periodically woke up, were no different than she ordinarily experienced except for the incessant barking of her next door neighbor's collie, Dollie. She must be barking at everything that moves including the branches on the trees, Nelda thought. But she was afraid not to investigate. Reluctantly, she pulled on her robe and was feeling around for her slippers when the barking stopped. Nelda sighed, pulled off her robe, patted her feather pillow smooth and went back to sleep.

A mocking bird singing in a tree next to Nelda's bedroom window woke her up. Slipping into her robe and slippers, she hurried to the kitchen to grind the Colombian coffee beans. She knew the beans should be ground right before you make the coffee for the best taste. When that was taken care of, she rushed to the back door to see how Sugar had fared during the night. She stepped out on the back porch and called his name. No dog appeared. Hurrying out into the yard she called louder, still no Sugar, only Dolly from next door acknowledged her call. Finally, Nelda ran to the back gate; it was open. What was she going to tell Sally? Sugar was gone.

She turned to find Sally standing on the back porch. "Now, please don't get too upset Sally, but Sugar's gone. I can't imagine how that back gate came open, because I saw Dennis latch it."

Sally's eyes filled with tears. "We've got to do something Nelda. That poor baby, I know he's scared to death. His tags aren't even for this area. . . I won't rest until we locate him."

"Don't worry, let's get dressed and walk the neighborhood. As soon as the dog pound opens, we'll call to see if they have him."

"The dog pound? Oh my God! They'll kill him before we get there. I heard they are so overcrowded that they put them to death right away." Sally wrung her hands in despair.

Nelda could see she had to take control, before her friend went into hysterics. "Sally, get dressed. Now! Five minutes; that's an order."

Five minutes later they were walking down the street looking for Sugar. Nelda had a travel mug filled with coffee, but Sally was too worked up to drink anything.

"Now if you were Sugar, Sally, where would you go?"

"I wouldn't go anywhere because I would be perfectly content. Sugar had everything he needed, plenty of food and love."

"He might want to visit other dogs."

"All that amorous stuff has been fixed. That dog wants only to associate with humans."

They called and looked for forty minutes in all directions, but no Sugar. Finally, Nelda decided to call some neighbors, so they traipsed back home.

"He's such a beautiful dog; I just know someone stole him. No more Sugar." Sally moaned with tears streaming down her face.

"Stop saying that Sally. Believe it or not some people are not terribly fond of dogs, that's why we should call the pound as soon as it opens at 8:00 a.m."

"It's almost that time now."

"I've got time to call a couple of neighbors before then."

On the eighth call Nelda received a positive response from the Hillmans who lived across Sandy Creek several blocks away.

Sally was beside herself with happiness. She stood with her hands clutching Nelda's arm. "Well what did they say, tell me quick."

"They heard their dog barking, got up to see what it was all about, and that's when they saw Sugar, all wet from wading the creek. They opened the garage door, lured him inside with dog bones, then closed the door."

"Is he all right? What were they going to do to him?"

"Nothing, they were waiting until the animal shelter opened, so they could take him there."

"I'm so thankful. Can we go get him now?"

"Yes."

"Do you want to move your car so I can get mine out?" Sally inquired. "He might get yours all messed up if he's wet."

"Oh no, I'll grab an old blanket to spread out in the back."

"Let's hurry; I know he's scared."

Sally and Nelda scurried to Nelda's old wagon. They were rolling down the street when Nelda realized her friend hadn't buckled up.

"Put your seat belt on, Sally."

"Why? we're only going a few blocks."

"It's the rule in my car, humor me."

Things were looking a lot brighter now with Sugar safe. Sally even managed a grin as she pulled her seat belt in place.

Nelda picked up speed after the first couple of blocks. She always gave the engine an opportunity to flex its pistons before she pressed hard on the accelerator. Now with increased speed, she made a sharp turn onto Sandy Creek bridge. Suddenly, the car shuddered and shook as though it was coming apart. Nelda panicked as she struggled to keep the car on the road. "Sally," she shouted, "hang on... stopping fast." She hit the brakes and the old car spun out of control. Sally screamed as the car broke through the guard rail and dove off the side. Hissing and grinding noises issued forth from the car as it hit the water. Nelda's left side bounced off the window and then all was dark.

The cold creek water, and the sound of Sally's soft moans brought Nelda back out of darkness. Her eyes examined the interior of the car. Both were still strapped in their seat belts, but the car was on its side. Sally was partially hanging from her seat belt, and Nelda lay below in the slowly rising water. Nelda realized that even though the creek was shallow, she was in danger of being submerged.

"Sally! Sally! can you hear me?"

"Ohoo," moaned Sally, opening eyes partially filled with blood. She put her hand to her forehead, and winced when she found the source of the red, warm fluid. "I ..I...think I'm all right...except for this gash on my head. How..How about you?"

Gingerly, Nelda tried to move each limb, and found that she could without too much discomfort. Cold creek water covering her legs caused Nelda to respond quickly.

"I'm fine, We've got to get out of these seat belts; can you unfasten yours?"

"I think so, but when I do I'm going to fall on you."

"Let me try first. Then I can get out of the way."

Nelda frantically tried to unfasten the belt, but realized that something had happened to the release mechanism. Sally had better luck. Easing herself out of the strap, she carefully avoided Nelda by climbing to the back seat.

"Good," shouted Nelda. "Now open that back door."

"Un..lock it," Sally cried.

The release control was under water. Nelda pushed on all the control buttons, but the door remained locked. She heard Sally shriek in despair.

CHAPTER TWELVE

The Escape

Nelda wanted to shake Sally, but couldn't reach her. Instead, she answered her shriek with as much assurance as she could muster.

"Sally, neither one of us is going to die from this. Now what I want you to do is crawl back to the front seat and get the scissors out of the glove compartment of the car."

"What are you going to do?" Sally asked wiping some of the blood out of her eyes.

"I'm going to get myself out of this safety belt, then I'll break a window open, so we can call for help."

Sally carefully crawled back into the front end of the car making sure she avoided stepping on Nelda.

Even though she was desperate, Nelda tried to lighten up the situation for Sally's sake.

"Be careful when you open that pocket, because it's like Fibber Mc Gee's closet."

The door opened easily, Sally held back the deluge of miscellaneous objects with one hand as she reached into the compartment with the other and located the scissors. She carefully withdrew them, then slammed the door shut before handing them to Nelda. Cutting through the seat belt with dull metal scissors took considerable time and effort. Nelda's hand ached from the extended exertion. Finally the belt was haggled in two. She was free!

"It's going to be all right now," she said smiling weakly. "I'll crawl into the back and get the car jack to break out the glass, then we can call for help. People going to work will certainly be able to see or hear us."

Nelda found it painful to climb into the back of the station wagon, however she was satisfied that no bones were broken, not even her ribs. Her concern now was for Sally's head wound.

"Can I help you, Nelda?" called Sally, standing where Nelda had been sitting.

"No. I'll have this jack loose in a minute."

Nelda freed the jack from the compartment under the floor and barked out instructions. "Sally, get down behind the seat, I'm going to break out this side window."

Nelda shielded her eyes with sun glasses and wrapped her head in the beach towel she kept in the car. She then swung the jack up toward the window. The first blow bounced back harmlessly. Nelda increased the velocity of her swing with the second blow and was rewarded with cracks running in every direction. However, it wasn't until the third blow that the glass finally gave way. Pieces of glass fell like hail inside the car.

It took several minutes for Nelda to break off all the jagged edges in the window opening. Now there was a safe place for her head to slip through. Only then did she realize there was another problem.

Sally saw her hesitate. "What's the matter, Nelda? Are you too short to stick your head through the opening."

"You guessed it. Maybe I can stand on the spare."

Nelda unbolted the tire she found in the spare compartment. It was a little doughnut, but it would do. After lifting it out, she leaned it against the side of the tilted seat, then balanced herself on top of the tire. With this added height, her head barely cleared the window frame. Two cars whizzed by without hearing Nelda's cry for help. She knew her best bet of being rescued would be a jogger. Nelda waited patiently, and was soon rewarded with the sight of an overweight female runner. Nelda never thought she would be so happy to see bouncing fat. The jogger looked down on the station wagon in amazement. She made little, high pitched, nervous noises as she answered Nelda's call for help.

"Aeeh...aare you okay down there? Anybody hurt?"

"Not seriously. Go call Sheriff Moore for me; he'll know how to handle this. We're going to be fine."

"No ambulance?"

"We don't need an ambulance, just call John Moore, please! Tell him Nelda Simmons needs him."

The woman turned and ran back in the same direction from which she came. Sally and Nelda breathed sighs of relief even thorough they were chilled from standing in cold creek water which now partially filled the car.

While they were waiting for John, Nelda had time to think about her wrecked car; sadness filled her heart. Like all her possessions, she had taken great care of this car, knew all it's idiosyncrasies; it was a part of her life. If something was wrong with it, she would have known about it. Something was amiss and she intended to get to the bottom of it.

She didn't dwell long on the condition of her car. Her old friend was her greatest concern. Sally might have a concussion from her head injury and at best she'd need some stitches to close the wound.

Smith's Wrecker drove up about the same time as Sheriff Moore. An ambulance, sounding its siren, whipped in behind him. John, oblivious to the cold water and mud that encased his shiny boots, didn't waste any time wading out to the car.

"I told that silly jogger not to call an ambulance. We don't need one," said Nelda, speaking to John.

"I called them," John answered. You and Sally could have had a spinal injury. I just didn't want to take that chance."

"I'm fine, but Sally's head needs some attention. Just help us out; we'll go to the hospital and get Sally checked over."

"I've already called Walter Goodman. He'll meet you at the hospital in Smitherton.

You might as well go in the ambulance. I'll take care of your car and we can talk when you get back home. I want to know all about this wreck."

Sally and Nelda were carried to dry land with the help of John and the medics. Nelda saw Sam Smith, the driver of the wrecker, poking around in the woods. He came running back to them babbling excitedly, his old denim shirt flapping in the breeze.

"You shore is lucky to be alive Mrs. Simmons. Lookee whot I dun found way over here in dem bushes."

Smith led them across the bridge where they followed a trail of flattened grass. There lay Nelda's left front tire.

"I knew there was something terribly wrong with the car," Nelda said. "All at once it spun around. I couldn't keep it from plunging over on its side."

"Somebody loosened the lugs on the tire. That's the only way this could have happened," John said with a grim face.

Nelda and Sally were both shivering. The shock of the accident plus the cold water treatment was finally setting in. The medics took over; wet clothes were removed and both women were wrapped in blankets. John waved them off with Nelda's promise to call when she returned home.

* * *

Sally, lying in a hospital bed, fingered the large bandage on her head as she talked to Walter and Nelda. "It's ridiculous for me to spend the night in the hospital."

"I'd rather not take any chances with that head injury. That was a pretty nasty jolt to your head, and I want you here for observation." Walter declared.

"Do you actually think this big bandage is necessary for five little stitches?"

"Probably not. I'll see to it that a smaller one is used tomorrow."

"Walter and I are leaving now, Sally. I'm going straight home, get into your car, and pick up Sugar. I've called the Hillmans and explained what happened. They're taking good care of him until I get there."

"Thank you. Keys are in my purse. You'll be here early tomorrow to bail me out won't you?" Sally said soulfully.

"You bet," Nelda said with a forced smile as she patted Sally's arm. "You just follow the doctor's orders." Nelda felt remorse at having to leave her good friend alone.

A light rain was falling as Walter and Nelda made their way to the car. Walter carefully worked his way out of the parking lot. Soon they were on the highway headed home. He then turned his attention to Nelda, clenching his hands to give him courage for what he wanted to say.

"Nelda, you and I have been friends since my high school days. I've always admired and respected you because you told the truth and stood up for what you believed in even though your decisions were sometimes unpopular."

"What are you getting at Walter? Just come right out with it. Do you think I'm meddling where I shouldn't?"

He squirmed in his seat, then ran his fingers around the inside of his collar. Walter had forgotten how direct Nelda could be.

"I know you believe that someone at the clinic is responsible for both the Coldsbys' deaths, but I'm sure none of us are capable of murder. It had to be someone from the outside."

Nelda's head shot up with renewed energy. "Who have you been discussing me with, Walter?"

"Well, uh-Violet and I talked about it. Sue was there too."

"What was said?"

"Just that you and the Sheriff should look outside the clinic for the murderer. But after today, I'm convinced you should get out of it altogether."

"You do know what my answer is going to be to that don't you?"

"Yes," Walter answered and then bit his lower lip as if to keep himself from saying more.

"What else is bothering you?" Nelda wished he could lighten

NELDA SEES RED 99

up every once in awhile and not be so doggone serious.

"It's not any of my business. If I wasn't so fond of Sue I wouldn't say anything, but Steve Morris is not good for Sue. He's hot headed, has no real ambition, and most important of all, he's not making her happy."

Nelda smiled to herself at this unneeded revelation. Walter was showing an interest in her niece. She was sure it wasn't just an employer's interest. This thought was very pleasing to Nelda, but the interest required a lot of ground work.

"I think Sue is having some second thoughts about her relationship with Steve," Nelda answered. "I advised her to go slow with any thoughts of marriage, however these things must be worked out by the two of them."

"Marriage is certainly a big step in anyone's life, especially if you expect it to last a lifetime," he said.

Nelda thought at this point Walter had stopped talking about Sue. He had some reservations about his own marital plans.

Each was caught up in their own thoughts for the rest of the trip. Nelda found herself dozing off just as they reached the city limits of Stearn.

"We're almost there. Nelda, are you planning to attend the funeral this afternoon?"

"Yes, I'm going with Sue. Does she know about my wreck?"

"No, not unless the sheriff told her. I'll explain everything to her and tell her you still intend to go. You sure you feel up to it?" Walter said as he drove up in Nelda's driveway.

"You said yourself that I'm fit as a fiddle. Will you be there?"

"All the employees at the clinic will attend. I'm closing the clinic at 2:00 p.m.; the funeral is at 4:00 p.m."

"Thanks again Walter," Nelda said hurriedly getting out of the car. She could hardly wait to change out of her shoes and clothes. The hospital had made an attempt to dry them, but they were still damp and smelled like pond water.

Nelda looked down at her watch as she hurriedly undressed to shower. So much had happened in such a short time. She was amazed that it was only a little after noon.

* * *

Sugar was still locked up in the Hillman's garage. Doris Hillman heard him bark as Nelda drove up. She was delighted to finally get rid of her uninvited guest. She opened her front door before Nelda had a chance to ring the door bell.

"Nelda! good to see you all in one piece. Is your friend going to be all right?"

"Yes indeed, and we are so grateful to you for taking care of Sally's dog. I hope he wasn't too much trouble."

"Not at all. I'm happy that he came here instead of going somewhere else."

"What time did you discover him in your yard?"

"It was about 2:30 a.m., that's when old Spot started making so much racket we couldn't sleep."

That's about right thought Nelda, she remembered looking at her bedside clock when the neighbor's Collie started barking. It was 2:00 a.m. then, and Sugar needed time to get to the Hillman's house. Someone had deliberately set him free so he wouldn't bark while her car was tampered with. Nelda shivered even though she was standing in the sunshine.

Nelda thanked Doris and started home with Sugar. She even allowed the Lab to plant a few wet kisses on her cheek. When she arrived, she secured her back gate with a strong lock, put fresh water on the back porch for Sugar, then turned her attention to dressing for Joan's funeral. She decided on her new black suit. Nelda didn't perceive herself as being old fashioned, but she would never dream of wearing bright colors to a funeral. She shuddered at the thought of how some townspeople would dress.

Sue didn't disappoint her. When she arrived she was wearing a navy blue dress with matching accessories.

"Oh Aunt Nelda!" Sue said throwing her arms around her aunt. "Are you really all right? I'm so sorry about Sally and your station wagon."

"I am too Sue, but we better discuss it on the way to the mortuary. Let me just switch to my black purse."

She started looking for her billfold in her damp purse and came across the group picture from the clinic.

"Sue, I've been meaning to ask you. Who are these people on the back row?"

"Why, Aunt Nelda, I thought sure you'd recognize Dennis."

CHAPTER THIRTEEN

Chanel Connection

Nelda thought it was a fitting day for a funeral. Dark clouds covered the sky and lightening was flashing in the distance as she and Sue drove into the crowded parking lot at the mortuary. God couldn't be happy with this one.

Scores of people hovered in the vestibule waiting to be seated. Nelda recognized most of them as she moved in next to Violet and Walter. Grasping her hand, Violet gave her a bright smile. Nelda, not knowing how to react to this unexpected display of affection, finally smiled weakly and withdrew her hand.

She noticed that Violet's face was void of all makeup except bright red lipstick, and her body was clothed in a discreet two piece black checkered suit. Was this new image for Walter's sake? One would think from Violet's demeanor she was one of the chief mourners.

Nelda scolded herself for being so cynical and spoke to them warmly. "I'm glad both of you came. I'm sure Mrs. Coldsby would have liked that."

"She was a wonderful lady and this town will miss her," Walter commented. His face suddenly took on a concerned look as he spoke to Nelda in earnest. "You will go home after this and go to bed won't you? You've had a traumatic day."

"I'm fine, and yes I will go home after this. I'll probably turn in early."

They didn't have time for more conversation. Nelda and Sue were seated in the back of the chapel. As they waited for the ceremony to start they listened to musical strands of "Amazing Grace," one of Nelda's favorite hymns.

Three of the last people who entered were Dennis, Marcie and Lola Gibbons, Marcie's mother. Nelda had never seen Dennis dressed up. He looked handsome in his light blue suit, very mature too. It was the hair, she decided. She knew it sounded silly, but with every strand of hair in place he looked older, certainly more serious. Nelda knew Dennis couldn't play a part in these murders, or could he? The thought was too perplexing.

As the minister droned on, Nelda found herself feeling dizzy. Stale air mingled with the aroma of funeral flowers made her quite ill. Just when she had decided she must leave, the funeral was over. Nelda rushed outside, not waiting for Sue. She stood under the porch awning watching the rain come down in sheets, breathing in the fresh-washed air. She was disgusted with herself for not bringing an umbrella. Finally, she saw Sue edging her way toward her accompanied by Sheriff John Moore.

"Aunt Nelda, couldn't you even wait for me? I had a horrible time trying to locate you. John was looking for you too."

"I'm sorry Sue. I just couldn't take the sickening perfume from those flowers any longer."

John, dressed in his sheriff's uniform, looked at Nelda with concern. His face wore a worried frown. "I wanted us to go back in and have a talk, but if you're not feeling well let's do it tomorrow."

"Heaven's no. I feel better now. Sue you go on; John will give me a ride home."

"Okay, Aunt Nelda, I'll call you later." Sue waited until Carol Scrubbs came by with a large stripped umbrella and quickly ducked under it. They moved briskly toward Sue's little car.

"You need to ask Dennis some questions, John. Why don't you nab him when he walks to his truck."

"Why?"

"Here he comes now. Just detain him with the excuse that you want to know if he saw anything suspicious last evening. I'll explain the rest when we go inside."

"Dennis," John called. "Could I speak to you inside for a minute?"

Dennis stopped and turned back. "What can I do for you, Sheriff?" He and Marcie exchanged wary looks before he waved her on. Reluctantly Marcie let go of her mother's arm, opened up a big black umbrella, then both disappeared in the dispersing crowd.

"Ms. Simmons, Marcie was just telling me about your accident. Is Ms. Feddington going to be all right?" asked Dennis, displaying real concern in his voice.

"Oh, I'm sure she'll be fine. But the reason the Sheriff detained you is to find out if you could give us a clue as to what happened yesterday." Nelda explained.

The three of them entered the mortuary. John asked the director if there was an office they could use for a few minutes. He directed them to a small conference room next to the chapel.

John instructed Dennis to sit outside the room, then he and Nelda went inside. "What's this all about Nelda? How is Dennis going to help?"

"I'm not sure. Dennis just happened to be at every place that bad things happened. Could be coincidental, but listen to this: Dennis keeps the grounds around the clinic, was with me when I found that comic book in my closet with a Latin note attached, mowed Joan's lawn right before I found her floating in the pool, and was at my house last evening, just hours before my accident."

"Hmm, you're right. With Dennis being at the scene of each crime, even if he wasn't involved, he should have noticed something."

"That's what you should find out," Nelda said.

"Well look, before we talk to Dennis let me explain some other things." John took some papers out of his pocket and gave Nelda some estimates on fixing her car. "Your station wagon is not worth repairing. You're just going to have to get another vehicle."

Nelda fought back the tears. What a sentimental old fool she was. She answered John with no emotion in her voice. "Guess I'll be busy for the next few days looking for a new car. What other good news do you have for me?"

"Joan drowned, but not before she downed the powerful muscle relaxant which was probably mixed in her drink."

"Just as we thought: something in her drink! It's uncanny isn't it. Either the murderer is very clever or lucky not to have any witnesses to two murders and an attempted one." Nelda felt completely drained.

"Let's hear from Dennis," John said opening the door and beckoning for Dennis to come in.

"How do you think I can help you? I've already told you everything I know," Dennis said, sitting down in a chair next to Nelda.

"Well," said John leaning on the desk with his arms folded. "Maybe not. Now let's go back to when Albert Coldsby died. You were taking care of the clinic grounds at that time, right?"

"Yes, but that day I was working down the street mowing the Stearn's Savings and Loans' grounds. It was 6:00 p.m. when I loaded up to go home."

"How did you know the time?" asked Nelda.

"Marcie Gibbons went by and waved. That's when I looked at my watch, packed up and left."

"Tell us again about working at Joan Coldsby's house right before she died." John requested.

"I stopped working right after Dr. Goodman's visit at 4:00 p.m. He stayed about fifteen minutes, then left. Dorsa, Joan's maid, gave me a glass of ice water while I was loading my tools. I remember her commenting that she was tired, and glad she'd be going home in about an hour." There was no one else around that I could see. I never did see Mrs. Coldsby, just her car in the open garage.

"How did you know about my accident, Dennis?" Nelda asked.

"Marcie told me about it. She said somebody unscrewed the

lugs on your car, the wheel came off and Ms. Feddington was hurt. Somebody must have done that during the night. Too bad you didn't have the dog outside. He would have barked and warned you."

"They took care of that, Dennis; they turned him loose," Nelda spoke with fire in her voice.

"Oh no! Did you get him back?"

"We did. That's where we were going when we lost the wheel, to pick him up."

"I'm sorry I wasn't more help," Dennis declared, rising from his seat.

"You might have been more help than you think." John said. "Did you say Marcie was going down Elm street after work the day Dr. Coldsby was killed?"

"She lives on Hickory in the opposite direction," Nelda said.

"I recall her saying she went right home," John said more to himself then to any one else.

Dennis covered his face with his hands. "What have I done?" he moaned.

"What's wrong Dennis? Do you know more than you're telling us? You've got to come clean," John declared.

"Okay," Dennis said with a firm commitment in his voice. "Marcie came by to tell me she was going home and I followed her there. We've been seeing each other for the last six months."

"What!" Nelda said. "But, Dennis, you're so young."

"I thought you, of all people, would understand, Nelda. I know there's an age difference of fifteen years, but would you be upset if I was the older one? No, I don't think so."

Nelda nodded in agreement. "That's true. Society still frowns on the woman being older. I know that's not right."

John finally reacted to Dennis' statement. "Are you saying that you and Marcie were together at her home when Dr. Coldsby was murdered?"

"Yes, but Marcie didn't want everyone to know about our relationship, because she's afraid of what people will say."

"You mean no one knows about the two of you?" Nelda asked.

"Only her mother, and she thinks we're just friends."

"Dennis, you should have told me about this relationship when I questioned you earlier," John said in a tense voice. "I'll expect you in my office tomorrow at noon to make a formal statement."

"I'm sorry, Sheriff. I wanted to tell you, but Marcie wouldn't hear of it. She still thinks our age difference is too great. She wants to keep our relationship quiet until she can be sure we're doing the right thing."

"Are you talking about marriage?" Nelda asked.

"Yes, even if it means moving away."

"All right, Dennis, you can go on home now, but I'll see you and Marcie tomorrow, and I'd better hear the truth about the whole situation," John said in a disgruntled voice.

Dennis closed the door to the office gently as he left. Nelda and John sat without speaking for a minute. Nelda knew the age difference between Marcie and Dennis was a real problem for Marcie. If this romance finalized in marriage, they would probably have to leave town. A small community like Stearn wouldn't be able to handle their situation without ridiculing them.

"You were right, Nelda, he did know more than he's told me, but I bet you never figured it would be that piece of information."

Nelda looked thoughtful. "I think they'll have a few bugs to work out in that romance. I hope they can pull it off."

"Let me get you home; you look like you're going to collapse."

Nelda didn't deny it as they left the funeral home and headed for her house. There were still a few chores do before retiring: Sugar needed attention and food, the flowers needed watering and she had to have a report from Sally.

The brown dog heralded their arrival by barking loudly as John pulled up in Nelda's driveway. His barking stopped as soon as he saw her, but it triggered a tail-swinging bout. Sally was right, this is a people dog, Nelda thought.

John insisted on going in the house with Nelda to make sure everything was in order. "My Deputy is going to patrol this area tonight, and don't you hesitate to call if you hear the slightest noise outside."

"Thanks, John. There's something else I need to ask you. Mary Sanchez, Berto's wife, desperately needs for him to come back home and wants you to reassure her that you won't arrest him for the murder of Coldsby."

"You know I can't rule him out as a suspect, but I'm certainly not going to lock him up without more evidence. That threat to kill Coldsby is not enough to hold him, however I need a statement from him."

"I promised I'd bring her to see you next Tuesday about 2:00 p.m. Is that all right?"

"Good, 2:00 p.m. would be fine. Have a good evening, Nelda."

After John drove off, Nelda busied herself with Sugar before calling Sally's hospital room. She was surprised to hear someone else's voice on the other end of the line. What she heard sent her into tears. The nurse who answered said Sally was doing fine and her phone had been removed from her room, so that she could rest without being disturbed. Nelda knew everybody was disturbed every thirty minutes in a hospital by nurses coming in to poke, probe and make you swallow things. She deeply resented the fact that she couldn't even have a firsthand report from her old friend. Realizing she had to end this miserable day, Nelda put Sugar out, checked the locks and went to bed.

* * *

Nelda woke to traffic sounds and sun streaming through the slats of the Venetian blinds. She looked at the bedside clock and was amazed to find she had slept until 8:00 a.m. Sitting up in bed was a painful chore; every movement caused Nelda to groan. The last time she was this sore was when she fell in a skiing accident. Grimacing, she made her way slowly to the kitchen. Coffee and a hot shower always made her world a lot brighter. And it worked today too.

After Nelda and Sugar had breakfast, she decided to take the neglected brown dog for a walk. Actually the walk would be good for both of them, because she needed to exercise her sore muscles before she went to get Sally.

"Come on old boy. Let's put this leash on and we'll be off. This time you'll have a little guidance with your stroll."

Sugar seemed to know what was coming when Nelda opened the back gate, but he wouldn't keep his head still long enough for her to clip the leash on his collar. He hopped up and down, causing Nelda to work her already strained muscles. They ended up near the side of the driveway in a low grassy area. After finally leashing the dog, her foot stepped on something hard. She reached down and picked it up. It was a well-used tube of lipstick. Chanel, "Midnight Red"! Who did she know that used this brand? No one. *Several familiar faces with painted red lips floated through her mind.*

CHAPTER FOURTEEN

Latin Warning

The evening sun made long shadows on Nelda's back porch. She busied herself repotting a red begonia while Sally fidgeted nervously in an old rocking chair.

"I swear to you, Nelda, this week has seemed like a month. If you keep me cooped up in this house one more day I'm going home. My head has healed and we have no earthly reason for not going out."

Nelda didn't answer right away. She wrestled a water hose away from Sugar in the backyard and coiled it neatly on a stand by the outdoor faucet.

"Really, Sally, you're beginning to sound like a teenager. Do you think you have to go somewhere every night?"

"I know you've been sitting home on my account," Sally said, "but now it's time to get out. What about us shopping for your new car?"

Nelda straightened up and pulled off her working gloves. Her snapdragons had never looked more beautiful. She wondered if Marcie's mother would appreciate a bouquet of them.

"Nelda, you haven't heard a thing I said."

"What's this I've found in my pocket?" Nelda responded, holding up two tickets.

"Well, what is it?"

"Tickets to the pop concert in the park tonight," Nelda said.

"You sneaky old devil. That's what Sue was doing over here at lunch. You had her buy those tickets, didn't you?"

"Only because we got a deal. The Smitherton Symphony Orchestra is going to present 'An Old-Fashioned Pops' and the clinic is helping to sponsor it. Our tickets were half price."

"I would have paid full price to get out. What time will it start?"

"Six. You better get prettied up," laughed Nelda. No one could be happier to get out than Nelda; she had a new car to buy and lots of people to talk to. She felt like her life had been on hold since Sally got out of the hospital.

They were going to take a picnic supper so Nelda went in to see what she could find to put into the old picnic basket she'd had forever. She found her favorite foursome: baked chicken, cold slaw, potato salad and banana pudding. In no time Nelda had the basket ready to go.

"Better take a sweater," Nelda called to Sally as she passed Sally's bedroom. "It's windy and chilly in the park when the sun goes down."

It was five-thirty when they left in Sally's car, just enough time to get there and get settled before the entertainment started. Nelda felt like a bird let out of a cage; she gazed down the open road with eager anticipation.

"What's on the program, Nelda?" asked Sally as they drove down the street.

"At seven some local dance groups are going to perform. The concert doesn't start until eight."

"Will Sue be there? You know, she could have come with us if she's not bringing her young man."

Nelda pursed her lips. "They're kinda on the outs now and I hope the romance keeps going in that direction. She couldn't come with us because she had to work late, but I'm sure she'll ride over with one of her friends."

Most of the conversation on the way to the concert was centered on possible replacements for Nelda's old station wagon. Nelda decided she'd definitely look at the Ford Windstar because it had received high consumer ratings. Soon they arrived, parked, and approached the amphitheater loaded down with lawn chairs, picnic basket and a red plaid blanket that smelled slightly of moth balls.

The amphitheater was constructed in a natural valley near a creek and surrounded by a water filled-moat. Some of the spectators were already having their evening meal. They were scattered in small groups on the side of the grassy hill adjacent to the theater. Nelda smelled fried chicken and wished she had a large greasy piece of it. It was tough trying to keep on a healthy diet. Sometimes she wished she'd never heard anything about cholesterol.

"Here's a good spot, Nelda. We're right in front of the orchestra, yet far enough back not to get blasted."

Nelda quickly spread their blanket, set up the lawn chairs and opened up the picnic basket. Sally went to a concession stand to buy diet Cokes as the last rays of sunlight slipped away. They ate their supper to the strands of the "Emperor Waltz," taped music designed to keep them entertained until the dancers arrived.

It was almost seven before the show started, then Nelda wished it hadn't. "Look at those children dancing to that rap music. It's disgraceful," she said.

"All those suggestive dance steps. I think the voice with the music, if you want to call it music, is saying Jesus loves me," Sally commented.

"It's no wonder we have teenage pregnancies with all that going on. I can't imagine parents paying for their children to carry on so." Nelda frowned in disgust.

She spotted Sue several yards away with several clinic employees. They were making their way toward them. Nelda was glad for the distraction. The group consisted of Sue, Carol, Violet, Marcie and an older gray-headed woman.

"Hello," called Sue, "It's good to see both of you out. Sally, did Nelda surprise you with those tickets?"

"You bet, it was a pleasant surprise, I think."

Nelda laughed. "We're not sure about the pre-concert enter-tainment."

"Guess you know now why we came near concert time," Marcie said. She then pointed to the older woman. "This is Mother's sister, Molly Snider, from Aspen, Colorado. I used to spend some wonderful holidays with her, and this time it was her turn to visit us."

Both Nelda and Sally acknowledged the introduction. Nelda wondered if this visit was related to Marcie's mother's mental con-dition. Alzheimer's disease could be so insidious.

The newcomers arranged their lawn chairs while Nelda con-tinued talking.

"Didn't you allow any men to come with you? The fresh air would be good for them too."

Violet, who looked very stylish in a navy blue jumpsuit and matching sandals, answered her question.

"Walter took Elizabeth Gomez, our new clinic doctor, to a medical meeting. He'll be here late. I don't know about any other men. Maybe they think it's not manly enough."

"Rubbish," Carol commented. "Shelby would love it if he weren't so ill."

"How is he doing?" asked Nelda, feeling guilty because she hadn't visited him again.

"They're trying out an experimental drug on him and it seems to be working."

"I'm so glad, Carol," Nelda said. "Do you ever see Will Campbell?"

"His sister removed him from the hospice last week and took him to Mexico. Some last effort to save him. There's a doctor there that claims he has a cure for cancer and she didn't see what Will had to lose."

"I'm sorry we didn't get to tell him good-bye," Sally said.

Nelda shook her head and was silent. Maybe there was a miracle cure out there somewhere, but she really didn't expect to see Will again.

Small gyrating bodies made several rolls on the floor and thus ended the dance class' last number. Nelda and Sally applauded because it was over. Then, members of the orchestra started warming up. Presently the conductor, dressed in a Nehru jacket, came sailing in. Everyone rose for "The Star Spangled Banner."

Nelda thought the concert was wonderful. Accomplished musicians played musical scores composed by Strauss, Fuick, Sousa and Smith. She found herself keeping time to the music by using her rolled up program as a baton.

At break, Nelda walked over to the concession stand with Marcie to buy a drink. She didn't know if Marcie would say anything about her relationship with Dennis, but was hoping she would.

"Well, Nelda, tell me truthfully, do you think it's absolutely disgusting that I'm carrying on, as my Aunt Molly calls it, with a man fifteen years younger than I am?"

"I guess I was a little taken back when Dennis told us, but only because I'm still thinking of Dennis as my high school student. I know that you're not a vamp who snares younger men for your enjoyment. Dennis seems totally in love with you and I assume you feel the same way."

"It all started because I was so lonesome. When I worked late at the clinic, he'd visit with me and gradually we just slipped into this wonderful relationship. He really is a bright man, very sweet. But the people in Stearn will never accept our age difference."

"You don't have to stay here."

"Oh don't I? My work is here, Dennis is in school and Mother is my sole responsibility. Lets face it, Nelda, maybe God didn't intend for me to marry. I'm always on the outside looking in."

Her eyes welled with tears and Nelda couldn't think of words to console her. Marcie pulled a tissue out of her pocket. When she did, Nelda caught a whiff of strong perfume. She knew that scent, but for the life of her couldn't recall the name of it.

Intermission was almost over when Nelda spotted Dennis. He strolled up to the group, said hello, then sat down on the grass next to Marcie. She smiled at him and no one seemed to think anything of it. Nelda could tell the clinic employees didn't know how serious this romance had become, or maybe they were just more understanding than the townspeople. No sly glances or smirking smiles were exchanged between the clinic employees.

Walter and the new clinic doctor, Elizabeth Gomez, joined the group before the concert ended. Nelda offered them her blanket to sit on. They gratefully accepted and sat down. Violet snuggled in between Walter and Elizabeth. The temperature had dropped and those who didn't bring wraps were beginning to feel the chill.

The rest of the program flew by. Nelda beat her makeshift baton to "The Sound of Music," *Star Wars* medley and "God Bless America." So engrossed was she in the music, that for this brief time she didn't even think about the murders.

Finally, with a standing ovation from the crowd, the concert was over. Nelda and Sally gathered their belongings, said their good nights and hurried, with other spectators walking in the same direction, toward Sally's car. Nelda was taking no chances of another attempt on their lives. Sally's old Volvo was built like a tank. Thank goodness it had locking hub caps, and a hood that was almost impossible to open unless released from the inside. They both inspected it before opening the doors and loading up.

On the way home, Sally was full of conversation. "Nelda, did the sheriff ever tell you where those phone calls Dr. Coldsby made in Aspen came from?"

"Yes, Hotel Jerome and Sardy House. Why did you think of that?"

"Marcie's Aunt Molly is from Aspen. I was just wondering if Marcie might have been visiting her aunt when Coldsby was there."

"The thought did cross my mind. I might take Mrs. Gibbons some of my flowers, and when I do I'll get better acquainted with Molly."

"I bet you will," Sally said grinning.

When they arrived home, Nelda and Sally greeted woman's best friend. While Sally reestablished her bond with Sugar, Nelda walked into the kitchen and dumped the basket on the kitchen table. Her rolled up program fell to the floor. She left it there while she fixed the coffee pot for the next morning.

Sally walked into the kitchen and picked up the program. "What have you written on this program Nelda?"

"What do you mean? I didn't write on it."

"There is something written in Latin on the side of your program. I'm afraid I can't translate it. See if you can."

Nelda stared at the words *finem respice* without speaking. Her hands were clenched as she faced Sally.

"Well, you taught Latin. Tell me!" Sally demanded.

"It means *consider the end.*"

CHAPTER FIFTEEN

Night Horror

Nelda walked slowly down a long hospital hall staring into the open doors as she passed. There was no perceptible sound except the beating of her own heart. She heard a rhythmic thump, thump, thump as she warily approached each room. The last door was closed. Loud laughter rang out as the door opened with a bang. Nelda stared in disbelief at what she saw. Gathered in the small room were all the employees from Coldsby's clinic. Slanted, piercing eyes of the employees were focused on her. Their wide mouths were shaped in sardonic grins. Suddenly, as if by signal they parted and exposed the naked body of Albert Coldsby lying on his own examination table. A Latin book lay across his genitals. Nelda backed away and screamed.

Sally rushed into Nelda's bedroom. "Nelda!, Nelda! wake up," she said as she shook the bed. "You're having a bad dream. Everything is fine."

"What? Oh my God!" said Nelda as she struggled to sit up. "Thank you, Sally, for waking me. It was the most horrible nightmare I've ever had."

"You want to talk about it?"

"What time is it?"

"6:00 a.m."

"It's time to get up. Let me clear my mind and have a cup of coffee, then I'll tell you about it."

Nelda struggled into her robe without bothering to find her slippers, then headed for the kitchen. Sally was already pouring the coffee. They didn't say anything until they were seated opposite each other at the kitchen table.

"We're going to get away from here for a few days, Sally. Both of us need a change of scenery and I know just the place to go."

"Was that nightmare about the murders?"

"Yes, it was terrible. I saw all the people from the clinic gathered around Albert's naked body and there was a Latin book covering his 'you know what'. All the employees taunted me with their laughter."

"Good heavens, Nelda. You're right, we do need to go somewhere for awhile. What about Sugar? I don't want to put him in a kennel."

"Sue will take care of him. She can just stay in this house at night and look after him."

"Where did you want to go?"

"To the coast. Just looking across the ocean puts me in a better frame of mind. However, there're two things I need to do first."

"What?"

"I promised Mary Sanchez I would go with her to talk to John. Another biggie, I've got to get another station wagon. Right after breakfast let's go look at the new Ford wagons. I've read the consumer guides; I know what I'm looking for."

"Sounds good."

After dressing and breakfast, they checked Sally's old car for possible tampering, loaded up and headed for the Ford dealership in Smitherton. Nelda hoped they had what she was looking for, because she didn't have time to waste. Thirty minutes later they drove up to the agency. The new car lot was loaded with station wagons in several different colors. She immediately fell in love with a Ford wagon in jade-green.

A young, suntanned salesman dressed in a short sleeved, white shirt and faded blue Dockers' pants found them peering into the interior of the car.

"My name is Ned Brooks. May I help you?" he asked.

"You sure can, Ned. I'm Nelda Simmons; this is Sally Feddington. Now tell me everything you know about this station wagon."

He kind of smiled and looked at the car for a second. Nelda supposed he was thinking about his sales pitch for old ladies.

"Well, it has all these things listed here on the side window plus keyless entry. Let me open it up and I'll go over everything with you."

"Good. And tell me about the wheel covers. Do you have any that lock?"

"Yes, they're available."

"Now give me the bad news."

"You mean the lowest price to you?"

"Exactly. And without a trade-in."

In the next two hours, Nelda took a test drive, then haggled with the dealership owner over the cost of the car, using her young salesman as a mediator. Finally, she thought she had brought him down as far as he would go. She signed a contract and Ned promised to have the car ready the next day, so she drove away satisfied.

"Well," Sally said, as they drove away, "I'm excited for you Nelda. I admire your bargaining ability. I would have given up after the first counter offer."

"They knew I did my homework, Sally. I made a dozen calls to Ford dealers all over the state. It gave me a pretty good idea of what to expect."

"What do you have planned now?"

"Let's go home. You can start packing for the coast, and I'll use your car to meet Mary Sanchez over at John's office after lunch."

* * *

Nelda eased Sally's old car into one of the visitor's spaces in the County Sheriff's parking lot. Mary Sanchez was already there stand-

ing under a tree. She stood there twisting a large white handkerchief in her hands.

After Nelda got out of the car, they exchanged greetings. As
they walked toward the office, Nelda talked to her in reassuring
tones. "Don't be nervous, Mary. In light of what else has happened, I don't believe your husband is a suspect any more."

"I really need him at home," she said in a shaky voice, "but am
afraid for him too. He should not have run away. Can they do
something to him for doing that?"

"Don't worry. You can trust John Moore to give you an honest
answer. Ask him what to expect."

John saw them come in and smiled. "Good to see you, Nelda.
And you must be Mrs. Sanchez?" he said, shaking Mary's hand.
"Come into my office so we won't be disturbed."

They sat down facing John at his desk. Nelda explained the
situation to John.

"Mary wants her husband to come home from Mexico, but is
afraid you will arrest him. If she has your assurance that he won't
go to jail, she thinks he'll come back."

"Is Roberto a citizen of this country?" asked John. He made
notations on a pad.

"Oh yes," Mary answered while gripping the arms of her chair.
"He was naturalized many years ago. All my close family belongs
to this country, but we still have many relatives in Mexico. My
husband was afraid when he found out you were looking for him
and ran away."

"If he didn't kill the doctor, he has nothing to worry about,
however there were some people that heard him threaten to kill
Dr. Coldsby." John gave Mary a stern look.

"It was just talk," Mary said, tears welling up in her dark eyes.
"He was mad, because he thought the doctor could have saved our
David. Instead, he turned him away because our daughter, Theresa,
couldn't pay."

"I believe his threat was just talk too, Mrs. Sanchez, but we
still need a statement from him. If he comes in and tells me what

happened that night, I won't lock him up. Of course if we discover later on that he had a hand in the murder, we'll arrest him." He tapped on his pad for emphasis.

Mary squirmed in the chair. "I understand. I'll send him a message right away. Thank you, Mr. Moore, for seeing me."

John and Mary stood, but Nelda wanted a few more minutes of John's time. "Mary, I'm going to stay here for a while. I would like to talk with the Sheriff about something else. You send word to Berto right away."

"I will and thank you for meeting me here. I hope to see you again soon." Mary walked to the door and gave Nelda a sweet smile before closing the door. Some of the worried wrinkles from the woman's round face were gone now.

Turning back to face John, Nelda settled back in her chair. "Bought a new station wagon today," she said.

"And I bet I know what kind. It was a Ford product wasn't it?"

Nelda had to laugh. Had she ever bought any other kind? No, never. She supposed that was kind of narrow minded, but it wasn't because she hadn't looked at other models. Even when her husband was alive, they always ended up with a Ford.

"Prettiest jade-colored Ford you've ever seen. I'm picking it up tomorrow and then Sally and I are going to the coast."

"Good. You two be careful. I'm glad you're getting away for a few days."

"Have you made any headway at all on the case?"

"No, it seems as though we've come to a stone wall. I sent a picture of Coldsby to the Aspen police. The hotel managers recognized him but couldn't remember any details about his stay."

"John, how are you coming along with the background checks on the clinic employees?"

"Slow. The information just dribbles in," he said, beginning to pace.

"Well, don't ask me why. But I have the feeling Coldsby's murder might be related to something that happened several years ago." She straightened the papers on his desk.

"Yes, I've asked for copies of the clinic personnel files. I'll check them out. Now what's wrong with you? You seem nervous."

"When we got home from the pop concert last night, I had another Latin phrase written in red on my concert program. I guess it did upset me because I had a dream about it last night."

John snapped his pencil in two. "For crying out loud, Nelda, why didn't you call me last night? What did it say?"

"It was too late and what could you have done about it? Be reasonable, John. Anyway, I'm telling you now. The phrase is *finem respice.* Which means *consider the end.*"

John slapped the desk with his hand. "Of all the nerve! The dirty murderer is right under our noses and I can't figure out who it is. Makes me so blasted mad. Was anyone from the clinic there?"

"Just about all of them. There was Marcie and her Aunt Molly, Sue, Walter, Carol, Violet, Dennis and the new doctor, Elizabeth Gomez."

"I'm surprised Roberto and Steve weren't there too," said John bitterly. "That would have made it a full house."

"Calm down, John, the reason I'm taking a trip is to get away and sort things out. I'm sure there are clues here and we're just missing them."

"There might be a chance you'll be followed and they might make another attempt on your life."

"No, they'll probably think I'm running away. That's what the murderer wants me to do, not be here to gather any more information."

"Call me when you get there. Do you know where you're going to stay?"

"Cousin Wilber has a beach house on Galveston Island. I'm sure he'll let us use it if no one is there this week."

"Keep in touch and I'll get right on those personnel files. I'll call the clinic now and pick those files up tomorrow."

Nelda drove home to a cheery Sally. Binoculars, towels, an ice chest, suntan lotion and two beach chairs occupied the kitchen floor. Sally was sitting in the middle of the clutter making out a list.

"How long are we going to stay on the coast?" she asked.

"Less than a week. I think we'll be ready to come home in four or five days."

"Good, you sure you want to go in your new car? That salt air won't do it any good. We could use mine. It's so old it might be revived in salt air."

"No thanks," answered Nelda. "I noticed your air conditioner doesn't blow cold air. That old buggy needs to be in the shop. Why don't you take it and leave it at a garage while we're gone? They could give it an overall inspection so you won't be stranded on the highway someday."

"Great idea, Sally agreed. "

Nelda called Sue and then Wilber. When she finished the conversations, she spoke to Sally. "We're all set. Sue will be glad to take care of Sugar, and Cousin Wilber said the beach house is all ours. The key is taped to a beam downstairs."

"What can we do in Galveston?" asked Sally. "I'm not one to sit on the beach and look at all that dirty sand and water."

"You haven't been there since they put Moody Gardens in, have you?"

"No, what's that all about?"

"It's a botanical garden utilizing animals and nature. You're going to love it, especially the Rain Forest and the 3D-IMAX. With 3D glasses on, it seems you're right in the middle of what's happening on the screen."

"I remember seeing something like that in.... now let me think. It was 1953. The movie was a monster thriller called 'House of Wax'. We had to put on these funny glasses, made the monsters seem to come right at you. Almost scared me to death."

"Well," said Nelda. "I'm sure they've improved it in forty years." She was a little miffed that Sally could remember the exact year that 3-D movies came out and she, herself, didn't have a clue.

"And I'm sure," Sally continued, "we're going to be able to

identify all kinds of water and shore birds." She added Peterson's bird identification book to her long list.

Nelda smiled. Sally's enthusiasm was getting to her now and she couldn't wait to be off. They went to bed early. She mentally stacked luggage and beach chairs in the back of her new jade Ford without producing a scratch.

At 4:00 a.m. the ringing of the telephone jarred Nelda awake. She answered it reluctantly, expecting bad news. She knew from experience, no one ever called with good news at this hour.

"Hello," she whispered, still lying down.

"Aunt Nelda, it's Sue. There's been a fire at the clinic."

"That's horrible. How bad is it?"

"It started in Marcie's office. All the files are gone."

Nelda sat up straight squeezing the telephone receiver. "Personnel files too?"

"Yes, everything."

Nelda sighed, she had been right. *The clues were in the past.*

CHAPTER SIXTEEN

Gun Attack

Nelda couldn't go right back to sleep after Sue called about the fire. She lay there trying to put everything into perspective. It was a gut feeling, but she was confident the murders were committed by an employee of the clinic and maybe an accomplice. It was someone who had a lot to gain by Coldsby's death or held a mighty big grudge. As for Joan Coldsby, she was going to supply information that would lead to Albert's killer: that's why she died. The fire was meant to destroy evidence in someone's records that would help us identify the killer. Stealing just one file would be too obvious. It was better to destroy them all. Nelda knew the critical information about the killer would never be put back in the file.

She'd sort it out when she got to Galveston, but now sleep was what she needed. Nelda found herself trying an old exercise she knew to help her fall asleep. She cleared her mind and started concentrating on relaxing her body, starting with her feet. After a few minutes of concentration, her toes relaxed and she could feel a pleasant, tingling sensation in her feet. Nelda moved slowly up her body with the same relaxing technique. She had just worked her way up to her arms and was dozing off. Then, the smell of fresh coffee drifted into her bedroom. She pulled the covers over her head and didn't get up until she heard Sally talking to Sugar.

"You ol' dog you. Come here so Momma can give you a hug,"

Sally said, putting her arms around Sugar's neck. His tail beat fiercely on the table leg, threatening to turn her coffee over.

Nelda couldn't believe Sally was up first. She threw back the covers on the bed and rushed into the kitchen, dodging the ice chest and lawn chairs on the kitchen floor.. "Were you calling me an ol' dog?" she asked.

"No, you're an old, tired cat. What do you mean sleeping till 7:00 a.m. on the first day of our vacation? We've got to hit the road." Sally poured coffee for Nelda.

"I had trouble going to sleep, and then the phone rang at 4:00 a.m. Did you hear it?"

"Goodness no, who would call at that hour? Come fix your coffee."

"It was Sue," said Nelda as she stirred sugar in her cup. "She called to tell me there was a fire at the clinic, and all the personnel files were burned up in Marcie's office."

"You think that was intentional, don't you?" I can tell by the look on your face we're not leaving on our trip today." Sally's face was all frowns.

Nelda took a sip of her coffee and watched Sally with amusement. Sally was like a kid when it came to being disappointed, Nelda thought. I'm not going to disappoint her; we're leaving today.

"You're wrong," Nelda answered. "But, we can't go until we have something to go in. They're going to deliver the station wagon at 9:00 a.m. You got your bag packed?"

"Yes sir, Captain."

Nelda pointed to the hall. "My bags are out there."

"As soon as I get a bite to eat, I'll get dressed and we can carry all this stuff out to the driveway," Nelda said. "You know I've been thinking, why not take Sugar with us? He'd have fun on the beach and when we need to leave him he'll be comfortable in the air conditioned beach house." Sugar's tail pounded Nelda's leg when she mentioned his name.

Sally's face lit up like one of Nelda's glass suncatchers. "Oh, he would just love that! You sure your cousin won't mind? Some people can't stand to have an animal in the house."

"Not Cousin Wilber. Right now he and his wife have one of those little white poodles that sleeps with them."

"Well," said Sally shaking her head. "Don't you think that's a little too cozy?"

"Not if you saw his wife at bedtime," laughed Nelda. "He's probably glad there's something between them. She's so oiled up at night with face cream I'm surprised she doesn't slip out of bed."

"You've convinced me," said Sally. "I'll just get his belongings and add them to the pile in the driveway."

Nelda had her usual oatmeal and then went to dress. She planned on wearing her white walking shorts, tennis shoes and a yellow knit shirt. She should have gotten a new bathing suit, but couldn't find one that covered up enough of her body. She considered women's bathing suits disgraceful. What had happened to their design? Why, they're no bigger than a sling shot and looked like one too.

By the time they carted everything on Sally's list outside, Nelda wondered if there was anything left in the house. They probably wouldn't use half the stuff they piled in the driveway. Nelda decided she'd load the essentials in first. Everything else could go in the garage.

Sally was perspiring profusely from all the exertion. It's no wonder, thought Nelda, looking at her friend's attire. She had on a frilly collared blouse with three quarter sleeves and a skirt that almost swept the ground.

"I hope for your sake, Sally, you packed shorts and short-sleeved shirts. If you didn't, you're going to be in for a rough time. Galveston is about as hot as it is here with more humidity in the air."

"I've got a little bit of everything," Sally said.

"I can believe that," said Nelda looking at the mound of Sally's luggage.

It was after nine before the station wagon arrived. Nelda looked it over carefully before the driver left in another vehicle. There were still two small scratches they hadn't taken care of. She made note of them on the delivery form before she signed it. The mechanic promised to remove the scratches as soon as Nelda brought the car in.

Sally started placing things in the car as soon as the back was opened, but Nelda stopped her. "Now, let's do this right or we won't have room for Sugar. Besides that, I want to spread some sheets in here to protect the inside."

"You load up then," Sally said looking at the perspiration stains under her arms. "I'm going in to change into something cooler. I just might go topless."

"That should cause a few wrecks," chuckled Nelda as she struggled with the mound of suitcases, blankets, beach chairs, coolers and beach umbrellas. She got everything inside except the chairs. They would just have to do without those or rent some, that was that.

She went into the house to call Sue about their decision to take Sugar. Nelda was surprised to learn from Sue that the fire had done considerable smoke damage to the interior of the clinic and the clinic would be closed until the following Monday. Sue was happy about the situation.

"It's going to be like a mini vacation, we're being paid for time off."

Nelda was not pleased to hear the clinic would be closed, because she suspected the murderer was having a vacation too. Better get in touch with John before she left. John's phone was busy so she decided to call later.

Trying to cast off the dark spell, she hummed to herself as she helped Sally load the dog. Then they were off. Nelda loved the feel of her new car and played with some of the buttons on the dash. She pushed one that showed the number of miles she could travel before the gas tank was empty, and then another that gave kph. Surrounded by glass was a wonderful feeling too. She imagined it was like riding in a bubble.

"What route are we taking to Galveston?" Sally asked.

"We're going State Hwy 6 all the way to Lamarque, which is only eight miles from Galveston. It's a four hour drive from here to Cousin Wilber's beach house on West Beach."

Because of light traffic, Nelda skimmed along smoothly with her cruise control set on the speed limit. She and Sally were perfectly content to sit back and listen to a collection of old melodies on the radio. Sugar was a good traveler, but Nelda was taking no chances. After two hours she stopped at Mc Donald's, so the dog could have a bathroom break.

While Sally walked him around, she hurried into the restaurant and got some burgers, cokes and fries to eat while they traveled. As she paid for their food and drinks, she caught the fragrance of the same perfume she had smelled at the concert. The perfume Marcie had on her tissue. She finally recognized it as Chanel No. 2. Nelda looked all around the dining area, but could find no familiar face.

As she returned to the car her dark mood returned. Should she tell Sally that the employees at the clinic were having a holiday? No, she decided not to worry her.

It was 3:00 p.m. before they turned into the driveway of the beach house. It was a small house with the living area upstairs and parking below. The neat house had two bedrooms, family room and one bath. It was adequate for the two of them. Nelda looked all around. There seemed to be only a handful of beach houses occupied. She should have been happy at this revelation, but Nelda couldn't shake off the idea that maybe someone wishing them harm had made the trip ahead of them. These thoughts will never do, thought Nelda. We're going to have a good time. With that affirmative decision she smiled at her companion.

"Well here we are Sally, smell that sea breeze? I'm just itching to put on my straw hat and go for a long walk on the beach. How about you?"

"That would be fun. Sugar can get some exercise, so he won't go bananas when we leave him alone."

When Nelda opened the beach house, stale, hot air blasted

her face. "Phew! Good thing we planned a walk. I'll get that air conditioner going. Got to get rid of some of this hot air and stale odor."

"Wait!" sang out Sally. "Let me grab Sugar's leash and we'll be off."

It was only a five minute walk to the beach. Sugar, his excitement mounting, was out in front pulling Sally along. Sally and Nelda scurried up the steps leading to the beach. They could smell dead fish before they could see the water.

"Oh no!" Nelda exclaimed, "would you look at the condition of this area."

Both of them stared in disgust. Seaweed and debris covered most of the beach while large globs of oil added to the dirty look of the sand.

"This is the worst I've ever seen it," Nelda said shaking her head sadly. Do you notice the kinds of things that come out of this water?"

"There's proof of illegal dumping here," Sally snorted indignantly. "I see syringes, rubber gloves and all kinds of medical garbage on this beach."

"The hospitals are paying companies to get rid of this stuff and all they're doing is going out and dumping it into the Gulf," Nelda said.

Sugar didn't seem to mind what was on the beach. He was fascinated with the water.

Sally unclipped his leash. Finding himself free, he ran through the shallow water chasing a sea gull.

Sally shook her head. "Tomorrow we'll investigate another part of the beach. We may have to pay a little something to walk on a clean sand, but I can't stand this."

They walked on down the shore line following the dog. Nelda noted that they were alone on this part of the beach and she certainly knew why. If they didn't have to exercise Sugar, she wouldn't be here either.

After walking several hundred yards down the beach, they

NELDA SEES RED 131

turned back. Nelda looked toward the steps they had used to come over the fence. She saw someone in a red shirt watching them with binoculars. The figure disappeared back over the fence before Nelda could distinguish any features. She suddenly shivered in the quickening breeze.

"Let's go unpack, Sally," she shouted into the wind. "We have the 3D IMAX Theater on our list for tonight and I'd like to shower first."

Sally agreed and called for Sugar to come. Reluctantly, the dog covered with wet sand made his way over to her. Just as Sally bent to snap the leash on him, he tried to shake the sand and water off. The result was a face full of sand for Sally. Nelda doubled over with laughter. Now, all three needed a bath.

While they hurried back to the beach house, Nelda looked in every direction for someone in a red shirt. All she saw was two teenage girls in string bikinis running along the street toward the beach. Disgraceful, Nelda thought.

After they unpacked, showered and dressed, Nelda and Sally watched the sun disappear into the bay from the balcony of the beach house.

"That was so beautiful," Sally sighed.

"Thank goodness man hasn't been able to put their garbage on the sun." Nelda said.

"Sure, right, but they have managed to destroy the ozone layer."

"Well let's leave the worries of the world for a while and think food. How does a seafood platter at Guido's sound?"

"Now you're talking. I'm ready to go," Sally answered.

Sally filled a bowl of water for Sugar and they drove to the restaurant. Even at this early hour they had difficulty finding a place to park. The place was packed. Nelda found herself studying everyone dressed in a red shirt. After a twenty minute wait, they were seated on the patio outside.

"Why are you staring at that man in the red shirt?" asked Sally

"I didn't think it was that obvious," Nelda responded. "I saw someone looking at us with binoculars on the beach and whoever it was had on a red shirt."

"You think someone followed us here?" questioned Sally.

"Of course not. Probably a bird-watcher on the beach. I don't know why I stared at the man in here, except it's just my nature to be suspicious."

The waiter came to take their order. They both ordered the seafood platter and iced tea. Nelda diverted Sally's attention away from suspicious characters to what they would be seeing in the lobby area of Moody Gardens.

"Have you ever seen what the first hot air balloon looks like, Sally?"

"No, are we going to see one of those?"

"Yes, right in the lobby is a replica of the very first one made in 1783. I bet that was a scary ride. "

The waiter brought their dinner. Talking ceased while they devoured stuffed crabs, fried shrimp, trout and potatoes. It all tasted so good with mounds of tarter and red sauce. Nelda decided not to even think of the cholesterol she was consuming.

It was close to show time when they finally paid their bill and made there way to Moody Gardens. Nelda parked as close as she could to the entrance. She was happy to find the parking lot well-lit with a security guard on patrol.

"This movie better be exciting, Nelda, or you might catch me napping."

"I've heard some good things about this one," Nelda said, hurrying Sally along. "It's all about underwater creatures. With the 3D glasses, it seems like you are swimming with them."

After buying their tickets, they hurried to look at the hot air balloon then decided the modern ones were prettier and safer. At the entrance to the theater, they presented their tickets and were given 3D glasses to wear. Both women made their way to the center of the theater. Nelda found it hard to visualize a picture filling the giant screen in front of them. Finally the picture started.

Long strands of seaweed seemed to float around Nelda while small schools of brightly colored fish swam up and over her head. Nelda had the sensation of being there in the ocean with them.

Suddenly the scene changed. The great white sharks, baring their razor sharp teeth, charged through the water a little too close to Nelda even for simulated action. One great white in particular was closing in closer and closer when Nelda saw red out of the corner of her eye. Turning her head for a closer look, she saw a revolver pointed straight at her head. Nelda screamed and bright lights swam before her eyes. *Funny, she thought, no pain and no bang but liquid was flowing down her cheek.*

CHAPTER SEVENTEEN

Man Overboard

"Get that bright light out of my eyes!" yelled Nelda. "You're blinding me."

"I'm sorry," the movie attendant said, turning off his flashlight. "I heard some screaming over here. Is anybody hurt?"

People all over the theater were standing up and craning their necks to see what all the ruckus was about. When Nelda's pupils finally returned to normal, the first thing she saw was a pint sized boy in a red shirt leaning over her seat. His mother clutched a black water gun while she spoke to Nelda.

"It's Timmy's fault! I've warned him a thousand times not to shoot people with that toy. Believe me he won't do it again." She grabbed her young son by the arm dragging him screaming from the theater. The young attendant asked everyone to sit down, then quietly made his way back down the aisle.

"Are you okay Nelda?" questioned Sally.

"Sure I'm fine." Nelda wiped her face with a tissue. "But I'm afraid I feel like a fool. In the dark that kid's gun looked like the real thing. When the water started running down my cheek, I thought sure it was blood."

"Do you still want to watch the rest of the movie? We can leave if you want to."

"Good heavens no! I was thoroughly enjoying this when I got the shower, so let's stay for the rest."

But Nelda couldn't relax for the rest of the movie. It wasn't like her to get upset over such an incident. The unsolved murders were beginning to make her edgy. She was glad when it was finally over.

On the way out Nelda spotted two familiar figures waiting in line for the next show, Dennis and Marcie dressed alike in jeans, red polo shirts, and sneakers. Nelda noticed the tip of Dennis's left sneaker had dark sand on it. Was it strange that they were here too? Why shouldn't they be here, she reasoned. The clinic is closed until next Monday and Galveston is certainly a tourist attraction. She waved to them and headed their way while Sally waited for her.

"Hey, you two," greeted Nelda, "taking advantage of that holiday huh?"

"Hi," Dennis answered, "Sue told us you were going to be here. How's the movie?"

"It's different, you're going to like it." Nelda looked at Marcie. "Did anyone else from the clinic come with you?"

"Carol and Violet are here. We've all rented 'By The Sea' condominiums. Walter is coming down tomorrow. After he finishes some business at the Medical Center, we're all going deep sea fishing. Don't you want to come with us?"

"No thanks," I remember being terribly sea sick on my last deep sea fishing excursion, but what about Sue?" questioned Nelda.

Marcie sighed and bit her lower lip before she spoke. "Well, I didn't want to say anything Nelda, but I think Sue has had it with Steve. She told me she's making a clean break with him this week."

Hallelujah, Nelda thought to herself. At last Sue was getting some smarts and breaking loose from a ne're-do-well. She'd learn more details when she got home. Out of the corner of her eye she could see Sally nervously tapping her foot. Right now she'd better find out what Sally's problem was. She hurriedly told the two good-bye and walked outside with her friend.

"What's wrong Sally?"

"I'm worried about leaving Sugar too long without a trip out-side. You know I keep him out most of the time."

"We'll be home in fifteen minutes. I had to see what was going on with the clinic group."

Soon they were in the station wagon making their way to the beach house. As Nelda sped along, her mind was busy with the few clues she had to the murders.

"I know you're trying to figure out which person from the clinic is the killer," said Sally interrupting her thoughts.

"You don't blame me do you? We're going to have to wind this thing up soon or they'll have to put me away."

"Tell me, who do you really suspect?"

"At this point, I can't rule any of them out except Sue and Steve."

"But Nelda, Steve was the only one that can be placed at the crime scene where Albert was shot. His fingerprints are on the door facing."

"I know, but neither Steve or Sue could have been involved in Joan's death; they were on their way back from the races. I'm sure both murders were done by the same person."

"Or persons," Sally said.

"Well, I've been thinking about two people being involved," Nelda said. "Could Dennis and Marcie be working together? Or maybe Violet and Walter? Is it possible that Walter wanted the business so bad he committed murder?"

"Why would Dennis and Marcie want them dead?" questioned Sally.

"Marcie wasted a lot of good years with Albert. She could be bitter. Is it possible she talked Dennis into committing murder for revenge?"

"It all sounds like the work of a demented person," Sally said.

"That's what worries me," Nelda complained. "The reason for their deaths might be off the wall and the case never solved."

"Don't forget there was an attempt on your life?"

"And how could I forget it? You were the one that had to go to the hospital. I still get goose bumps thinking about how close we came to being killed. I was certainly getting close to some piece of evidence that would have helped solve the case. If I only knew what."

"Here we are!" Sally sang out in her high pitched voice. "Sugar will be delighted to see us."

Sally hurried up the stairs with the key while Nelda checked the storage area downstairs to make sure it was locked. She heard Sally making a big commotion upstairs. Puzzled, she hurried to see what it was about. As soon as she stuck her head in the door, she knew. The odor coming from the living area told the whole story.

"Oh Nelda," whined Sally, "Sugar is so sick he's thrown up all over the house. Now he has diarrhea."

"Something he ate on the beach," Nelda said, taking command. "You take him downstairs while I clean it up. Maybe he'll be all right in a little bit."

"I can't leave you with this mess can I?"

"You're going to have to, because he may still be sick. Just do as I say."

"Okay, come on you poor sweet dog. Let's go downstairs until you feel better."

Nelda worked feverishly for the next two hours scrubbing the place with Lysol. She opened all the windows and turned on the fans. Finally, when she could breathe without gagging, she went downstairs to see how Sally and Sugar were doing. She found Sally sitting on the bottom step with Sugar at her feet. Both were asleep.

"Sally," Nelda said shaking her gently. "Come on up now and go to bed"

It was after midnight before the three of them settled down. Sugar seemed to be resting comfortably on the dog bed Nelda had bought for him. As soon as Nelda dozed off, she was awakened by the dog scratching on the front door. She wrapped a robe around her body and ran downstairs into the yard with Sugar. She was not a second too soon, he had to go. Nelda decided she was not about to repeat the cleaning binge again. She climbed the stairs, retrieved the leash and tied Sugar to the lamp post, but she couldn't just leave him by himself. There was just one thing to do, she'd get in the station wagon, so she could check on the sick canine every once in awhile. She let the back seats down in the wagon and stretched out on the bed that they formed. "Oh goodness," Nelda mumbled, "this would be first class if I only had a pillow." She found a partially deflated beach ball under the seat that made a perfect cushion. Five minutes later she was asleep.

Nelda woke up when she heard Sugar barking. Forcing her weary eyes open, she heard a car driving slowly up the driveway. Now what am I supposed to do? moaned Nelda. I've nothing to defend myself. I'll just lay low and see what's going to happen. Her heart raced as footsteps made crunching noises in the shell-strewn driveway. All at once Sugar stopped barking. Had someone delivered a death blow to the poor sick dog? Not able to be still a minute longer, she sat up and found a face staring into the wagon. Headlights from the car in the driveway partially lit the inside of the wagon where Nelda was sitting. The figure on the outside let out a scream, "Aunt Nelda, are you all right?"

Nelda opened the car door and grabbed Sue by the arm. "You almost scared me to death young lady. What are you doing here in the middle of the night?"

"I might ask you the same question. Don't tell me you're trying out the bed in your new car."

"Sugar was sick from eating something bad on the beach. We had to put him outside until he got over it. Who is that in the car?"

"It's Walter. I hitched a ride with him so I could go deep sea fishing with them tomorrow. But I'm so unhappy because I've told Steve it's all over between us." With that Sue started crying.

"Why don't you just wave Walter off. We'll hash this out in the morning."

"Oh sure, he's probably wondering why I stopped by your van. He just wanted to make sure I could get in the beach house."

Sue ran back to Walter's car and spoke to him. Nelda watched as the car backed out and went on down the street. She wondered what part Walter might have in this split between Steve and Sue.

Since Sugar was resting quietly, Nelda decided that it was time to try spending the rest of the night inside. Leaving a pan of water for him to drink, she and Sue climbed the steps together. For the third time that night she made another attempt to get some rest.

This time a wristwatch alarm was chiming away. It just had to be in the wee hours. Nelda stumbled into the living area where Sue was sleeping on a hide-a-bed. "For heavens sake Sue, why is that thing going off in the middle of the night? I'm going to have to die before I get any sleep."

"I'm sorry Aunt Nelda, but Walter is picking me up in a few minutes. We're supposed to be at pier 19 before 7:30 this morning to go deep sea fishing."

"Should I fix you some breakfast?" said Nelda peering out the window. In the glow of the street lights, she noted the wind was causing the fronds of the palm trees to dance, not a good sign for this type of excursion.

"No, we'll eat on the boat."

Ha, thought Nelda, she'll be doing just like poor old Sugar when the waves get rough. Aloud she asked, "What's the name of the boat you're going on, and when will you be back?"

Sue had slipped on blue jeans, a white sweatshirt and was busy lacing up her deck shoes. She was surprisingly cheery for someone who had a broken heart. "We're leaving on the New Buccaneer. We'll return around 7:30 p.m. The boat furnishes everything."

"Does that include sea sick pills?"

"Now, you know Walter is going to take care of us. He's already packed the medicine we'll be taking. I'm going to finish up in the bathroom. Why don't you and Sally meet the boat when it comes in. We'll eat out together?"

"We'll do that if I can get a nap this afternoon."

Presently Nelda heard Sugar barking and knew Sue's transportation had arrived. Sue gave her a peck on the cheek before running down the steps with a hat and jacket in her hands. Nelda, with no envy in her heart for that trip, fell back into bed.

* * *

Nelda and Sally stood on Pier 19 peering intently into the darkness. It was 8:00 p.m. and still no sign of the New Buccaneer. They could see other boats struggling to make it up to the piers. The wind had picked up, causing the water to be choppy. Nelda's impatience turned into deep concern when she heard the sound of an emergency vehicle pulling up to the pier. Two men in white uniforms hopped out with a stretcher. They stood waiting on the pier ready to receive someone.

"Why are you here?" asked Nelda, edging close to the pair.

"There was a man overboard on one of the party boats. They fished him out, but they're still going to need our help."

Lights from an approaching boat could be seen on the horizon. Nelda and Sally, bracing themselves against the gusts of wind, waited soberly for it to come closer.

"It's the Buccaneer!" Sally said, "I see the name on the side."

"Thank God," Nelda said, "I hope they're all okay."

As the boat's crew threw out their lines to secure the boat, Nelda saw a great deal of activity on the vessel. Several people were milling around a body stretched out on one of the benches that surrounded the cabin of the boat. As soon as the gang-plank was secured, the medics made their way to the deck taking their stretcher with them. Nelda could see them lifting an inert body dressed in blue jeans and a white sweatshirt. She slumped against Sally and closed her eyes. *It was Sue.*

CHAPTER EIGHTEEN

The Die Is Cast

As the medics lifted Sue onto the stretcher, her hand moved. Nelda started taking regular breaths then and cried silently. Walter Goodman rushed up to Nelda as Sue was loaded into the emergency vehicle. His face was lined with worry and looked pale in the weak light cast by the pier lamp.

"Nelda, Sue fell overboard," he said in a weary voice. "She almost drowned, but she's going to be all right."

"Are you positive?" asked Nelda.

"Her lungs had some water in them, so she needs an overnight stay in the hospital to make sure there are no complications," Walter said.

"Do you know how it happened?" asked Nelda.

Walter shook his head. "We were all too seasick, even with the Dramamine we took, everyone was leaning over the side throwing up. I...I guess she just lost her balance. Can you stay with her Nelda?"

"You shouldn't have to ask." Nelda said as she fought to keep the Gulf wind from stripping away her sweater. "Sue is the nearest person I'll ever have to a daughter."

"I'm coming to the hospital later," Walter said. "I've got to take the others back to the motel."

Nelda wanted to ride in the vehicle with Sue, but the tall, lanky medic in charge, who introduced himself as Sam, talked her out of it.

"Her life is not threatened. We're not going to go over the speed limit on the way to the hospital. Why don't you just follow in your car?"

Nelda nodded her head and did as she was told. She and Sally followed as close as possible. There were no problems keeping up. Nelda was silent with worry as Sally tried to make conversation.

"Sue was so fortunate to have Walter on board when they got her out of the water. I'm sure he knew just how to treat her, but what a pity to end a holiday like this."

Nelda listened to Sally prattle. It wasn't her niece's condition that bothered her now, because she was convinced that she would be okay. Somehow she got the feeling that the fall was no accident. She hoped Sue would be able to explain what happened when they got her to the hospital.

* * *

Nelda almost pulled her hair out in the next few hours getting Sue admitted and established in a private room. By the time she filled out all the papers she was beginning to look as exhausted as the patient. The emergency room doctor reaffirmed Walter's opinion that a few hours observation was necessary for Sue. If things went well, she'd be released the following day. Finally, Nelda and Sally were alone with Sue in the hospital room.

Sue was exhausted and was having a hard time keeping her eyes open . "I'm fine Aunt Nelda, just a little water logged, but I sure was scared when I went overboard."

"Maybe you shouldn't talk now. Just get some rest," Nelda said.

"No, Aunt Nelda, I want to talk about it. Someone... pushed me overboard."

The look on Sue's face was not of fright, but sadness. All the workers in the clinic were like family. Was it be true that one of them was trying to kill her? What could be the reason?

Nelda felt hopeless rage. It was like the enemy was the invisible man and could strike without being seen or leaving a trace of evidence. When would it end?

"If you feel like it Sue, go ahead and tell me exactly what happened from the moment you got on the boat," Nelda said.

"There were six in our party: Marcie, Dennis, Walter, Violet, Carol and myself. We were all acting crazy and having fun. After we traveled several miles out in the Gulf, two crew members gave us fishing poles with bait and stationed us all around the boat rail. I couldn't believe the size of the waves, they were as big as mountains. It was the motion of the boat and looking at those huge waves that finally did us in. One by one, we laid the poles down and started throwing up. It was awful. I think we were all sick...I wanted to die."

"When I looked out the window this morning," Nelda said, "I just knew you'd all be seasick, but didn't the Dramamine have any effect?"

"Walter said we waited too late to take it. At any rate, it didn't seem to help any of us. So there I was leaning as far over the rail as I could when I felt this jolt. I looked around, but all I saw was a blue slicker. Everybody was issued one. Then I was bumped again harder, my hands came off the rail. I...I lost my balance and the next thing I knew I hit the water."

"It's a wonder the boat's propeller didn't grind you up, " Sally said in horror.

"I guess if I'd been standing in the back I'd be fish bait now."

Nelda shuddered and held Sue's hand. "Who discovered you were in the water?" asked Nelda.

"Walter. He was looking for Violet and just happened to hear me fall in."

"Didn't all of you have life jackets on?"

"Sure, but I was screaming as the waves washed over me. I didn't have sense enough to close my mouth. I swallowed and breathed in lots of water. Walter was afraid I'd have an electrolyte imbalance from taking in all that water."

"How long were you in the water?" Nelda asked.

"About twenty minutes, it seemed a lot longer. I just feel all washed out." Sue yawned and grinned at her play on words.

Nelda marveled at the resilience of her young niece. Sue was making a joke about the attempt on her life. She felt the murderer was striking out at her by attacking Sue. She'd have to protect her, but how?

There was a tap on the door and a pretty, redheaded nurse came in. "Okay folks, I'm afraid Ms. Grimes needs her rest. She's been through quite an ordeal."

"Sue," Nelda asked, "would you like for me to spend the night with you?"

"No, Aunt Nelda. I'll be fine. They won't try to kill me here."

They said their good-byes, but Nelda felt uneasy. She'd take Sally home and then come back, since she wouldn't be able to sleep anyway. A good talk with John would help too.

As they drove back to the beach house, Nelda outlined her plans to Sally. "Sally, I'm going to call John when we get back to the beach house and then go back to the hospital and spend the rest of the night there."

"You're not going to be able to follow Sue around until this case is solved."

"I know. I've got to come up with a scheme, but this is the best I can do right now."

On the way back, Nelda stopped and picked up a vegetable pizza. It was a far cry from the sea food dinner they had expected to eat.

As soon as they arrived at the beach house, Nelda ate two pieces of pizza before she jotted down what she wanted to say to John.. She was sure she had a plan to learn the killer's identify.

Nelda called John; he answered on the second ring. "John Moore here."

"John, this is Nelda. I'm sorry I didn't call as soon as I got here, but I've had to do a lot of thinking and planning. Have you anything new to tell me?"

"Not much, we're down to five suspects: Carol, Marcie, Dennis, Walter and Violet. I think the murders are connected to something that happened in the past. We're going to investigate each person's activities for the last few years. Hopefully, we'll find something there. Did you know they're all in Galveston now?"

"That was another reason I called. Sue went deep sea fishing with all five of them. Somebody tried to kill her by pushing her overboard.

"My God! Is she okay? Did she see who pushed her?"

"No, she's all right, but is spending the night in the hospital because she swallowed lots of water. I'm worried sick about future attempts on her life. I'll ask Walter if she can have a few weeks off. The next time they may not fail."

"Why Sue? She doesn't know anything does she?"

"Not that I know of. I think it's my meddling they're trying to stop."

"Why they?"

"I'm not sure of the gender or the numbers involved, so that's the reason for it."

"Are you going to be in Galveston the whole week?" questioned John.

"I'm going to talk it over with Sally, but probably not. There's too many things to do back in Stearn."

"I'll talk to Sue as soon as she gets back home," John said. There is a chance that she could be mistaken about somebody pushing her overboard. It could have been an accident and whoever it was didn't want to admit it. The fishing boat must have been rocking pretty bad."

"That's a possibility; Sue is pretty emotional, however she seemed sure she was being forced over," Nelda responded.

"Did she report this to anyone besides you?"

"I don't think she did, because Walter didn't know about it. He was with her until the medics took over."

"Ask her not to say anything to anyone until I have a chance to talk to her. You think she'll be home tomorrow?" asked John.

"Yes, that's her plan," Nelda replied.

John and Nelda said their good-byes. She finished her pizza, gave Sally a word of caution about locking up, then headed back to the hospital. Driving into the parking lot, she could see that visiting hours were not over. It was difficult finding a place to park near the entrance, which didn't bother Nelda. The parking area was well lit and she could see several people in shouting distance.

Sue's room was on the third floor near the elevators. After riding the elevator up, she made for the nurse's station. A buxom nurse in a crisp, white uniform was filling out reports. She looked up without much enthusiasm as Nelda approached. The name tag pinned to her pocket read Mary Niles.

"What can I do for you?," she said, tapping her pen impatiently.

"My name is Nelda Simmons. I have a niece, Sue Grimes, in room 310. I want to spend the night with her and I'd like to have a chair recliner placed in her room."

Mary looked through the patients' folders until she found Sue's chart. She studied it for a minute and then looked up. "You know it's not necessary for you to stay with her. We're going to watch her closely."

"I appreciate that," said Nelda, but I promised her mother I'd look after her." Nelda failed to mention that the promise was made when Sue was five, the year her mother, Nelda's sister, had died.

"We'll find a chair for you," Mary said.

Nelda thanked her and went on down the hall until she came to 310. The door was ajar with the main light switched off. Nelda tiptoed into the room and found a screen around Sue's bed. When she peeped around the screen, she was surprised to find a man standing near the window.

"Hey there!" Nelda shouted, "what do you think you're doing?"

Nelda's screaming woke up Sue who cried out in fright. The man threw up his hands and spoke above the noise of the women.

"For God's sake Nelda it's me, Walter. I just came by to check on Sue and I wanted to see if she was awake."

"You shouldn't have done that Walter, we're all on edge. It

would have been better to check on her at the nurse's station," Nelda said in an irritated tone.

"It's all right, Aunt Nelda; it's not like you to get upset like this."

Nelda was immediately ashamed of her outburst when she looked into Walter's face. He seemed to have aged since the murders took place. There were shadows under his eyes and he had lost weight. His body appeared to be sagging under the weight of his problems. She wondered if Violet was the cause of his condition.

"I'm sorry, Walter, but what was I to think when I saw a man standing by her bed?"

"You see, Aunt Nelda is upset because someone deliberately pushed me overboard."

Oh Oh! thought Nelda, the cat's out of the bag now. John wouldn't be happy that Sue spilled the news, but maybe it was better this way.

Gazing at Sue in disbelief, Walter sank down in a chair. He closed his eyes and took several deep breaths before speaking. "John Moore is not doing enough to solve the murders. What will it take to get him going. Another death? Why would they want you dead Sue?"

"To make me stop probing," answered Nelda, holding Sue's hand.

"You'll have to stop now, Nelda," Walter said sharply. "You can't endanger Sue's life."

"I tell you what you can do, Walter. Give Sue a few weeks off. There's a place I know she'll be safe until this mess is cleared up."

"It's done, Nelda. I...we'll miss her, but it's the best thing to do," answered Walter. The lines in his face softened when he looked at Sue.

"Just a minute," said Sue pulling her hand away from Nelda. "You're talking about me like I'm not here. I guess I have something to say about taking time off. I just can't afford it. Besides, where would I go?"

"Could we talk about this later, Sue?" asked Nelda. "I'm sorry I didn't discuss it with you first. I guess worry clouded my reasoning."

"I'm sure things will look brighter tomorrow, so why don't both of you get out of here and let me get some sleep?" Sue said, lying down.

"Of course," Walter spoke quietly smiling at Sue. "We'll talk tomorrow."

Nelda waited until Walter was out of the room before she told Sue she'd be spending the night. Sue didn't bother to argue just turned on her side and closed her eyes. The recliner was brought in and Nelda stretched out with a light blanket covering her legs.

Nurse Mary was right about them looking after Sue. Every three or four hours a nurse quietly slipped in to monitor the patient. Nelda watched each entry and exit with caution.

* * *

The clatter of food carts rolling down the hall caused Nelda to sit up with alarm. She then realized night had long since faded away. The sun's rays streaming through the partially closed venetian blinds were making horizontal patterns on the floor of the room, and Sue was sitting up in bed brushing her hair.

There was a knock on the door. A cheerful, little blonde attendant placed a covered tray on the table beside Sue's bed and left. Nelda followed the attendant outside to see if she could get a cup of coffee. When she returned with her coffee, Nelda found Sue staring at a slip of paper.

"What is it, Sue? asked Nelda.

"I found this note when I lifted the lid of my tray. It's written in Latin; what does it mean?" she said, thrusting the paper in Nelda's hand.

Nelda read the red printed message aloud. "*Alea jacta est;* it means the die is cast."

Both women stared at the paper in dismay. Nelda reacted by rushing out to find the cafeteria attendant. She was working her way down the hall with the breakfast cart.

"Excuse me," Nelda said. "Is the food on this cart brought up in an elevator from the kitchen?"

NELDA SEES RED   149

The girl looked at Nelda oddly. "Yes, I use a service elevator to bring the food up."

"Then you leave it in the hall as you deliver food to each room?"

"Certainly, is there something wrong with the breakfast?"

"No, I was just wondering if a person would have an opportunity to slip a note under the cover of someone's food."

"If they walked down the hall while I was in a room, they could. The patient's name is written on a slip of paper attached to the tray."

"Did you see anyone you didn't recognize on the floor?"

"No."

Nelda thanked her, then rushed to the nurse's station. A tired looking nurse with steely gray hair was studying patients charts. "How can I help you," she asked?

Nelda explained the situation and asked if she had seen any strangers. She gave a negative answer and Nelda knew to investigate further would be fruitless. Disheartened, she headed back to Sue's room clutching the third warning in her hand.

CHAPTER NINETEEN

Midnight Red

As soon as Nelda pulled into her own driveway from their trip to Galveston, she knew what she had to say. "Sally, I've been thinking about your visit here. It's time for you and Sugar to go home."

Sue, sitting in the back seat, expressed shock at Nelda's seemingly rude behavior.

"Aunt Nelda, what are you thinking? How can you be so rude?"

Sally grinned. "Sue, I've known your aunt for a long time. She doesn't hurt my feelings in the least. I'm just getting in the way of her investigation, so she's decided to send me packing."

Nelda faced Sally and gave her a loving pat. "Someone is trying to get me off the case, that's why they're going after those close to me, like Sue. You'll be next."

"And you'd be able to spend more time investigating if you didn't have to entertain me," Sally said.

"Sally, you and Sue listen carefully. The murderer works at the clinic, and I have a feeling he or she is getting desperate. Sue, I want you to go home with Sally so she can drive you to the airport. You'll fly to Denver where Cousin Richard will pick you up.

He's pleased to have you spend a few days with him and his wife, Shelly. Remember, we don't want anyone here to know where you are. Don't tell a soul."

"I'm not going," Sue said. "I'm not leaving you here to battle this thing alone."

"But I'm not alone. John is here to help me. It'll all be over in no more than a couple of weeks."

"What about my job at the clinic?" asked Sue. There were deep circles under her eyes and her usual neat appearance was gone; it was replaced by windblown hair and wrinkled clothes.

"Walter will be happy to get a temporary helper to take your place for a couple of weeks. He seems worried about you too, but remember no one at that clinic is to be trusted," Nelda said emphatically.

"And if it's not over in a couple of weeks, then what?" Sue looked at Nelda with tears in her eyes.

Nelda put her arms around Sue and hugged her. "It will be over, baby, I promise you."

"Well goodness," said Sally. "I guess we've both been given our travel orders. Let's unload, then you and I will pack, Sue, and be off tomorrow morning bright and early."

Unloading was a tedious chore; everything was full of sand and they were emotionally and physically drained. Nelda drove Sue home, but promised to come back in a couple of hours to pick her up. All the suspects were still in Galveston, so Nelda felt safe in leaving her for this short time.

Big John's Auto Repair delivered Sally's old car all spruced up and ready to take on more mileage. Nelda felt a twinge of jealousy, because she really missed her old station wagon. She wished in some ways she still had it.

When they returned with Sue's luggage, Sally was putting the final touch to a garden salad to go with a large supreme pizza she had ordered.

"I hope you don't make a habit of eating food like this pizza," Nelda said to Sally. "Look at that conglomeration of stuff on top of the crust; it's oozing enough fat to raise your cholesterol level ten points."

"Well you just eat the salad you old grouch, because Sue and I are going to enjoy all the goodies on this pizza."

Nelda couldn't resist, it looked and smelled so good she had two pieces while Sue and Sally sat there grinning at her.

After supper, they packed Sally's car, listened to the news and went to bed early. What a joy to sleep in my own bed, Nelda thought. She had double checked the locks on the doors and windows and let Sugar sleep inside. Maybe, just maybe they could all get a good night's sleep. Goodness knows they all needed it.

* * *

As she waved good-bye to Sally and Sue after breakfast, Nelda stood in her driveway with a lump in her throat. She felt all alone, but knew she had done the right thing sending them away. All she had to worry about now was rooting out the killer and keeping herself safe.

Deciding to write down some of the information she and John had gathered about the murders, she went back inside and set up a large chalk board on an easel in the dining room. She figured it would take her till noon to organize the information then write it down. John needed to be in on this too, so she invited him to come over at 1:00 p.m.

First, she wrote Dr. Albert Coldsby's name on the board and made a side bar that listed facts about the case. Coldsby was found naked and dead on top of an examination table with his clothes neatly folded on a chair. A Latin message was taped to his chest. No sign of forced entry and the cause of death was a single bullet through his heart fired from his own gun at close range.

On the other side of his name, she made a second side bar listing all the people who might want to kill him and had the opportunity to do so. The names included everyone that worked inside the clinic: Marcie Gibbons, Walter Goodman, Violet Rosin, Carol Scrubbs and Sue Grimes. She then included the names of Steve Morris and Dennis Toliver. They were suspects from the outside that had motives and access to the building. The last name added was Roberto Sanchez, big motive but no access.

Skipping down, Nelda listed possible clues: powder burns and lack of forced entry indicated he was shot by someone he knew; a woman sent the murder weapon to the sheriff; he died between the hours of eight and nine; all suspects disliked him and had no iron clad alibis.

On the bottom of the board, she wrote the name of Joan Coldsby and the cause of her death and underneath she wrote a possible motive for her death.

Joan Coldsby drowned because of a muscle relaxant in her drink.

Reason for death: Joan was going to give information related to his murder.

Nelda then listed other clues and some related incidents to the deaths: Three warnings in Latin; Chanel lipstick in driveway; the smell of Chanel; attempted murders by loosening the wheel lugs of her station wagon; Sue's near drowning; burning of the personnel files; Coldsby's old telephone bills.

Nelda didn't know if the hodgepodge she had written on the board would be of any use, but it was a beginning. Maybe John could add or take away from it.

She had just finished a sandwich and glass of milk when the doorbell rang. Nelda looked out the window. She could see John standing there with his hands in his pockets, his head lowered in thought. She thought he looked thin, and a few gray hairs were beginning to crop up in his dark hair.

Opening the door, she smiled at him while giving his arm a squeeze. "Come in here," she said. "I bet you could use a big cup of coffee to keep you awake while we go through this information I've written down for us."

"Thanks Nelda, you're right as usual. Some of the town kids decided to go on a drinking binge last night. I haven't had much sleep."

"I hope you got them squared away," Nelda said, leading him into the kitchen.

"Sure did, it was quite a surprise for some of their parents too. I think they'll impose some curfews now."

John and Nelda took their coffee into the dining room. They sat facing the blackboard Nelda had set up.

"Let's start with your list of names, Nelda. I notice the last one on the list is Roberto Sanchez. I've eliminated him from my list. He's not guilty of killing Coldsby even though he might have the best reason of all. Berto told me he believes Coldsby let his grandson die."

"I'm glad to hear you say he's no longer a suspect. Let's go to the next name."

John shook his head sadly. "What a shame that Marcie wasted so much of her life on that miserable doctor. She kept waiting for him to divorce his wife. It never happened. Could a lady scorned be that vindictive?"

"It's happened before," said Nelda. But when did her affair with Coldsby end? When did her affair with Dennis start? I think if we knew more about that romance we could get a better feel for her part, if any, in these murders. I don't think we'll be able to rule her out as a suspect right now.

"And while we're talking about her we might as well talk about Dennis. He kept the grounds around the clinic as well as those at the Coldsby residence. By his own admission, he was mowing grass at a business near the clinic the same day of the doctor's death, and he was around the Coldsby house shortly before I found Joan Coldsby dead in the pool. In addition, he knew about me collecting old comic books. He could have easily slipped that horrible old comic with the warning in my collection."

"Dennis might be responsible for the other warnings too, but it's hard for me to believe this guy had a motive. Killing two people because Marcie couldn't snare the doctor just doesn't add up, however we can't rule him out as a suspect, or the possibility they're working together."

"Now we come to Walter and Violet," Nelda said, as she took a long sip from her cup. "When Walter was my student, he was an idealist studying hard so that some day he could alleviate human suffering. Do you think those years of clawing his way through medical school has turned him into a murderer? One that will do anything to get his own clinic? And Violet, what role does she play?"

John looked down at his notes before he spoke. "Tell me in all honesty, Nelda. Who gained from these deaths?"

Nelda sighed and looked away. "Yes, Walter did get the business, and I know he'll stay on our list and Violet too. Sue says that Violet will do anything for Walter."

"I think we can safely eliminate Roberto, Sue and Steve Morris," said John. He happily went to the board and erased their names. "Those three were not around when Mrs. Coldsby was killed. We know the two deaths are connected."

"Yes, it would be awfully hard for me to picture any of those three removing Coldsby's clothes and neatly folding them on a chair before they blew him away," Nelda grimaced as she spoke.

"But you can with some of the suspects can't you?" John asked.

"I suppose I could, but let's talk about Carol Scrubbs now. She was eaten up with hate for Coldsby. I still can't believe how insensitive he was; at the lowest point in her life, he was going to throw her to the dogs," said Nelda.

"Did Carol kill him?" John asked.

"She had motive, opportunity, but did she have the nerve? Somehow I think her hard shell is just a front to protect herself from further injury. Her family has turned on her, her husband is dying and she's worried about her own health," Nelda said.

"Well there you have it. There are five suspects left on the board. All of them were on the boat when Sue was pushed overboard. They were also at the outdoor concert and know some Latin. Besides that, they were capable of loosening the lugs on your old station wagon." John paused and Nelda took over.

"There was definitely a woman involved. A woman called about the gun and men don't wear Chanel lipstick or perfume," Nelda declared.

John nodded and said "Well it looks like it boils down to this. It's either a woman working by herself or with a man, and one of them or both are connected to the clinic. I'm going to call the suspects in once more, then see if I can come up with something new. In the meantime, I'll press Walter for his personnel files as soon as they're replaced from the fire damage."

Nelda rose and stretched her arms. Her body ached from lack of exercise. As soon as John left she'd take a walk.

"I'm going to interview those people too," Nelda told John as she walked him to the door. "But I might be a little more subtle than you'll be," Nelda said smiling.

"Promise me you'll use caution, Nelda; this murderer has nothing to lose if he or she kills another. Call me if you turn up anything at all. Let's stay in close touch."

Nelda gave her word and watched him as he backed out of the drive. She looked across the yard at all the work that needed to be done in her flower beds. Soon she was engrossed in thinning out clumps of Lemon Grass to plant in another bed. The grass, with a citrus odor, was touted to keep mosquitoes away. After several hours of digging and planting, she noticed clouds were gathering overhead. If she wanted a walk, she'd better hurry or she would be walking in the rain. Slipping on a light jacket and securing her hair under a scarf, Nelda started out in the direction of Carson street. She knew Carol lived in a condo on the corner of Carson and Fifth Street, a good two miles away. She felt confident she could walk there and back before the first drop fell.

There were hardly any cars on the streets and why should there be, it was Sunday afternoon. She could imagine half the town dozing in front of their TV sets. As she approached Carol's apartment, the activity picked up. She noticed several cars parked out on the street. When she got closer she recognized one of them belonged to John. Her curiosity heightened as Deputy Carl Hanks pulled up in his old truck and got out. Quickening her pace, she called to Carl before he went inside.

"Hello there, what's going on here?"

Carl looked around startled. "Oh it's you Ms. Simmons, I didn't expect to see you here. Have you heard the bad news?"

"What bad news," said Nelda, walking toward him as it started to rain.

"It's about Carol Scrubbs. She's dead!"

"Oh...No!...how did it happen?"

"When she came back from Galveston, she went to visit her husband, Shelby, and found him dead. She just lost it...started blaming herself for leaving him...drove to the clinic, injected herself with a muscle relaxant ... her heart just stopped."

"That's terrible," whispered Nelda. "Who found her?"

"Dr. Goodman."

Nelda's warm tears mingled with the steady rain falling on her face.

CHAPTER TWENTY

Night Fright

Shelby and Carol both dead! Of course everyone expected Shelby to go, having AIDS and all, but Carol had her whole life before her, or did she? We'll never know, now. Nelda mulled these things over in her mind as she followed Deputy Sheriff Hanks into the apartment.

John was looking through some papers on Carol's desk as Nelda entered. He looked up in surprise.

"Nelda!" someone call you about Carol?"

"No, I was out walking and saw Carl."

"Did he tell you what happened?"

"Yes," she said shaking her head sadly, "was there a note?"

"No, she had a big emotional outburst at the hospice, blaming herself for his death, because she wasn't with him when he needed her. Then, she went over to the clinic and took enough of those muscle relaxants to kill a horse. When Walter found her it was too late."

"What are you looking for?" Nelda asked.

"According to Marcie, Carol had paid for two funeral policies to have herself and Shelby cremated. She doesn't recall which insurance company issued them, so I'm trying to find the policies."

"Did you notify her parents?"

"I did and they won't have anything to do with them, even after death."

"That's so pitiful. What about Shelby's folks?"

"I can't even find them."

"Have you just started your search for the insurance papers?"

"Yes, and it shouldn't take long to find them if they're here. The apartment only has three rooms."

"She might have put them in a safety deposit box," Nelda said, seeing a bank statement in John's hand.

"I guess I'll have to wait until tomorrow. Where do you suppose Carol would keep those policies if she didn't have a safety deposit box."

"Closet... in a box, under the bed, maybe even in the kitchen cabinet. I'll give you a hand in the search."

Nelda was impressed with the neat and orderly way Carol had kept her apartment. The floor was clean, not even a dust ball under the bed. The simple cotton curtains in the windows looked fresh. Nothing was stored under the bed, but she found a large brown box on the floor in the back of the closet. It contained a photograph album and some old text books. She opened up the album and was instantly saddened by the smiling faces of Shelby and Carol taken on their honeymoon. The album was a pictorial, chronological review of their life together. Halfway through the book, Nelda noticed a remarkable difference in the pictures of Shelby taken then and those in earlier years of marriage. His hair was longer, his clothes looked dirty and his smile seemed forced; Carol's picture was different too. Her face had taken on a solemn look and she had added pounds to her short frame. The few friends that appeared in the photographs appeared scruffy and malnourished. They looked like street bums. Nelda wondered if Shelby hadn't taken up drugs at this point in his life. This would certainly account for his state of health.

Closing the album, she perused the well-used text books stacked neatly in the box. There were several on bacteriology, virology and laboratory techniques. At the very bottom of the box, she discovered a small volume of pharmaceutical Latin. Nelda was taken aback by her discovery, but then she reasoned, why shouldn't Carol have a Latin book? Her degree was in science, so Latin was probably required. Thoughtfully, she replaced the box in the closet.

Before tackling the bathroom, she searched for John and Carl. Both of them were in the tiny kitchen and dinette area. "I didn't find a thing in the bedroom. Have you two had any luck?" Nelda asked.

"There's nothing that can help us in here," answered Carl, "even the cupboard is bare. Carol must have done a lot of eating out."

"She probably didn't eat anything here but breakfast," John said. "The people at hospice said she spent most of her free time over there. I guess that's why she felt so guilty when Doc Goodman talked her into going to Galveston for a couple of days. It's a shame Shelby waited until that time to die."

"Most folks don't pick their time to die, John. If they did, we'd probably have more folks on earth than it could support," Nelda said.

"We're almost through here," John said. "Are you going to tackle the bathroom?"

"Sure," Nelda answered walking out of the kitchen, "but it's unlikely she'd keep any papers, except toilet paper, in there."

There was a tiny medicine cabinet to one side of the sink, a towel closet and a small drawer under the built-in vanity. The towel cabinet contained three towels and wash cloths. One of the towels had Carol's maiden name on it. Nelda had to grin, because she knew if she had one with her maiden name on it, it would be considered an antique. Next, she pulled open the vanity drawer. This contained some Avon face powder, a jar of Clinique cream and several tubes of lipstick. All the lipsticks were well used tubes of Revlon. The medicine cabinet was bare except for a box of Band-Aids and tampons. As she moved the boxes over, the Band-Aid box fell on the floor and out rolled a tube of lipstick. Nelda bent to pick it up and gasp in wonder as she read the brand out loud, "Chanel."

* * *

The sun was setting and there were dark shadows on Nelda's back porch as she and John sat in grandfather rocking chairs trying to qualify what they had found. John had the lipstick and Latin book in one hand, and used the other hand to rub his chin, something he had a tendency to do when things weren't going well. Nelda feared he wouldn't have a chin left if this case didn't end soon.

"Well, what do you think, Nelda?"

"It's ludicrous! Carol didn't have enough money to buy bread much less Chanel lipsticks. Someone could have planted the lipstick and book after they found out she was dead. There was enough time, wasn't there?"

"Of course. How long would it take to go anywhere in this town?"

"It would certainly be convenient for the killer if you decided Carol was guilty. That would be the end of that," Nelda said. "Case closed." Nelda got up to inspect a wilted begonia flower and yanked off the wilted flower.

"You don't think she's guilty?"

"No, but I didn't think she would take her own life either. I thought I knew her well when she was my student; but maybe I didn't. What happens to their bodies if no one will claim them?"

"The county will see to it that they get a decent burial, but I'm still in hopes of finding the cremation policies."

"What happened to her handbag and where is her car? The policies might be in there."

"Her handbag was virtually empty, just a driver's license and Exxon credit card. There were no papers in the glove compartment of the car. Tomorrow we'll examine the laboratory at the clinic. Maybe she has the policies there," said John getting out of the chair and walking toward the steps.

"What's the shade of that lipstick, John? I want to see if it's the same shade as the one I found in the driveway after my car was tampered with."

John held the lipstick out in the fading light and identified it as Midnight Red. The one she had found in her driveway was also

Midnight Red. Both being the same shade couldn't be just a coincidence could it? Had someone replaced the lipstick they lost and put it in Carol's cabinet?

"I don't know what it means John, but I do know if I'm not in bed in the next two hours I'll probably fall on my face. Call me if you find the policies. I'd like to have a memorial service for them here. The thought of those two buried or cremated without a formal good-bye makes me want to weep."

"I'll call tomorrow as soon as I find out anything," said John wearily as he made his way out to his car.

Nelda went back inside and tried to watch the evening news, but couldn't keep her eyes open. She checked all the locks, got ready for bed and realized she hadn't called Sue to let her know what happened. She was torn between calling and not calling, but she knew that Sue wouldn't forgive her when she found out about the deaths.

Nelda picked up the phone and dialed Cousin Richard's phone number. He answered the phone and Nelda forced herself to chat for a minute and then asked for Sue.

"Sue, this is Aunt Nelda. I have some bad news to tell you about Carol and Shelby."

"What is it Aunt Nelda? Did Shelby finally die?"

"Yes, that and more. Carol killed herself when she heard the news." Nelda waited for the flood of tears and moans, but it didn't come, just sadness in Sue's voice when she finally spoke.

"She told me she was going to die when Shelby was gone; I didn't believe her. I'm sorry I wasn't there when she needed a friend. I'm coming home for the funerals."

"No, no," Nelda answered. Just hang on for a few more days with Cousin Richard. You can't help Carol anymore. Coming back would just expose yourself to the murderer."

Sue gave a soft little moan. "Promise me you'll call me if anything at all happens."

"I promise," said Nelda, realizing she'd won the battle. "One more thing before we say good night, do you know where Carol kept her insurance policies?"

"Yes," Sue laughed through her tears. "She kept them in the cabinet locked up with the drugs. She used to say it was cheaper than a safety deposit box and just as safe."

"All of you had a key to that closet?"

"No, she was the only one besides the doctors. When we wanted something out of there, she made us sign for it."

"Well thanks for that good information, at least their wishes can be carried out. I'll talk to you in a few days and please, please don't let anyone know where you are."

Nelda couldn't believe a bed could feel so good. She went right to sleep and didn't wake up until she heard the telephone ringing.

"Hello," she managed to say in a cheerful voice even though her mouth felt like a dry well.

"Nelda, I know I didn't wake you because you're such an early riser," came John's reply.

"Sure," laughed Nelda, not bothering to tell him she'd over-slept. After all she did have a reputation to keep up.

"You want to meet me at the clinic this morning? I'm going to look for those policies."

"No need to search, I know where they are. I talked to Sue last night and she said they were locked up in the drug cabinet."

"That's great; I'll go over and pick them up."

"I'd still like to meet you there, because I'm going to invite all the employees to a memorial service for Carol and Shelby."

"I'll be there at ten," he said.

"I have a plan in mind that I'd like to share with you," said Nelda as she glanced toward the window where sunlight danced on her collection of glass paperweights displayed on a marble top table. "I'll tell you about it when I see you," she said cradling the phone.

Nelda went to the kitchen for coffee and started taking mental notes of everything that had to be done before there could be a memorial service. She had to find out if Carol belonged to any particular faith, arrange for a speaker, order food and drinks and see about seating the friends who would attend.

* * *

John and Nelda drove up at the same time. The parking lot was full of cars and Nelda wondered how they were getting along with Sue's temporary replacement.

"That was really good timing," John said, as he approached her with a smile. "Let's go on in and get this over with; nothing I hate worse than a doctor's office."

"That makes two of us, but it's not like you were here because you're sick, John. Just feel sorry for the people that are here because they have to be."

"Good point," said John looking down at his cowboy boots.

Nelda cringed as he rubbed the toe of one boot on his pants leg. John had a thing about his boots; the pants could be dirty, but the boots had to shine.

They walked to the office together, lost in separate thoughts. Nelda broke the silence as John opened the door for her.

"Hopefully, Carol left a will, so the things in her apartment can be disposed of. Maybe even instructions about their funerals."

"That would be nice, but there doesn't seem to be many worldly goods to worry about," commented John.

They made their way to Walter's office and found him waiting for them. He seemed especially glad to see Nelda; Sue was on his mind.

"Nelda," he said after greeting them, "when are we going to get Sue back? Do you have a number where I can reach her?"

"Sorry, John, but I'm sure she'll be calling us in a few days. How is her replacement working out?"

"The place is in shambles. I didn't realize how much we depended on Sue and Carol. I almost feel like shutting the place down and taking a trip myself."

"Things will be back to normal before long, you'll see. It will just take some time to replace Carol."

John turned their attention back to the reason for their visit. "Walter, I need to get into your drug cabinet and retrieve Carol's papers."

"I have them here for you," Walter said, producing a large manila envelope. Violet found them yesterday when I asked her to get some drug samples for me. I never dreamed Carol had her personal things stashed in there."

John opened up the envelope and discovered the burial policies, but there were no wills. Nelda could tell he was disappointed that there were no other papers. She turned her attention to Walter.

"Tomorrow night, Walter, I'd like to host a memorial service for Carol and Shelby at my house. Could someone here furnish me a list of people to call? Did she belong to a religious group?"

"Not to my knowledge, but I'm sure Marcie or Violet would know her friends and call you with a list, or even make the calls for you. I'm happy that you're doing this for them. What time do you want to have it?"

"I think 8:00 p.m. would be about right. It would give all of you a chance to go home, change clothes and relax a minute."

"I'll have Marcie make the calls and then call you. Shouldn't be but a handful of people, maybe fifteen, the staff at the hospice and people here at the clinic."

"Thanks, Walter, I'll be expecting Marcie's call. See you tomorrow."

"Happy to do it ....and listen...when you hear from Sue, please tell her we miss her." He gave Nelda a sad little smile.

They walked outside, but not too soon for John or Nelda. They both took deep breaths of fresh air to clean the antiseptic odor of the clinic out of their nostrils.

"What was this plan you wanted to discuss with me?" John asked.

Nelda leaned against a tree for support and tried to speak convincingly. "I think Joan was going to say that the solution to the murders is in Aspen. Let's start a rumor tomorrow night that I'm going to Aspen, because someone there will help me identify the killer. Then, we'll see if I have any visitors after the memorial."

"You mean set yourself up as bait? I can't let you do that."

"I didn't mean to be in the house by myself. You could be

inside and Carl staked outside. You know it's worth a try John; we haven't gotten anywhere so far."

John stood there rubbing his chin and finally gave a big sigh. "O.K., provided I spend the whole night inside with you and Carl will be hiding outside."

"Agreed, so I better get home to prepare for tomorrow." Nelda adjusted her blue jean skirt before getting into her new station wagon. Her memory of the old wagon was beginning to fade. Now she wondered why she had waited so long to get a new car.

* * *

Before the service started, John answered questions about the murders when asked by several individuals. He also made sure the news got around about Nelda's proposed trip to Aspen.

Twenty pairs of eyes watched Walter Goodman walk up to the makeshift podium in Nelda's living room. Nelda glanced at the card table displaying a wedding picture of the departed young couple beside a vase full of roses. The flowers were sent by Shelby's nurse, Rose Washington.

"Tonight," Walter said, "we're gathered here to remember our friends, Shelby and Carol." He spoke for a few minutes and then sat down. One by one friends of the couple rose to give their remembrances of them. Nelda wiped away tears and wondered about the cold hearts of their parents.

At 10:00 p.m. she said good-bye to the last mourner and started putting things away. It was 11:00 p.m. when John returned and tapped on the back door; an hour later all the lights were out; Nelda's kitchen window was slightly opened; the neighborhood was silent, and the waiting had begun.

"Remember, Nelda, "if someone climbs in the window, make sure he is all the way in before you budge an inch," John whispered.

"I'll be tempted to run in there, but I'll wait for you to make the first move."

It was still dark outside. Nelda and John, stretched out on lawn chairs in Nelda's dining room, suddenly awakened to the rustling of bushes under the open window. They both listened intently as the window was raised with soft scraping noises, followed by light footsteps across the kitchen floor. John grabbed his gun and rose quietly from the chair, but Nelda pulled him back down.

"More noises in the bushes," she whispered.

After several seconds of bumping and fumbling at the window, a man's head and shoulders appeared in the window opening.

"Stay right there!" shouted John with his gun pointed at the window as Nelda flipped on the powerful spotlight held tightly in her hand.

"Don't shoot! don't shoot!" shouted the intruder as the rays illuminated his face.

"My God!" shouted John, "I could have killed you Carl. You should have waited outside."

"But someone climbed through the window and I thought you might be asleep," Carl answered.

John turned and ran for the front hall just in time to hear the front door slam. Anxiously, Nelda and Carl followed John into the front yard. However, the early morning visitor had disappeared.

"If it was daylight, we might have a chance of catching the intruder, but not now," Nelda said. "He or she is long gone."

John shook his head in disgust as he pointed the spotlight toward the heavy shrubbery. After a thirty minute search in the area, they gave up and went back inside. The culprit had left no self incriminating evidence in the house or outside the window, not even footprints.

The night was wasted away and all Nelda's trap had snared was an inexperienced deputy. *She moaned in the darkness knowing the murderer was one step ahead.*

CHAPTER TWENTY-ONE

"Three Blind Mice"

Nelda sat brooding on her back porch, not bothering to see that her hanging baskets of English ivy could use a drink of water. The phone rang and she was tempted not to answer it, but then she realized cutting herself off from the outside world wouldn't make up for the faux pas that happened after the memorial. She answered on the fifth ring.

"Nelda, this is Walter. Hope I didn't catch you working in your garden. I just wanted to thank you for having the memorial for Carol and Shelby. It was a wonderful thing for you to do and we all appreciate it."

"I wouldn't have had it any other way," Nelda responded. "They were just two people caught up in a web without a means of escape. At least we provided some dignity to their lives."

"Yes, I'll never forget them, but I'm not forgetting Sue either. It's been a week now since we've heard from her. Is she all right? When is she coming home?"

Nelda noticed a certain edge to his voice; it was just short of being frantic. She realized that there was more than an employer interest here. She wondered what had happened to the Walter/Violet romance.

"She's going to be fine; it'll just take a little time, Walter. You realize the events of the last few months have taken its toll on her physically and mentally: the breaking up with Steve, and near drowning. It was time she took a break so she could pull herself together."

"I'm sure that's true, but I...we...really miss her and need her. I don't even know where she is."

"You can be sure she's well taken care of and will contact you soon. In the meantime let's let her rest. By the way, how are the plans for your marriage coming along? I haven't heard anyone speak of it lately."

There was a long pause on the other end of the line. Nelda wondered what thoughts were going through Walter's mind. His romance had all the signs of going sour, but she knew Violet had too much invested in Walter to give him up without a struggle.

"I guess you could say it's on hold. With all that's going on, I'm not exactly ready to make plans for the rest of my life."

Nelda caught a bit of aggravation in his tone. She decided it would be better if she didn't extend the conversation on this topic.

"Thank you for calling, Walter. I'll pass the news on to Sue that everybody misses her."

"Listen, Nelda, before Sue left the clinic, employees bought tickets to Stearn's Little Theater to see Agatha Christie's play "Three Blind Mice." Since Sue is not here, why don't you come with us? I picked up the tickets today. We're meeting in the lobby at 7:30 p.m."

"Well, how sweet of you to offer! You know how I love anything to do with a mystery. I'll be there."

Nelda twisted her wedding band around her finger, something she had a tendency to do when she was excited. Here was another chance to be around the suspects, and see how they would react to her now that they thought she was going to follow up leads in Aspen.

As soon as she hung up, Nelda made a beeline for the bookcase. She searched the shelves until she came up with the volume that contained the short stories of Agatha Christie. There was a big smile on her face as she sat down to reread "Three Blind Mice". She was disappointed to find that neither Jane Marple nor Hercule Poirot was in the story.

When Nelda read a Christie mystery with Miss. Marple in it, she always felt ...well...inadequate. How was it that Miss. Marple, given a few clues, could solve a crime from her rocking chair? Why couldn't she, Nelda Simmons, do the same? If she only had the insight of those two super sleuths, her own mystery would be solved. Nelda shook her head and smiled. It was ridiculous for her to think of Jane Marple and Hercule Poirot as real people.

Time to get back to the real world. She called John to tell him she would be attending the play. He said that, because of the stakeout fiasco, he was making unscheduled checks of her house from now on. They were so close to the murderer this morning. Nelda bit her lip in frustration.

* * *

Watching the local news at five, Nelda learned that the Little Theater was having its twenty-fifth anniversary reception before the performance. This would certainly alter what she planned to wear to the performance. Instead of a pantsuit, she chose a long, violet blue dress that reminded her of the skies in Aspen. Everything she did now reminded her of the unsolved case. Those phone calls from Aspen by Coldsby had to be a clue and she knew she would be the one to check it out.

At 6:30 p.m. Nelda was decked out in her best clothes. She felt like Mrs. Astor. Sailing out of the house, she slid into her new station wagon. There was nothing she enjoyed more than mingling with people and being entertained, except of course, solving mysteries

A few minutes later Nelda arrived at the theater. She parked under a street light as close as she could to the entrance. Her small purse was strapped around her waist, freeing her hands to carry a long, black, unopened umbrella. An umbrella serves two purposes thought Nelda, protection from rain and from assault. Sometimes she wondered why women lived longer than men did, because they had a lot more aggravation: childbirth, rape, unequal pay and bad hair days just to name a few.

An old downtown building had been converted into the theater. Nelda entered a softly lit lobby where clusters of people were visiting while sipping on cheap champagne. She recognized Olga Triskey, the founder of Stearn's Little Theater. Olga and Nelda had worked together for several years on the Arts Council and were on first name basis. Olga was the nearest thing to a movie star Stearn had. She was standing in a corner surrounded by admirers; a bright pink dress covered her voluptuous body. Nelda wondered how she had reacted when cast in the role she was playing tonight. Olga was playing the part of an obnoxious, overbearing, middle-aged woman who's killed off at the end of the first act.

Nelda was admiring the four-tiered cake displayed on a side table when she felt someone tap her on the shoulder. Turning, she realized the clinic staff had arrived. Most of them reminded her of characters in her old *Archie* comic book. Dennis, looking uncomfortable in his light blue sports coat, was a ringer for Archie; Marcie, in a tightly fitted white, silk dress would make a stunning Veronica. Violet, dressed in a sea green gauze gown, could double for Betty. But fortunately, Walter, looking tired in a navy blue suit, was not a Jughead. Nelda thought that Clark Kent, in her *Superman* comics, would be more in line for Walter's look-alike character.

"It's so nice to see all of you," Nelda said, "I know we're going to enjoy this play."

"We'd enjoy it more if Sue was with us. Is she ever coming back? Her replacement is just not the same," Marcie said.

Nelda looked in the faces of each one. They were all looking at her with half smiles on their lips, waiting for an answer. It was hard to believe that one or perhaps two of these seemingly wholesome-looking people were wanted for murder and attempted murder. If she could only read their hearts for the truth. Nelda knew the killer would strike again until he or she felt safe.

"Just a case of nerves after the boat incident," she answered. "She'll be back with us soon."

"Are you really going to Aspen to look for clues to the Coldsby murders?" Dennis asked. "I'll be glad to go with you."

Marcie frowned. "You're not going by yourself are you?"

"I haven't finalized my plans for that trip."

"Nelda, it's not safe for you to go there," Violet said looking to Walter for confirmation. "Why don't you let the sheriff handle it?"

"I believe that's enough advice for Nelda," Walter said irritably, giving Violet a hard look. "I've known her for a long time and she doesn't use bad judgment. I think we're forgetting what we're here for. How are the bubbles, Nelda?"

"Haven't had any, Walter, but the year and label on the bottle doesn't look promising," she said grinning.

They chatted for a few minutes before Nelda excused herself to have a word with Olga. She approached the circle of admirers around the founder.

"Nelda, darling, it's so good of you to come to our little celebration and to see "Three Blind Mice". Twenty-five years, it's been a lifetime since the theater was started. Do you remember?"

"Of course I remember. I helped with the fund raising and my husband, Jim, had a small part in the first production," Nelda said wistfully.

While they were reminiscing, the other people in the group wandered off to refill their glasses, and graze on the finger food arranged at the far end of the room. Nelda found herself alone with Olga.

"Olga, how do you manage to get killed off in the play?"

"Ah ha, I see you've read the story. I'm hung from a rope at the end of the first act, very dramatic."

"The play must be a little different from the story Agatha Christie wrote?"

"There is some difference, but basically it's the same. Three orphaned children, two brothers and a sister, were sent to a farm by a social worker...the officer is the part I'm playing...then the youngest child, Georgie, dies from criminal neglect and ill-treatment at the hands of the farmer and his wife. The farmer dies and the wife goes to prison. Several years later the oldest orphan, Jim, sets out to kill the three people that he thinks are responsible for his brother's death...hence the tune 'Three Blind Mice'."

"Olga, I better stop talking and let you get back stage."

"Darling, I didn't know it was time," she said, looking at her watch. She gave a little scream, gathered up her skirt and ran.

"Break a leg," Nelda called after her before rejoining the clinic group.

Lights dimmed as patrons took their seats. Nelda's seat was on the end, next to the aisle. Walter, Violet, Dennis and Marcie occupied the next four seats.

The play started violently with the murder of the farmer's wife, who had just gotten out of prison. Nelda followed the play carefully, looking for all the clues that might help someone, who didn't already know who the murderer was, solve the mystery.

Olga, as Mrs. Boyle the retired social worker, played her part beautifully. She was bossy, arrogant, insulting and someone the audience might wish dead. Nelda knew it was time for Mrs. Boyle to die when darkness enfolded the theater. She slipped from her seat and headed for the powder room to beat the crowd before intermission.

When she entered the powder room, she found it empty. Nelda looked around and found nothing had changed in the last twenty-five years. There were still damp cement floors, a disinfectant odor, dingy stalls and a long unframed mirror hanging over the chipped vanity and lavatories. She promised to have a word with Olga about helping with a few renovations.

Entering a stall at the far end, Nelda heard the sounds of a squeaky door and high heels as someone entered the room. She listened as the tapping of the shoes drew near, stopping in front of the stall she occupied. Nelda held her breath and waited. Finally, the steps receded to another part of the room. She heard the door squeak again. The voices of two young girls could be heard over the hum of old florescent lights that needed replacing.

Nelda seized this opportunity to come out of the stall. As she turned and lifted her head, she gazed into the blue eyes of Violet Rosin, who stood in front of the mirror with a lipstick in her hand.

"I thought that was you in the last stall, Nelda, but was afraid to say anything."

"Yes, I wondered who might be sneaking up on me."

"Well, just needed to put a little more Midnight Red on," said Violet turning back to the mirror.

Nelda glanced at the top of the lipstick lying on the vanity table. The label read Chanel! Violet lied to John, she told him she used Clinique makeup.

As if reading her mind, Violet said, "This lipstick was a birthday gift from a patient, isn't it beautiful?"

"Yes indeed. That patient must have thought a lot of you. When was your birthday?"

"Last month. I don't know who to thank for the lipstick. They sent it through the mail, with a bottle of cologne and no return address. I just know Walter did it, but he says not."

"That is sort of...strange," mumbled Nelda, wondering who was covering their tracks with so many expensive lipsticks.

"Great play! I'll see you back in the theater, Nelda. I'm going to find Walter and make him buy me a drink."

Violet put the top back on her lipstick and hurried out of the powder room. Nelda moved more slowly, her mind feverishly trying to sort out the information about the Chanel lipsticks. Each lipstick she encountered was the same shade and brand...there was a connection.

Out in the lobby, Nelda spotted another familiar face. John was standing alone near the entrance to the theater. She hurried over to fill him in on the lipsticks.

"Hello, John, just couldn't keep away from the entertainment could you?"

"I just wanted to make sure the only murders that occurred were on stage. How's the play?"

"It's great, but let me tell you the latest on the lipstick saga."

"Don't tell me you discovered the mystery behind the lipsticks? When I interviewed them, the women at the clinic said that they didn't use Chanel cosmetics.

"Yes and no to your question. In the powder room, Violet was applying Midnight Red Chanel lipstick. She claims she received it through the mail for her birthday and made no bones about it."

"So, either someone is trying to frame her, or she's pretending to be framed."

"There you have it. It wouldn't surprise me to discover that Marcie claims she too received a Midnight Red Chanel lipstick. That would make Carol, Violet and possibly Marcie in possession of the same name and brand of lipstick found in my driveway."

"I'm going to ask Marcie now," John said emphatically.

The lights were dimming as a warning for everyone to go back to their seats for the second act. Nelda knew it was bad timing for John to question Marcie.

"Could I just ask her for you? They're returning to their seats and I'm sure she'll answer that question for me."

"That's fine, I need to check the area downtown. We'll talk tomorrow."

They both looked toward the entrance to the theater and found Walter watching them with a puzzled expression. John walked away as Walter approached Nelda.

"What's going on, Nelda, what's the Sheriff doing here?"

"I guess he was just making his nightly rounds. See if he was needed in anyway."

"Any new development in Coldsby's murder?"

"He didn't tell me if there was."

Nelda still considered Walter a suspect even though she hoped and prayed he had nothing to do with the murders.

"We better get back to our seats," Walter said. "The second act will start shortly."

The second act was as good as the first and the actors got a standing ovation.

Nelda said goodnight to John and Violet then accepted Dennis' offer to walk her to her car. There was no moon, only the faint

glow of the street lights. She noticed the night people were beginning to circulate. A homeless old man was making a tent out of a
cotton blanket under the awning of a deserted building, and two
derelicts, with brown bottles in their hands, weaved down the
sidewalk.

"I'm glad you're with us, Nelda, because this old downtown
section is scary," Dennis said. "That was a treat to watch the play.
It was a winner, even though you girls will probably look under
your beds tonight before you go to sleep," he laughed.

Nelda didn't know exactly how to ask the question about the
lipstick, but knew it had to be soon because they were approaching her car. She decided to be straightforward with her inquiry.

"Marcie, do you remember when you were questioned by the
sheriff about the type of cosmetics you used?"

"Of course. He never did tell me what it was all about. He
asked me if I used Chanel lipstick, which is a joke. A tube of Chanel,
according to Violet, cost over twenty bucks."

"How does she know?"

"She received a tube for her birthday, then went out and priced
it."

"Did you receive such a gift too?"

"No, the only thing I have in Chanel is a perfume sample.
Maybe someday I'll be able to buy their makeup. It's a lovely
lipstick don't you think?"

"Yes, yes it is."

"What's it all about, Nelda? Was one found where one of the
murders was committed?" asked Dennis with a strange look in his
eyes.

"No, in my driveway after my car was tampered with."

"I think the sheriff had better concentrate his efforts on the
beautiful Violet," Dennis said with hardness in his voice.

"Dennis!" Marcie said sharply. "What a horrible thing to say."

"Well, let's face it. The murderer is a woman and Violet is the
obvious choice."

"Why? Asked Nelda.

"So Walter could have the business."

"It would probably be a good idea if you kept that opinion to yourself, unless of course, you have some evidence," Nelda said.

"Of course he wouldn't say this to anybody else," Marcie said. "I don't think we should start accusing each other."

Nelda opened her car door and then turned to Dennis. "I hope you're not holding anything back, Dennis. And if any information turns up, please let us know."

"Okay, I'm sorry I popped off. Goodnight, Nelda."

Was he really sorry for spinning threads of doubt? Nelda had no answers. The mystery of the Midnight Red lipsticks loomed larger than before. She said goodnight, buckled up and drove home.

CHAPTER TWENTY-TWO

Sue's Heartbreak

Gale force winds, lightening and heavy rain made sleep impossible for Nelda. She usually enjoyed a thunderstorm, thinking about all the impurities washed from the sky and life giving water falling on the earth, but somehow this one seemed sinister. She heard the pipe chimes on the back porch ringing furiously, crescendo after crescendo coming from them. Nelda feared the chimes and hanging baskets would blow away. As she lay in her comfortable bed, wondering if she should brave the storm to rescue them, her concentration was broken by someone banging on her front door.

"Who in the devil would be out in this kind of weather?" she mumbled to herself as she wrapped her old terry cloth robe around her thin frame. She rushed to the entry hall, flipped on the front porch light and peered through the side glass panel. A familiar figure stood outside clutching a red umbrella turned inside out. It was Sue!

Nelda hurriedly opened the door and pulled Sue inside. "Sue what are you doing here in the middle of the night? Why did you come back?"

Sue's clothes were drenched and water dripped from the rope-like curls of her hair onto Nelda's hardwood floor.

"Is that all you have to say Aunt Nelda? Aren't you glad to see me? Coming home in that storm was no picnic; I thought we weren't going to be able to land."

"Why didn't you call and let me know you had decided to come home? Who met you at the airport?"

"I called Walter. I didn't want you to have to get out in this weather. My luggage is still in his car. He wanted to bring it in for me, but there wasn't any sense in him getting drenched too. I'll get it tomorrow."

"Well, I'm glad you came here instead of going home."

Sue stood there shivering in her soggy clothes, head bowed. Nelda felt ashamed of herself for being so insensitive. She grabbed Sue and squeezed her hard; more water gathered at Sue's feet as Nelda drew back. Sue laughed as they sloshed through the water to Nelda's guest bedroom.

"I'll get you some pajamas while you dry off. It's a good thing I keep an extra toothbrush around. You'll be fine for tonight."

Nelda laid the pajamas on the bed while Sue was in the bathroom, then she went back to the entry, wiped up the water and threw the red umbrella on the front porch. Now that she was up, she might as well inspect her plants and chimes on the back porch. She walked to the back porch door, turned on the lights and peered out. The wind had died down, but the damage done to her plants made her want to wring the weatherman's neck. He hadn't predicted this storm on the evening news. Most of her hanging plants were now on the ground, and she couldn't see her chimes anywhere. Well, there was no point crying about it. The damage was done. She turned out the light and went back to the bedroom to see what else Sue needed.

Nelda's pajamas were too short for Sue. She had rolled up the bottoms and was busy towel drying her hair. Her wet clothes were in a heap on the bathroom floor.

"Let me have those wet clothes, Sue. I'll just put them in the washer and they'll be ready for you when you get up tomorrow."

"Thanks Aunt Nelda. Do you feel like talking or do you want to go back to bed?"

"No, let's go in the kitchen and have a cup of hot chocolate and you can tell me why you decided to come back without calling me."

They walked to the kitchen. Nelda mixed the coca with milk while Sue got the cups from the cabinet. After heating and pouring the liquid in the cups, they sat facing each other across the kitchen table.

"Now, Aunt Nelda, you know if I had called, you would have told me to stay put. I was tired of sponging off of Cousin Richard, also bored and worried about my job. You don't know how happy Walter was to hear from me. I just want to get back to a normal life."

"I do have some idea about Walter's so-called feelings, but you should know that all those people at the clinic, with the exception of the new doctor, are suspects in the two murders, not to mention two attempted murders."

"I'm a big girl, Aunt Nelda. I just can't hide forever. Have you ruled Carol out as someone who could have killed them?"

"No. Did you ever see Carol or Violet use Chanel lipsticks? Carol had a Chanel lipstick in her medicine cabinet called Midnight Red, and Violet claimed someone sent her the same shade of lipstick through the mail for her birthday."

"I didn't know about Carol's lipstick, but I do remember when Violet received hers. You'd have thought someone gave her the moon. She showed it to everybody."

"You or Marcie ever receive one?"

"I sure didn't and Marcie never said so if she did. Was this the same shade dropped in your driveway when they tampered with your car?"

"Yes."

"What does it mean, Aunt Nelda?"

"Someone is trying to muddy the water by having more than one person with that particular shade of lipstick."

"I see; they could have mailed the lipstick to Violet and slipped the lipstick in Carol's cabinet after she died or perhaps it was Carol that murdered them. I know she hated Dr. Coldsby."

"She left no suicide note. I suppose she could have accidentally dropped the lipstick in my driveway and sent Violet a tube of lipstick the same shade to confuse us," Nelda said.

NELDA SEES RED   181

"It seems odd to me," said Sue getting up to rinse her cup, "that Carol could buy such an expensive lipstick. She was always complaining about being broke. Shelby's medical bills were horrendous."

"That thought crossed my mind too," Nelda said thoughtfully, "but it might have been a gift or an urge to buy something nice whether she could afford it or not. I know somebody like that," she said, smiling at Sue.

"I know you're talking about me, Aunt Nelda, that's why I need to go back to work."

"Will you do me one big favor for just a little while?"

"You know I will. What is it?"

"Stay with me at night for a couple of weeks. I'm not convinced the murderer is Carol."

"I'm not a baby, Aunt Nelda!"

"I know. Maybe I'm the one who needs some babying!"

"Well, if it puts your mind at ease I'll do it." Sue said, squeezing Nelda's hand.

"Thanks, now when are you going back to work?" Nelda asked, putting the washed cups in the cabinet.

"Tomorrow, so I better go to bed and get some sleep."

"I know I acted like a sore head when I saw you standing on the porch Sue, but I'm really happy to see you and glad you'll be staying with me for awhile."

Nelda kissed Sue on the cheek and went on down the hall. She quickly brushed her teeth, pulled back the covers on her bed, turned off the light and got into bed. The rain had stopped and she could see the faint glow of the moon through her window. The warm drink made her drowsy and the sinister feelings she had experienced earlier were gone. Maybe things do happen for the best. She felt good about Sue being with her for the next two weeks.

* * *

Nelda woke up earlier than usual. No coffee aroma, the electricity had gone off during the storm. She hurried to the kitchen and turned on the coffee maker. But something else was bothering her, then she remembered. It was Sue's clothes. They forget to put the wet clothes in the dryer. Sue wouldn't have anything to wear this morning. She ran to the laundry room, opened the washing machine and pulled out Sue's white jeans. Oh no! she hadn't checked the pockets and something blue had stained the outside of the pocket. She pulled a crumpled blue ticket out of the pocket. It was a ticket stub from the Silver Queen Gondola in Aspen. What was Sue doing there? Of course Denver was not that far away from Aspen. She'd find out about the ticket when Sue woke up. She quickly worked on the stain, managed to get most of it out and put the clothes in the dryer. By that time she could smell the coffee brewing. Nelda went to Sue's room.

"Sue, it's time to get up," she called. "May I come in?"

Nelda heard a muffled assent from Sue. So she got a flowered housecoat from the closet and put it on the edge of the bed. By that time Sue was sitting up and stretching. All at once she looked at the clock and gave a little cry of dismay.

"Oh no! I've got to wash my hair and iron my clothes. I'll be late for my first day back."

What's new? Nelda thought. Sue was indeed back home. "Don't worry, I'll do your clothes," she said. "There's a hairdryer, shampoo and conditioner in my bathroom. Go on in there and get started."

Nelda couldn't wait for Sue to finish with her hair so she could ask her about the motel accommodations in Aspen. It was years since she had vacationed there and even then it was known as the rich peoples' playground. She was sure the prices for meals and rooms had not come down.

Nelda was putting the finishing touches on Sue's clothes when Sue, now wide awake, bounced into the laundry room with shiny blonde curls.

"Aunt Nelda, you're such a doll to do my clothes for me. You know I couldn't do without you."

"I know," Nelda said handing over Sue's clothes and putting the ironing board away.

"I've fixed you some breakfast, too, while you were washing your hair. Get your clothes on and we'll visit while you eat."

"Now, Aunt Nelda, you know I just have toast and coffee for breakfast. I couldn't possibly eat more than that."

"That's not enough, but I won't force a nutritious breakfast on you. Just come on in the kitchen when you're dressed."

In a few minutes Sue entered the kitchen, smiling as she posed a question for Nelda. "Aunt Nelda, I need to go to my apartment, and pick up my car. Would you drive me over to my place?"

"Will I have time to get dressed?" Nelda asked.

"Your housedress will be fine, but when we get there you better wait to see if my car will start."

"Sit down and eat your breakfast. We'll worry about your car after you've had something to eat."

Nelda had gone to great lengths to squeeze fresh orange juice for Sue. Squeezing oranges was something Nelda hated to do. She wouldn't do it for herself. It took six oranges to make a small glass of juice.

"Fresh orange juice! Are you trying to spoil me?"

"No, make you healthy. Now, tell me how you happened to be in Aspen. I found a gondola stub in your pants pocket. Did you spend the night there?"

"I sure did," said Sue drinking her orange juice faster than it took Nelda to squeeze it. "Did you know Cousin Richard's company owns a lodge in Aspen? It's just wonderful, located on the side of Red Mountain, and has six bedrooms."

"No I didn't know that. I thought it was a cabin. His computer consulting company must be doing better than I thought. How does he use the lodge?"

"To entertain the people he does business with, a promotional thing especially in the winter. It's not fancy, real rustic with a big wood burning fireplace. Lucky for me there was no one there. Cousin Irene went with me, but she could only stay for a couple of days. There are tons of things to do in the summer there. It's not just a winter resort town. I would really like to go back."

"How long will it be vacant? Did Cousin Richard say?" Nelda asked as she passed Sue some of her strawberry preserves.

"No, but I had the feeling that it wouldn't be used for another month," Sue answered, heaping the preserves on her toast. "Humm, good strawberries," She said, licking her lips.

"Who takes care of the lodge when no one is there?" Nelda asked.

"An old semiretired detective friend of Cousin Richard, Jake Cohen, he lives over the garage and oversees the place for free rent. Why all these questions about Aspen?"

"I'm going there to see if I can find any clues to Albert Coldsby's death. Before Joan was murdered, she had some information that would link Albert's death to his trips to Aspen. There were some old telephone bills with Aspen charges on them. Calls that were made from where Coldsby was staying. I'm sorry the murderer arrived before I did."

"Such nasty business. I sure wish I could go with you. We could have some fun even if you were investigating the case. Why don't you call Cousin Richard and see if the lodge is available for you to stay there?"

"I guess I could. I'm sure he wouldn't mind if he's not entertaining."

"You know he wouldn't," Sue said, taking a last sip of coffee. You and Uncle Jim practically raised him."

Nelda couldn't help but smile thinking of the good times she and her late husband, Jim, had with Richard on summer vacations. Even then she had known he was destined for success. At twelve, he could plan a vacation for the three of them and make all arrangements.

"Well we didn't exactly raise him, just gave his parents a little relief each summer."

"He hasn't forgotten it, all he did was praise you. Hey, we better go," Sue said glancing at the kitchen clock and getting up. "I'll just take another cup of coffee with me."

What a break if the lodge is not in use, thought Nelda as she hurried to the bathroom, ran a comb through her hair and applied some lipstick. It sure would help her budget to stay at Richard's place in Aspen. Of course she'd insist he accept some payment. She wouldn't take advantage of him because he was a relative.

Sue continued her chatter on the way to the apartment. Nelda decided that Sue's stay in Colorado had done her some good. She seemed relaxed and in good spirits.

When they reached Sue's apartment, Nelda waited in the driveway. Several seconds after Sue entered her apartment, she came running out signaling for her to come in. Nelda couldn't figure out what it was all about. Entering the open door, Nelda found Sue sobbing in the middle of the room.

"What in the world is happening?" Nelda said to no one in particular. She started running toward Sue, stumbled over a smashed coffee table, side-stepped a broken lamp and then stopped. Sue's furniture had been demolished. All the padded furniture was slashed, cotton and foam stuffing lay everywhere. Bric-a-brac, the entertainment center, and end tables were crushed, piled high in the corner of the room. "It looks like this place was hit by a tornado!" Nelda exclaimed. Even the drapes were shredded.

Leading Sue by the hand, they moved to the bedroom and found more of the same destruction. A demon-driven person had slashed the mattress, overturned Sue's desk, poured paint on her clothes and torn the sheets out of her photograph albums. Some of the pictures were cut in small pieces and tossed like confetti around the room. The kitchen fared no better, everything was in ruins.

Sue could stand no more. She sat down on the floor and put her head down crying piteously. Nelda ran to the bathroom for a wet washcloth. The first thing she saw as she opened the door was a message printed in red lipstick on the bathroom mirror over the lavatory. *Odi et amo* read Nelda out loud, then mumbled the translation, "I hate and I love." *She touched her finger to the writing and cringed when she held her finger to the light, knowing full well the shade of that lipstick.*

CHAPTER TWENTY-THREE

The Latin Connection

Nelda sat in John's office trying to peer over the stack of magazines and books piled high in front of her. Frustrated, she finally got up and perched on the corner of his desk. The clutter didn't bother her today; she was beyond that. The important thing was to find out if anyone had left fingerprints in Sue's apartment.

"Only Sue's," John said. "The perpetrator wore gloves."

"Surgical gloves!" Nelda said clasping her hands together. "How about the neighbors? Did you question them about any noises they may have heard?"

"We canvassed the whole apartment complex. The neighbors on either side didn't hear anything at night, and they both work during the day. A woman three doors down heard some banging at noon one day last week, but she thought it came from the new apartment complex under construction."

"Well, so much for witnesses," Nelda said.

John nodded and glanced down at a notebook in which he had written all the Latin expressions left behind. "Read these phrases to me Nelda, and let's see if we can make any sense out of them."

"All right John. A note was left on Coldsby's body, *pro bono publico*, which means "for the public good." It gave a reason for killing him. Then, the first warning, *caveat lector*, "let the reader beware," was written on a horror comic book and slipped in my home after the antique show.

John chimed in, "If I remember correctly, the caption on the cover of the comic was 'Dead Men Don't Talk.' Mrs. Coldsby had some information about Coldsby's murder for you and the killer made sure she didn't talk."

"Right! The next one was written on my program at the outdoor concert. It reads *finem respice,* which means "consider the end.""

"That was right after your tire lugs were loosened and you and Sally were almost killed in your old station wagon."

Nelda gave an affirmative nod. "The next phrase *Alea jacta est,* "the die is cast," was slipped under the lid of Sue's tray after someone tried to kill her on the fishing trip."

John massaged his neck with his hand, puzzled over the expression and then spoke. "It has to mean the murderer can't turn back."

"Exactly, the guilty party will have to play this out to the end. Whoever gets in his or her way will suffer."

"You've sure suffered," John said looking at Nelda, "but you're not giving up are you?"

"No indeed," Nelda said. "Let's go on to the next Latin phrase. This one was written in lipstick on Sue's bathroom mirror. The message reads *Odi et amo,* "I hate and I love.""

"That one completely baffles me," John said getting up and pouring strong, black coffee in two Styrofoam cups and handing one to Nelda. "What kind of a message is that?" He asked.

"I suppose it could have two meanings, as far as this case is concerned," Nelda said as she took a sip of the coffee and made a face.

John watched Nelda's obvious distaste of the coffee and grinned. "What two meanings could it have, Nelda?"

"It could mean someone both hates and loves Sue, or it could mean the murderer hates Sue and loves someone else."

"Nelda, I think I'll have to go with him hating Sue. He certainly couldn't love her if he tried to kill her and destroyed her apartment..... could he?"

"I'm with you, but are they trying to get at Sue because I'm involved in the case and they want me to back off, or is Sue a threat to the murderer?"

"How could Sue possibly be a threat to the murderer?" John asked.

"Suppose Sue has some information about the murders that she doesn't even know she has. They did destroy some of her photographs."

"Yes, and everyone of them was of the staff at the clinic. You might have something there, Nelda."

"There's so much we have to figure out. I think the whole reason for leaving those Latin phrases behind is to scare me off."

"You're probably right. I'm also thinking that the murderer must be proficient in Latin to come up with those meanings."

"Oh pooh! John. All he-or-she would have to do is open a Merriam Webster Dictionary to the section on foreign words and phrases and look for the phrase of their choice."

"I have one of those," he said, grabbing a dictionary from under some magazines on his desk. He opened it to the contents page, then flipped to the foreign words and phrases. "You're right," John said glancing over the list. "Every phrase is in the book."

Nelda stood up. "Now tell me exactly what the handwriting expert said."

John rubbed his chin. "The words were printed in block letters. He couldn't match them with anyone's handwriting."

"Thought out ahead of time," sighed Nelda.

She got her notebook and pen out of her purse, pushed the magazines and books to one side of John's desk and sat back down in a chair. John looked at Nelda, gave her a half smile, rocked back in his chair and got ready for the interrogation.

"Now tell me John, when you did your background check on Marcie, Walter, Violet and Dennis, what did you find?"

"It was interesting to see how those four people became involved with Coldsby. They're all so completely different."

"Go ahead and tell me about Marcie. She hasn't always lived here."

"No, she grew up in Denver and went to secretarial school there. She worked for an oil company in Denver for three years and then moved here. After settling in, she was hired by Coldsby and has been here ever since. When her father died years ago, she asked her mother to come and live with her."

Nelda drummed the pen on her note pad and waited for John to continue. He remained silent.

"What are you thinking about John?"

"The reason Marcie gave for moving to Stearn."

Nelda leaned forward as John spoke. This was the kind of information she should have gotten from John weeks ago.

"Marcie said she moved here because she had a friend that went to the university in Smitherton. She wanted to be near him." John shook his head and continued. "I couldn't find out what happened to this friend."

"It makes me wonder," Nelda said, "if maybe Albert Coldsby wasn't the reason for Marcie's move here."

"Albert and Marcie may have met in Aspen, a romance developed, and he ended up asking her to move here and be his secretary," John said.

"Did you ask Marcie if she had a love affair with Albert?"

John nodded. "Yes, there was an affair, but she said it ended years ago. She didn't give me specific dates, but I'm going to question her again."

"When?" Nelda asked. "I'd like to know all the answers before I go to Aspen."

"I'll do it today."

"Now about Walter, John. Let me see if I'm missing anything about him: he grew up in a very poor family, went through college by using scholarships and money from part time jobs, graduated from the University of Texas Medical School, interned at Houston Methodist, and accepted a job with Coldsby. He seems to have very high morals and is extremely ambitious."

"Humm," John said, "I wonder if high morals and great ambition are compatible in this day and time."

"For Walter, it certainly used to be, but I know people change," Nelda said.

"What do you mean by high morals, Nelda."

"He sets his standards by the Ten Commandments. There are no gray areas with Walter. An act or deed is either right or wrong."

"I don't have anything new on him," John said. "He has no concrete alibi for the two murders, but neither do the others."

"Okay, now let's talk about Violet. Here we have ambition personified in that she's going to get her man come hell or high water."

John laughed, got up from the chair, opened up a cabinet and retrieved a file on Violet. With his back to Nelda, he held the file by the open window and began reading his notes aloud. "Violet Gale Rosin is twenty-five and single. She grew up and graduated from high school in Phoenix and worked her way through nursing school in Flagstaff waiting tables. She came from an abusive family, and decided she wanted to get away from them. Dr. Coldsby advertised for a nurse in a medical magazine. She saw the ad, applied for the job and he hired her."

"How did you get that information?" Nelda asked.

"She told me about her life and I called to follow up. Everything checked out except the advertisement she was supposed to have read. She couldn't remember which magazine the ad was in."

"How was her family abusive?"

"Her father beat her mother and in turn, her mother beat the kids. The cops were called to their house several times. The family was in counseling for a while."

"Lovely," said Nelda shaking her head. "I don't blame her for running, but why here? Sounds sort of suspicious that neither Marcie or Violet have legitimate reasons for moving to Stearn."

"Well at least we know where Walter and Dennis materialized." John sighed. "They both grew up here."

"And were my students. But did I really know them?"

"Maybe you did at the time, but it's like you said, they may have changed."

"Dennis, wanted to be an adventurer; he reminded me of a knight who was out to slay a dragon." Nelda said. "He used to talk about all the places he wanted to go and the good he could accomplish. It seems odd he'd be stuck right here in this little town mowing yards."

"Maybe he did find his damsel and slay the dragon," said John. " Was it accident or intentional that he was nearby when each bad event took place?"

"Could it be possible that Coldsby still had a hold on Marcie when he died?" Nelda asked.

The young sheriff shrugged his shoulders as she knew he would. She closed her notebook and pushed her chair back in place against the wall.

"John, how about giving me a copy of those phone bills Mrs. Coldsby was going to show me before she was killed. I'll need them to do my investigating in Aspen."

"Alright. Here is a file I made up for you." He slid the folder across to Nelda. "I wish I could go with you to look for answers, but there is no way I can go now. It seems everybody from the D.A. to the local farmer thinks it's more important to catch cattle rustlers than a murderer. You sure you want to go on your own?" John asked. "I might be able to send my deputy."

"You keep him, I'm going," Nelda said with determination. "I'd also like to have a copy of all the picture fragments you found in Sue's apartment. There might be a clue in those photographs."

"They're in the file I gave you. When are you going, Nelda? I'll call the Chief of Police there and let him know you're coming."

"I don't know exactly when I'll leave, but I don't think it would be wise to call the police in Aspen. They may not want to cooperate with someone who's not a legitimate law enforcement officer. Besides, Jake Cohen the man taking care of Cousin Richard's lodge, is a semiretired detective. He'll be there if I need him."

"That's good. I feel better about you already. I'll call this Cohen and talk to him. Let me have his number."

Nelda opened up her address book, copied the number, and handed it to John.

"John, I'm going to pick up Sue at work. Be sure to let me hear from you after you talk to Marcie. I'm certain the gossip about her affair with Coldsby was true, but I'd sure like to know when it ended."

"Okay, I'll let you know as soon as I can. But about Sue, I can't believe how brave she was after her apartment was demolished." John said walking Nelda down the hall.

"I'm really proud of her. She pulled herself together, reported the damage to the insurance, and went to work."

"They didn't touch her car did they?"

"No, the battery was dead. Sue's car spends most of it's time in the shop," Nelda said as she gave John a final good-bye, got in her wagon and drove toward the clinic.

The shoulders of the open road were thick with purple thistle. It reminded Nelda of the beautiful book she had bought so she could identify the wild flowers in the Rockies. She was happy about the prospect of going to Aspen even though it was supposed to be a working trip.

There were so many things to do to get ready! She had to call the travel agency, shop for a few clothes and, above all, get her hair fixed. Nelda flipped the sun visor down and glanced at the attached mirror. She was appalled by what she saw. Her thin face was accentuated by long straight hair that reminded her of the straws in her whisk broom. That stringy hair would have to go; she'd get it whacked off tomorrow and permed. She looked down at her baggy blue jean dress and decided to start a Goodwill bag as soon as she got home. By this time Nelda was at the clinic and realized she had more important things to think about. What was she going to do with Sue while she was gone?

Nelda was surprised to see her niece standing out under a tree in front of the clinic.

"What's going on?" She asked as Sue climbed in.

"You're not going to believe this. My first day back and the air-conditioning system failed. Not only that, but the odor in the place is enough to make you sick, if you weren't already."

"What in the world happened?"

"That fire that somebody set several weeks ago shorted out the whole air-conditioning system and the odor coming from all that wet insulation in the ceiling is nauseating. The place will be closed down for a whole week while they tear out the ceiling and replace the damaged materials."

"What about the doctor's patients?"

"We canceled next week's appointments. The emergencies will be handled by Dr. Wiley across town."

"How did Walter take this setback?"

"He was upset at first, but now he's decided to call it our vacation time."

"Did you tell them about your apartment?" Nelda asked as they fastened their seat belts.

"They already knew about it. John snooped around here while I was filling out claims at the insurance office. He gathered more background information on everyone."

"He didn't tell me that. I don't suppose it helped him," Nelda said driving out of the parking lot.

"I tried not to think about my smashed possessions today," sighed Sue. Everyone here acted like it was just a case of vandalism. John didn't tell anyone at the clinic about the message that was left on the mirror. Neither did I."

"Do you want to go to your apartment and start cleaning up the mess or wait until tomorrow?"

"I'm tired. I guess I'll have the whole week to do that. All the rest of them are planning on renting a condo in Snowmass, " Sue said sadly. "I wish I could go with them." A tear formed in the corner of her eye.

Nelda swung her head around so quickly she was dizzy for a moment. "Snowmass! That's only a stone's throw from Aspen."

"I know," said Sue sadly. "But I don't even have money enough to replace my furniture, let alone go on a trip."

Nelda was excited, but tried to keep her eyes on the road. A plan was taking shape in her mind. No time to waste; she spun the station wagon around and headed for the travel agency.

"What's going on Aunt Nelda?" Sue said, surprised to see Nelda's sudden burst of energy.

"We'll be heading for Aspen at the same time the clinic staff arrives at Snowmass," Nelda said with a grim smile on her face. "I have a feeling we're heading for a showdown."

"I'm sorry Aunt Nelda, but you've lost me. What are you conjuring up in that twisted brain."

"We're going to give them a chance to finish us off in the mountains," said Nelda.

"Aunt Nelda, do you know what you're saying? I don't know if I want to be a sitting duck or not," Sue said, nervously twisting on a lock of her hair.

"Not to worry, Sue," Nelda said, parking by the Stearn Travel Service. "We'll do the setting up, and I assure you, we'll be in control!"

"Well if you say so, but I don't have the money to go."

"Sure you do," Nelda said opening the car door. "Let's go in and make our reservation. By the way, who thought of this trip to Snowmass?"

"It was Marcie; she was very emphatic about it. Wouldn't take no for my answer either."

That's interesting Nelda thought. Things were finally beginning to take shape.

CHAPTER TWENTY-FOUR

Aspen Bound

Nelda cradled the receiver of the phone with a satisfied smile and spoke to Sue. "We'll be leaving on Wednesday with your coworkers. I called Walter and got their schedule. Called Cousin Richard too. He said he'd be pleased for us to stay in his lodge and we can use his van."

"That's great Aunt Nelda," Sue said, eyeing the few garments she had salvaged from the wreckage in her apartment.

Nelda followed Sue's gaze to the clothes spread out on the bed. She knew what she had to do. "All right, grab your purse; we're going to the mall. I have to pick up a few things for our trip and so do you."

"I'm broke and you know it. Besides I already owe you for the plane ticket," Sue said biting on her bottom lip.

"Don't worry, you can receive your birthday present ahead of time," Nelda said with a smile.

"Four months early," laughed Sue. "This is ludicrous, but what the heck, let's do it!"

They chatted excitedly as Nelda made the thirty minute drive to Smitherton's new mall. Sue listed what she needed while Nelda made suggestions. When they arrived at the mall, Nelda parked in a shady spot under a tree. Soon they were rummaging through the counter of their favorite shop, Lands End.

Nelda could not believe how many colors in mock turtleneck

cotton sweaters they had to choose from. They finally narrowed their selections to chamois, plum wine and spruce. As they charged with the plastic, Violet and Marcie entered the store and started walking their way.

"Ah ha," said Violet, "are you ladies trying to buy all the pretty clothes before we have a chance to shop?"

Violet looked like she might be the cover girl for a Lands's End catalog. She wore a long, floral, paisley dress with burgundy mesh pumps. The ribbon tied around her blonde hair matched the pattern in her dress.

Sue smiled, but answered in an aggravated tone. "I guess you weren't paying any attention to me when I said all my clothes were destroyed by the vandals that broke in my apartment."

"We're sorry," spoke up Marcie, "that was a rotten thing for someone to do."

Nelda noticed that Marcie had lost weight and had a new hair style. The dress she wore was several inches above her knees. If she was attempting to look as young as Dennis, she had missed her mark. Marcie was a beautiful woman, thought Nelda, and didn't need to dress like a teenager.

"Isn't this crazy about all of us going to Colorado?" Violet said. "We've reserved rooms at Snowmass Village; where will you be staying?"

"We're going to stay at my Cousin Richard's lodge in Aspen, so we won't be far from you. It would be fun to go on some outings together," Nelda said.

Marcie turned a quizzical gaze toward Nelda. "You'll be there for more than fun won't you?"

"I'll be looking for leads in Albert's death, but it shouldn't take up all my time," Nelda said. She tried to read the expressions on their faces as she answered Marcie's question, but all she saw was polite interest.

"Since we're leaving day after tomorrow," Violet said, "we better get on with our shopping. I suppose we'll be done by then," she laughed as they walked away.

"Come on, Aunt Nelda, let's finish our shopping too. We've a long list, and I have a wrecked apartment to clean up."

It seemed that the appearance of Violet and Marcie had taken all the joy of shopping away from Sue. Nelda sensed Sue's usually trusting nature had at last turned suspicious toward her coworkers. It was sad, but she was happy that Sue would be on guard when they were around.

Nelda didn't blink an eye as she handed her Visa gold credit card to clerks in several different stores. Soon they were weighted down with everything from insulated underwear to a plush warm jacket in feather-weight fabric. She kept telling herself that the clothes could be used at home too, and were not just for a week in Aspen.

It was time for a breather and Nelda knew just where to take it. She and Sue headed for the coffee bar located near the main entrance and arrived just in time to grab the last of the little tables that were placed in the corridor of the mall. Sue told Nelda to sit still with the packages while she fetched two cups of "French roast" coffee to revive them for their return trip home.

As she waited for Sue, Nelda studied the flight bags in the store window on the opposite side of the mall. One was a combination carry-on bag and attaché case; what will they think of next? she mused. Just then she was startled by a finger tapping her shoulder and whirled around to find Walter smiling down at her. His hands were full of packages. Nelda could see a back pack and a pair of hiking boots bulging out of one package.

"Sit down a minute, Walter, and tell me if you're serious about using all the stuff you just bought in the short time you'll be in Colorado."

Walter answered Nelda with an affirmative head nod, but his eyes searched for Sue. He finally located her in the coffee line, so he dropped his packages on the floor, grabbed a chair and sank into it.

"This shopping is really hard work, Nelda," he said sighing. " I don't know how you gals can do this every week."

"I suppose some women do it every week, but it would be a little rough on my pocketbook. It's just special occasions and pure need that gets me out here," Nelda said.

"I'm glad you talked Sue into going to Colorado, Nelda. It just wouldn't be the same going without her."

By that time Sue was back with the coffee and she gave Walter a warm look. "Sorry I couldn't carry three cups, Walter. We'll guard your packages for you if you want to grab a cup and revive yourself with us."

"No, Sue, your company is all I want. I was explaining to Nelda how happy I am about the two of you making the trip to Colorado."

"I understand all of you are staying at Snowmass Village. Did you have any trouble getting rooms?" Sue asked.

"No," answered Walter quickly, "the men have a double room and the girls do too."

"I didn't mean to pry into your sleeping arrangements," Sue said in a bristly tone. "I was just thinking how nice it will be with all of us together."

Nelda felt like an intruder sitting at the table with Sue and Walter. There was quite a bit of chemistry between the two of them and she didn't know if she approved. What if Walter is psychotic, the love-hate killer? She sipped her coffee in agitation and was thankful when Walter's pager went off requiring him to find a phone.

"What's going on with you two, Sue? I've noticed a big change in your relationship with Walter. He certainly has become attracted to you."

"I was afraid you'd notice and I really don't know what my feelings are toward him. He's still engaged to Violet. It's like he's not free to have any feelings for me."

"You do have some feelings for him, Sue. I can tell by the way you act when he's around."

"It happens when he's not around too, Aunt Nelda. That's one reason I came back from Colorado so soon. I just wanted to be near him, so bad, and I know he felt the same way."

"I think there's a stumbling block between you two by the name of Violet."

"More like a time bomb, Aunt Nelda. I can't see her giving up Walter. It's like he's her property and the world would end tomorrow if it wasn't so. I'm not showing my feelings for Walter when she's around."

"Wise choice. If Walter wants to break his engagement, it will be his problem as to how he does it, but do you realize what an uproar that will cause?"

"Of course. She's the nurse he works with. Just thinking about the whole situation makes me think I'm crazy. I just got out of one bad relationship and now all I'm asking for is peace and tranquillity."

"Good girl! Let's go home, put these things up, and I'll give you a hand with your apartment. We'll have it cleaned up in no time."

* * *

The next morning, while Sue wrangled with the insurance adjuster about her damaged goods, Nelda went over to find out the results of John's talk with Marcie. He was talking on the telephone when she got there, but pointed his finger at the coffee pot. Nelda was overjoyed to find it empty and quickly brewed fresh coffee. By that time, John was off the phone and gratefully accepted a fresh cup of java from Nelda.

"Great looking duds you're wearing!" John said, as he pulled out a chair for Nelda.

"I may have to cut your salary."

Nelda gave a sarcastic laugh, but was flattered that John noticed her new, sky blue jumper and bright yellow blouse. Maybe she was right in upgrading her wardrobe. At least it did wonders for her morale.

"Thanks, John, now what about that conversation you had with Marcie? Did she tell you more about her relationship with Coldsby?"

"She did and was straight forward about it. Marcie said she knew she'd have to give me more details sooner or later."

"Well," prodded Nelda, "when did it start and when did it end?"

"Marcie met him when she was in nursing school fifteen years ago. It seems Coldsby was attending a medical meeting in Phoenix and that's how they met. They had several romantic encounters during the following year and then he opened his clinic and asked her to move here and work for him."

"When did it end?" asked Nelda, "and why? I know that woman still felt something for him when he died. She had tears in her eyes when she was talking to me about him. Imagine an illicit romance going on like that with no hope of marriage."

"She told me the affair ended two years ago and she ended it herself."

"I wonder," said Nelda, "why would she end it herself? That seems a bit strange to me. Unless, of course, he didn't love her anymore."

"Women!" John said. "Now I remember why I'm not married. I can't figure them out."

Nelda smiled and knew John's time would come, but he was right about one thing, he'd never completely understand a woman.

"I'll get out of your hair, John. I've a ton of things to do before I leave tomorrow."

"Don't forget, Jake will be looking after you in Aspen." I told him you might need his help."

"I'll talk to him when I get there. I might as well tell you that Dennis, Marcie, Violet, Walter and the new doctor, Elizabeth Gomez will be in Snowmass the same week Sue and I are in Aspen."

"Why? I hadn't heard about that."

"The fire that burned up the records in the clinic caused extensive damage to the insulation in the attic. It has to be replaced, so Walter closed the clinic for the week. They're all taking vacation time."

"You should plan on going to Aspen later. It's not going to be safe for you and Sue to be there when they are."

"It's going to be fine John. They're staying in Snowmass and we're staying at Cousin Richard's lodge in Aspen." Nelda didn't want John to know she'd planned to be in Colorado when they were there. He was a worrier.

"Well maybe, but you're still too close together.....Oh, one other piece of information I have for you, Nelda. We weren't able to tell, from clinic personnel handwriting samples, who wrote those Latin messages. They were all printed in block form."

"The killer or killers have been so clever. I didn't think they would allow us to identify their handiwork." Nelda said.

"Be careful and take care of yourself and Sue while you're gone. It wouldn't hurt to also have some have fun," John said as he walked out to the front door with Nelda.

"Bye, John. I'll keep in touch," Nelda said as her mind turned to another pressing problem. Who could she trust to take care of her plants?

* * *

It was 6:00 a.m. and Sue was having a hard time trying to get Nelda away from her plants on the back porch. It was so dark, Nelda had to use the back porch light to see how to water them. She sighed as she stepped back and gazed at the blooming red begonias.

"Now, Aunt Nelda, you know Martha Hillman will take good care of your plants. Remember how she looked after Sugar when someone let him out of the yard?"

"I know she will, but I still worry about them. It's only been a week or so since that rain storm turned most of them over."

"They look just fine. The new doctor, Elizabeth Gomez, will be here at any minute to give us a lift to the airport. We better get all our luggage out to the driveway. That commuter plane leaves in less than an hour for Dallas."

Nelda and Sue had tried to pack as efficiently as possible but there was a mountain of luggage anyhow; two garment bags, two Pullmans, a satchel tote and a beauty case. They would check everything in at the airport. Running to make connections in Dallas and Denver was no picnic. Nelda did remember that much from her last trip to Aspen.

Elizabeth drove up in a well-used Ford Explorer and they exchanged greetings. She was dressed in a blue jean skirt, a long sleeved cotton blouse and moccasins. With her short, black curly hair and olive complexion she looked like a Native American.

"Nice of you to pick us up, Dr. Gomez," Sue said.

"No problem, Walter told me Nelda would be on pins and needles leaving her new car at the airport. No one would want to steal my old bucket," Elizabeth said. ""I can hardly wait to land in those mountains." She opened up the back of the Explorer and they piled the luggage inside. "I'll feel right at home there."

"Aunt Nelda, I didn't tell you that Dr. Gomez was from New Mexico did I?"

"No, you didn't. Are you familiar with Colorado too, Dr. Gomez?" Nelda asked.

"Please, no 'Doctor.' While we're on vacation, I'm just Elizabeth. Of course I've been to Colorado many times, but never to stay in Snowmass or Aspen. When I was younger, we went to visit relatives and couldn't afford to stay in the resorts."

Thirty minutes later they pulled in the parking lot of the Smitherton airport. They were twenty minutes ahead of time. As they were checking their luggage in, Walter, Dennis, Violet and Marcie walked in empty handed. Nelda panicked!

"Did you decide not to go?" she questioned.

"Are you kidding?" laughed Dennis. "Those girls brought so much luggage we had to get here early to check it all in. We just came from eating breakfast, because we're on the peanut flight and it's a long way to Colorado. No real food till we get to Aspen."

The commuter plane arrived on time and they found themselves boarding the prop driven plane for Dallas. It was a noisy flight, so instead of talking most of the passengers buried their noses in a book or magazine. Nelda was amused to find that Sue was seated next to a good looking young man who came on to her while Walter looked on with displeasure.

When they reached Dallas, there was little time before departing for Denver. It seemed they were continually on the run until they boarded the commuter plane for Aspen. Nelda had forgotten how rough that flight could be. The ride was so bumpy all the drinks were quickly collected by the attendants and several passengers, including Dennis, were sick. Fortunately the flight became smooth a few minutes before they arrived at the Aspen airport. As they taxied up to the passenger entrance, Nelda noticed the ground crew members were all wearing jackets. Coming from short sleeves to jacket temperature would be a welcome change. She knew the Aspen mornings would be chilly and she welcomed the change.

"Better put that sweater on, Sue. This wonderful, cool weather might be a shock to your system," Nelda said smiling.

"It'll be great," Sue said. "I hated to leave when we were here before."

"Will you be able to recognize Jake," Nelda asked.

"Sure, I saw him every day for a week. You'll like him. He's very helpful."

Everyone gathered their belongings and walked down the steps to the ground and crossed the few feet to the passenger entrance. The cool wind blowing across the field invigorated Nelda. She grabbed Sue's arm and jogged to the entrance.

As they entered, Sue and Walter exchanged glances and a little smile played on his lips. Sue looked away and called to Nelda. "There's Jake, he's standing back of that group waiting to check in."

Sue and Nelda walked over to a tall man dressed in blue jeans and a red and white flannel shirt. "Aunt Nelda, this is Jake," Sue said.

Nelda looked into the bluest eyes she had every seen; they

were set in a round face with hundreds of reddish brown freckles the same shade as his hair. She instantly took a liking to him and was glad he would be in hollering distance from Cousin Richard's lodge.

Jake gave Nelda's hand a firm shake. "Good to meet you, Nelda. Richard and John told me to take good care of you, so let's get your luggage."

A few minutes later, they were all gathered around the luggage conveyer waiting for their bags to appear. Jake bought coffee for Nelda and Sue, because he knew it would be a lengthy wait. Finally, they saw their luggage coming around, and collected all of it but one piece. Missing was Nelda's satchel tote containing notes of the murder case, Sue's photos of the people from the clinic, and copies of Coldsby's phone bills. Nelda began to panic, then she heard Elizabeth call to her from where she was standing.

"Nelda, I think one of us picked up your bag by mistake. It looks like the one I loaded for you this morning."

"I believe it is mine," Nelda said, retrieving it. "I'll just check the numbers with my stub."

Nelda wanted to draw her hand back and scream, but she didn't. There were two stubs hanging from the handle. One had a set of numbers that matched those in her hand and the other stub contained a Latin phrase. She palmed the stub with the Latin phrase, pulled it off and stuck it in her pocket. *Nelda wasn't about to amuse a watching murderer or two by reacting to it!*

CHAPTER TWENTY-FIVE

Burden of Proof

Nelda, still thinking of red lipstick and Latin phrases, stared straight ahead at Marcie, Violet, and Dennis walking in front of her. Suddenly, clutching her coffee cup, she stumbled, spilling coffee all over Violet's new pink outfit. Some of the dark liquid flowed down Violet's arm and hand. Was this an omen of bad luck? wondered Nelda.

"I'm sorry! How clumsy of me. I guess I don't have my ground legs yet."

Hurriedly, she pulled a linen handkerchief out of her purse and put it in Violet's hand. Violet, looking very disgruntled, cleaned her arm and hand vigorously. Then she patted the wet spots on her new frock. When she finished, Nelda took the handkerchief back, looked at the stains on it with disgust and stuffed it in her purse.

The two groups parted ways with promises to get together for some outdoor activities in the next few days.

Jake loaded all their luggage in a an old Dodge van and they were off. Nelda caught Sue glancing at her as if expecting a flood of comments on the Aspen scenery, but Nelda sat strangely quiet. Finally, Sue broke the silence.

"Okay, now that's enough gloominess. What in the world is bugging you, Aunt Nelda? Pretty soon Jake will think we don't appreciate his company."

"I was just thinking about the tag someone put on my tote and wondering if I did the right thing letting you come with me."

"What tag? What on earth are you talking about?"

"I didn't want to talk in front of Jake, but I'm going to have to tell him why I'm here anyway," Nelda said.

"Well let's hear about the tag first, Aunt Nelda."

"Someone put a tag on the handle of my tote bag that had a phrase in Latin printed on it with red lipstick. The phrase was *onus probandi* and means "burden of proof.""

"In other words it's a message from the murderer telling you that even if you think you know who the murderer is you've got to have evidence?" Sue asked.

"Exactly," answered Nelda

"Ladies," Jake said, "don't leave me in the dark. What's all this talk about a murderer?"

Nelda responded, "I know John told you why I'm in Aspen."

"Yes, he did say you were coming here to find clues about a murder that occurred in Stearn, but he didn't say anything about the murderer following you here."

"I'm certain the killer is from the clinic where Sue works and will be staying in Snowmass, but I have no proof. That's what I'm here to get. I need to find someone that remembers the doctor who was killed and can identify his companion here in Aspen. I think that person murdered two people."

"That's going to be tough, Nelda," said Jake. "The turnover of workers in motels and restaurants is almost eighty percent since most of the workers are college kids. They're here today and gone tomorrow or as soon as they earn enough money to go back to school."

"Maybe someone in that twenty percent will remember him. I'm going to start with the places he stayed and then try some of the restaurants," said Nelda with a determined voice.

Sue asked, "Do you think, while you're doing all that, we could have a little fun?"

"We can," said Nelda, "but let's always be on guard so one of us won't be the next victim."

"I'm sorry our police force hasn't been much help." Jake said. "Well, we have no proof that any of the clinic people are involved. And because I'm not officially connected to the County Sheriff's Department, they probably couldn't help me. However, I'm grateful for your help, Jake."

"I'll sure do what I can. You can also count on my support at the lodge." He turned a grave face toward Nelda and his hands clenched the steering wheel. "If you and Sue don't mind, I'll move into one of the upstairs bedrooms until you leave. That way I can be sure you're safe while you're in the lodge."

"I wouldn't want to inconvenience you, but we'd certainly feel safer if you were near at night," Nelda said gratefully.

"It's settled. Now what do you think about our downtown Aspen? Do you have flowers as big as those in the wooden barrels over there?" Jake slowed and pointed to giant sized white petunias, and red geraniums blooming in front of a restaurant.

"Oh Jake! All the pretty shops with the beautiful flowers, it's like a picture postcard and just look at those mountains. I relax just gazing at them," Nelda said, sighing.

"Just wait, Aunt Nelda, till you see the lodge. It's right on the side of Red Mountain across from Aspen Mountain. You can see the mountains called the Maroon Bells from there. That's where we're going to have our picnic with the others."

"We've got to do some work first you know, visit hotels and restaurants," Nelda said.

"I know," said Sue, "but for right now let's sit back and watch Jake drive us up Red Mountain."

They arrived after several miles of twisting and turning up the mountain road. The two level lodge, made of rock and rustic wood, sat on a three acre lot. Nelda fell in love with the property and wouldn't go inside until she'd inspected the grounds. She walked through clusters of aspen and spruce trees to an open area where wild pink roses and giant red paint brushes bloomed in profusion. Nelda felt a sense of peace as she closed her eyes and listened to the cool breeze make musical sounds with the aspen leaves.

She put her cold hand into her pocket and felt the luggage tag with the Latin phrase. It reminded her that this was not the time to relax and enjoy the scenery. Thoughtfully she headed for the front door of the lodge which opened on the second level.

Jake and Sue waited for her in a large Spanish tiled foyer. It contained an indoor atrium filled with huge plants of philodendra, ferns and crotons. The layout on the first floor consisted of the kitchen, laundry room, large dining room, living area, two bathrooms and three bedrooms. Walking downstairs to the first level, she discovered three more bedrooms and two baths connected by a long hall. Nelda choose a corner bedroom for herself on the bottom floor. In this room, she visualized herself going to sleep listening to the wind in the aspens, and soothing water sounds from the stream running through the edge of the property.

* * *

The next morning Nelda was up early. She shivered as she slipped her old velour robe on and stepped into moccasin slippers. Taking her daily planner and Coldsby's telephone bills with her, she climbed the stairs to the kitchen. It didn't take her long to find the coffee and the coffeepot. While the coffee was perking, she opened the sliding glass doors to the second level deck and stepped out to view the mountains. Snow had fallen on them during the night, and their peaks were partially covered by a thin layer of clouds. The combination of trees, snowy mountains and violet blue sky was so beautiful it didn't appear real until she inhaled the clean smell of cedar, and heard two large Canada jays scolding her for disturbing their peace.

Coming in from the deck, she poured herself some coffee, and sat down at the kitchen table to map out her plans for the day. As far as she knew, during the past eight years Coldsby had registered at only two Aspen hotels, both on E. Main Street, the Hotel Jerome and the Sardy House. She searched for a phone book and finally found one after opening three kitchen drawers. In the front of the phone book, she discovered a map of the city and quickly located the two places. It wouldn't take them long to visit the hotels, but the restaurants would be another matter. There were scores of places to eat. Maybe Sue could help her determine where Coldsby would go for a meal.

She was on her second cup of coffee when Sue bounced into the kitchen, wearing a blue chambray shirt, flowered corduroy skirt, burgundy vest and black boots.

"My you look spiffy today," Nelda teased, "you're not dressing for me are you?"

Sue ignored her question. "I knew you'd be up at the crack of dawn," Sue said, smiling. "Where's Jake?"

"He's already gone to work, but he'll be in the lodge at night and I'm thankful for that," Nelda answered.

"All right, what's in the plan for today?"

"As soon as I get dressed and you have breakfast, we're going to talk to some folks at the two places Coldsby stayed while he was in Aspen. Then, we'll visit a few eating places. I was thinking you might suggest some places where Coldsby might have eaten. You know his taste better than I do," Nelda said.

"As a matter of fact, I have heard him talk about some good places to eat here. I'll try to remember them while you're getting dressed."

* * *

Nelda drove cautiously down Red Mountain in Cousin Richard's old Dodge van. Sue had a map of Aspen, borrowed from Jake, spread out in her lap. Hotel Jerome and Sardy House were only three blocks apart. Nelda decided she's try Hotel Jerome first because it was located to the right of the first red light. As Nelda approached the hotel, she was awed by its size. Sue was dismayed.

"Aunt Nelda, it's going to be an impossible task finding someone that remembers both the doctor and his companion. Look at the number of rooms this hotel must have. It would take us years to interview all the employees."

"Just take it easy Sue; we'll just walk in and see what we can find out."

"Are you going to start with the management?"

"No, John sent pictures of Dr. Coldsby to both places and they identified the doctor, but said they couldn't remember seeing him with anyone. He registered alone. What I plan to do is interview some of the people who worked here when he was a guest, four to eight years ago."

Nelda finally found a place to park and they walked into the lobby of the hotel. Sue picked up a brochure advertising the hotel and they sat in the lobby reading it.

"Listen to this, Aunt Nelda, Hotel Jerome has ninety-four restored rooms and is over one-hundred years old. There's also a Grand Ballroom, Board Room, restaurant and bar."

"A restaurant?"

"Yes, offering American food, whatever that means."

Nelda decided to make good use of their time. "The bar and restaurant sounds promising for finding out information, but it's too early to eat or have a drink. Let's go sign up for the downhill bicycle ride and lunch around Maroon Lake. You did want to do that with the others from the clinic didn't you?"

"Yes I do, Aunt Nelda. It sounds like a lot of fun. Let's leave the van here, because according to the map, we sign up at the corner of Hyman and Mill Street. That's only two blocks away."

"Let's get going and come back here for lunch."

When they went outside, they discovered it was raining, and made a dash for the car to retrieve their umbrellas. Jake had warned Nelda that there would be rain some mornings, but it wouldn't last long.

They walked briskly down Mill Street to the Blazing Paddles booth. The young girl in the booth flashed them a big smile and asked if she could help.

Nelda squinted at her through the rain and said, "We'd like to sign up for the downhill bicycle tour, but tell me what happens if it's raining tomorrow morning?"

"It's only raining for the flowers to grow," the girl said as she took their money and gave them tickets for the next day. "Just wait, you'll have a perfect day tomorrow."

Nelda laughed, because the rain had already stopped and Sue was closing her umbrella. They turned down Hyman street; Sue wanted her to visit a shop called Bright & Shiny Things. As they entered the shop, Nelda's eyes lit up when she saw the American Indian jewelry. She remembered how fond Sally was of silver concha bracelets, and made up her mind to buy Sally one if it was reasonably priced. Nelda was intently studying the different pieces when someone cast a shadow over her right shoulder. She turned sharply as Dennis jumped back.

"I'm sorry I startled you, Nelda. We were at the boutique next door, and I just ran over to see if you had signed up for the picnic and bicycle ride tomorrow."

Sue answered, "We did Dennis. What are all of you doing today?"

"Marcie and Violet wanted to shop, so I'm with them. The two doctors are visiting a hospital of all things. I dropped them off, and you should see the rooms in that place. Most of the hospital rooms have a picture window in them with a mountain view."

Sue grinned, "If you knew you'd have that kind of view in the hospital, it would make falling off a bicycle almost fun, wouldn't it?"

Nelda was not a superstitious person, but for some reason Sue's flippant remark about an accident bicycling gave her an uneasy feeling, so she changed the subject.

"Have the girl's been to Aspen before, Dennis?"

"Marcie told me she has, but I don't know about Violet. Why don't you come have lunch with us at Little Nell's restaurant? I hear the food is good."

"Thanks, Dennis, but Sue and I have some errands to run. We'll see you tomorrow."

Sue looked over at Nelda as Dennis went out the door. "You were a little antisocial with Dennis, Aunt Nelda, why?"

"I didn't want them around when we went to lunch at the hotel. They know we're here to investigate, and that's all I want them to know."

"I understand; well what do you think of the jewelry?"

"It's beautiful and I might come back to buy that bracelet for Sally, but I'd like to compare prices first."

They spent the remainder of the morning browsing through the shops in the Hyman Avenue Mall. At noon, she and Sue walked back to the big hotel. The bar wasn't crowded when they entered. Nelda insisted on sitting at the bar instead of a table, much to Sue's amazement.

"You've always wanted to be as inconspicuous as you could in a place like this. Why the change now, Aunt Nelda?"

"I'd like to speak to the older bartender and he's not waiting tables. I'll have to talk to him up here."

Nelda and Sue's order for two glasses of California white wine was taken by a young man who took an obvious interest in Sue. He barely glanced Nelda's way as he placed the glasses of wine in front of them. Nelda took advantage of the situation by asking Sue to engage the young man in conversation, find out the name of the older bartender and how long he had worked for the hotel. Sue found the answers were Nick Barnes, and ten years. Nick was gray-headed, at least fifty pounds overweight and looked dead tired. Nelda made her move when Nick had a break; he was resting at the end of the bar.

"Excuse me, sir, I wonder if you could help me?"

"I'm on break, lady, why don't you ask the other bartender for a refill?"

"No, Mr. Barnes that's not what I want. For the last three years, a doctor that I knew spent some time here on vacation. I just want to see if you can recognize him and anyone else in this picture."

Nelda placed the enlarged photographs of Coldsby and the other clinic personnel on the bar in front of Nick. He stared at them for a moment and then looked up at Nelda.

"The police have already been here and I told them he was here, but they didn't show me no group picture. What's in it for me, lady?"

"What would it take for an honest answer?"

"Fifty bucks might refresh my memory. It's been a while."

"Okay," said Nelda as she counted out the money. Please look these over carefully and see what you can do."

Nick shuffled through the pictures slowly, staring at each face. "This is the doctor," he said pointing to Coldsby, "he was in here every day before he went out to dinner, but there ain't no one else I can recognize in these pictures."

Nelda's face must have shown the disappointment. The big man spoke again.

"I'm telling you the truth, but I will tell you that he was with somebody. One of the girls that worked in here set her cap for him, but the doctor brushed her off. He let her know he had a female roommate."

"Is there anyone you know that could identify his girlfriend?"

"No, not if she didn't want to be recognized. As you know there are a lot of rooms in this hotel and the cleaning staff doesn't pay close attention to the goings on."

"Thanks, I believe you."

Nelda, downhearted, made her way back to Sue. They finished their wine and headed for the restaurant. Sue looked at her aunt's bowed head and tried to cheer her up.

"Don't worry, Aunt Nelda. Maybe one of the maids will remember her."

"No, I don't think so. I believe the woman he was with didn't want anyone to know about the affair."

"Maybe at the other hotel we'll have better luck."

Nelda went to lunch without an appetite, not really tasting the grilled, fresh tuna salad she ordered. She hurried Sue through her lunch, skipping coffee and dessert, hoping they would get to the Sardy House in time to talk to some of the housekeepers before they finished their shifts.

They paid their bill, climbed into the old Dodge and drove the two blocks to Sardy House. It was an old Victorian structure, much smaller than Hotel Jerome. Nelda didn't think a stranger could wander about the halls without being noticed. She was delighted to find it also had a restaurant. Now was a good time for dessert and coffee.

As they found a table in the corner, she looked the waitresses over. Most of them were young, they looked like college kids. She was about to give up the idea that she could find one who had been there at least five years ago, when she saw a an older Mexican woman cleaning tables and setting them with silverware for the next wave of customers. Nelda waited until she was at the table opposite theirs and then she made her pitch.

"Have you worked here long, Senora?"

"Many happy years I've worked here," she said in good English.

"I wonder if you could help me?" Nelda asked.

"I will if I can," she answered.

Nelda looked into the woman's well-worn face and decided to tell her the truth. "There was a doctor murdered in my hometown, and we know he spent summer vacations here several years ago. What we don't know is who the woman was that stayed with him. She might have some connection with his death. Would you see if you could identify the doctor and the woman?"

Nelda held her breath while the waitress took her time looking at each photograph. She shuffled them back and forth. Finally, she dropped the one of the Christmas party on the table.

"This is the man," she pointed to Coldsby, "and this is the woman," her fingernail tapped on the face of Marcie, "they were so in love."

"Have you seen them in the last three years?"

"No, they quit coming here."

Nelda got the waitress' name and address, slipped her six ten dollar bills, thanked her and turned back to Sue.

"You knew who he was with four years ago, Aunt Nelda? Marcie admitted she was in love and had an affair that lasted for fourteen years."

"But we don't know," answered Nelda, "who his companion was for the last three years."

Nelda began to worry about their safety in Aspen. She made up her mind to talk things over with Jake as soon as she got back to the lodge.

CHAPTER
TWENTY-SIX

Peace Be With You

As soon as Nelda got back to the lodge, she called the Aspen Police Station and asked for Jake Cohen. "I'm sorry, Jake is not here," said the desk attendant, "could someone else help you?"

"No, thank you," said Nelda. She banged the receiver down and beat on the counter in frustration. Where was he? She needed his help in identifying the visitor at Hotel Jerome. And would he help her set the trap for the killer tomorrow? The previous difficult weeks and the disappointment in Aspen caused Nelda to weep. Jake found her in the kitchen wiping her tears away with a paper towel.

"What's wrong, Nelda?" Jake asked with concern.

"Oh Jake, forgive me for this emotional breakdown. I'm afraid my frustration is showing. I called the police station to ask for your help, but you weren't there."

"I am now," said Jake, smiling.

"I'm glad," Nelda said, fighting back more tears.

"Look, don't be discouraged; I know I can help you. Just tell me what you want me to do."

"Thanks, because I'm at the end of my rope."

"What have you found out about the doctor's vacations in Aspen?"

"He's been identified as staying at Sardy House and Hotel Jerome. And I found out the identify of his woman companion at

Sardy House, but his companion at Hotel Jerome for the last three summers remains a mystery. Could you help with that?"

"It's a big place. However, I have a friend, Don Brown, who's daughter, Linda, works there every summer. Let me have one of those group photographs you mentioned earlier, and I'll see if she can identify anyone in the picture."

"Bless you Jake! "I know the murderer is in this group picture and is now on vacation here in Aspen."

"I'm concerned about your safety, Nelda. What are your plans for tomorrow?"

"We've all signed up with Blazing Pedals for the downhill bicycle run and picnic at Maroon Lake. I intend to entice the murderer to come after me."

"How?"

"By riding alone down the mountain. Will you be my backup?"

"You know I will. I'll always be close enough to hear a whistle."

"I don't have one."

"You will," he assured her, "as soon as I get back from town."

Nelda didn't feel quite as helpless as she did before. She handed the group picture to Jake with a good feeling about his ability to help her.

"I'll be back in a little while," he said.

She walked Jake to the door and watched him drive off. After that, she decided to rest for awhile; she was emotionally drained. As she made her way to her bedroom, she saw Sue coming down the hall.

"Where are you going in a bathing suit?" Nelda asked.

"Did you see the hot tub on the ground level deck?"

"No." Nelda shivered just thinking about going outside without a sweater.

"Well, it's great!" Sue said, "It'll melt away all your troubles. You'll sleep like a baby tonight if you relax in that steaming tub. Come on and try it."

"I didn't bring a bathing suit," said Nelda.

"Not to worry," Sue answered. "Just wear my one piece."

Nelda thought the plunging neckline on the electric blue suit was scandalous, but put it on anyway, tugging the scanty briefs up to the two big buttons that hooked them to the top. She laughed out loud when she saw her image in the mirror.

"You've still got it, Aunt Nelda." Sue giggled standing in the doorway.

"And you better hope you don't catch it," remarked Nelda. She grabbed the largest towel she could find and wrapped it around her shoulders as they headed out to the deck.

Sue carried the portable phone with her. Nelda bet Sue was expecting a call from Walter. Would this growing interest between her niece and Walter bring Violet on a collision course with Sue? Nelda hoped not, but how could it be avoided since they all worked together?

They lifted the cover of the steaming tub, laid their towels in chairs, and stepped into the hot water. It felt absolutely wonderful to Nelda. Sue was right; it was very relaxing and Nelda could feel her troubles floating away. Right before she closed her eyes and dozed off, she told Sue about Jake offering his help. Twenty minutes passed by before she was jolted awake by the telephone. When Sue said "Hello Walter," Nelda knew her niece wouldn't appreciate an eavesdropper, so she reluctantly left the hot water, wrapped the large towel around herself, and ran for the bedroom.

After Nelda dressed, she walked upstairs to the kitchen. Jake had promised to cook steaks for them outside, and she was going to prepare the potatoes and salad. While Nelda rooted around in the refrigerator for butter and salad dressing, a frowning Sue walked into the kitchen.

"Well, I can see that conversation with Walter didn't suit you," Nelda remarked. You look like you're ready to bite nails."

"I'm pretty upset right now," confided Sue. "Walter isn't going to tell Violet it's all over between them until we get back home."

"Why is he waiting?"

"He feels sorry for Violet and doesn't want to spoil her vacation."

"How naive does he think Violet is? asked Nelda.

"Of course you're right. She must know their relationship is in danger. I feel a little guilty, too, even though Walter said he never loved her. It was like she pushed him into the engagement, and made more out of their friendship than he intended. He was her prize."

Poor Walter, he didn't know how to deal with a possessive woman like Violet, Nelda thought, and now he's in a real mess. "Let's worry about Walter later. You make the green salad while I wash the potatoes for the microwave. Jake is back and the steaks are on the grill."

Jake had picked up a bottle of red wine to go with their steaks. The next couple of hours were spent in a flurry of conversation, sipping wine and eating good food. Nelda was enjoying herself in spite of her mission in Aspen. They were listening to Jake's plans for a hike in the mountains when the phone rang again. This time it was for Jake; it was Linda Brown.

"Hi Linda, thanks for responding so fast. Listen, I'm going to turn the phone over to Nelda Simmons because she's doing the investigating. I'll be talking to you later." Jake passed the phone over to Nelda.

"Hello, Linda, thank you for helping me. Could you identify the doctor in the picture?"

"Yes," answered Linda, "and even cleaned his room for a week last summer, but never saw his companion. All I can tell you about his girlfriend is she was young and slim."

"How could you tell?"

"By looking at her clothes."

"Well, that's not much help, but I appreciate your effort."

"There was one other thing; it's about her makeup."

"What about it?"

"Expensive, she used Chanel and plenty of it. She had it spread out all over the vanity."

Nelda felt light-headed. She thanked Linda and hung up.

"What was that all about, Aunt Nelda?"

"It was one of Jake's friends trying to help me identify the doctor's other girlfriend."

"Did she?"

"No, It's certainly a disappointment. Sue, would you mind cleaning up the kitchen? I'm cold, tired and discouraged. I think I'll go to bed and read."

"I'll help Sue," Jake offered. "I'm sorry Linda couldn't help, but there's always tomorrow!"

"Good night, Aunt Nelda," called Sue as Nelda went inside.

Nelda needed to assimilate the new information she'd gotten from Linda. Chanel lipstick seemed to turn up a little too often in this case, and Violet was the only one in the clinic to use Chanel. Was her claim that it was a gift true? If she was the killer, what motive could she have? She wanted Walter to have an interest in the clinic, but had no way of knowing Joan Coldsby would sell the business to Walter after her husband's death. If she had an affair with Coldsby here in Aspen, it must have been over. She was dating Walter when Coldsby was killed. Did Walter help her kill the doctor and his wife? Nelda couldn't believe it. He was a puritan, expecting everyone to know the difference between right and wrong. Even the girl he married was expected to have a similar standard of purity. Nelda felt her thinking processes were completely bogged down and her head ached. The only thing to do was take two aspirins and try to get some sleep. Sleep, however, didn't come until she looked out the window and saw Jake patrolling the lodge grounds.

* * *

The next morning, Nelda still couldn't get the Chanel connection out of her mind. Now suppose, she reasoned, the murderer was Marcie and she was trying to frame Violet. Could that be it? Maybe Violet came along and took over Coldsby's affections and Marcie, after giving fifteen years of her life to the doctor, decided to kill him, and frame Violet for the murder by sending her the Chanel lipstick. But that didn't make sense either; Marcie claimed to be in love with Dennis. With grim determination, she decided her next step in the case would be to use herself as bait on the downhill bicycle ride. She knew Jake would back her up.

Nelda thrust the problem aside as she dressed for the outing. She pulled on her khaki shorts, T-shirt with Aspen logo and Nike sneakers. Sue knocked on her door just as Nelda finished with her makeup.

"I'm not going, Aunt Nelda," Sue said, when Nelda opened the door.

"Why not?"

"There was a bus accident this morning involving fifty-two kids who came to Colorado on a mountain climbing vacation. They're bringing most of them to the Aspen hospital.

"Were any killed?" asked Nelda in dismay.

"No, but the hospital administrator needed doctors, so he asked Walter and Elizabeth to help. They canceled their plans for the day."

"What about the rest of our group; are they still going on the outing?"

"Yes."

"I can't see why you should change your plans just because Walter isn't going. In fact, you'll have a better time without Walter, because you won't have to watch Violet fawning over him."

"I suppose you're right," Sue said gloomily. I'll go ahead and get dressed. But, I'm really sorry Walter and Elizabeth are going to miss out on the fun."

"Jake is going with us, Sue. He wants to help me if there is any danger on the bicycle ride."

"Good! I'm glad he's on our team."

A few minutes later the three of them gathered in the foyer. Jake silently handed Nelda a blue whistle attached to a long white cord. She put the cord around her neck and tucked the whistle inside her shirt, while Sue nodded in approval.

* * *

Nine vacationers, six of them from Texas, gathered together on the corner of Mill and Hyman streets where the guides were scheduled to pick them up. Marcie and Dennis were dressed like twins in blue denim shorts and red and white striped shirts. Violet appeared bubbly and happy in a one piece red culottes outfit. Everyone else in the group was dressed in T-shirts and white or khaki shorts.

Soon the Blazing Pedals bus whisked them away and deposited them on the shores of Maroon Lake.

"What a visual feast!" Nelda cried, looking at the masses of purple, red, and yellow flowers which covered the banks of the lake. She was glad she had remembered to bring her camera and color film.

Jake turned out to be a first rate guide for the Texas group. He helped them identify the wild flowers and pointed out the beaver lodge in the middle of the lake. At lunch time, they sat on a log cut down by a beaver. Jake proved it by showing them beaver teeth marks on the end of the log.

As they ate their sandwiches and fruit, Dennis asked Nelda a question.

"What kind of luck are you having with your investigation, Nelda?"

"Not as good as I had hoped, but I'm not going to rest until I find out who was with Coldsby at Hotel Jerome. There's certainly a connection between Coldsby's companion here and his murder. I think Joan knew who the girl was and that's why she was killed."

"When did he stay at Hotel Jerome?" asked Dennis.

"The last three summer vacations," answered Nelda, studying the expressions on all their faces. She saw Marcie had a pained look; Violet looked straight ahead with a half smile on her face; Dennis's eyes were bright with curiosity; and Sue looked worriedly over at her aunt. There was silence until Jake spoke up.

"Looks like lunch time is over; the guide is motioning for us to meet in the parking lot by the Blazing Pedals bus."

As they walked toward the lot, Sue spoke to Nelda under her

breath. "I really think you told them too much, Aunt Nelda. Now they know as much as you do."

"One or two of them know more than I do," Nelda said softly.

"Look at this," Jake said pointing to the dozen or so mountain bikes standing in the parking lot, "we have quite a few bikes to choose from. We can all find one that suits us."

Nelda couldn't remember the last time she rode a bike, but it was years ago. The only bikes she had ever ridden had three gears and now she was supposed to ride one with twenty-one. The guide assured her she could handle it. She choose a bike easy to mount and pedaled around in the parking lot. The gears would give her a few problems, but she started and stopped without a hitch.

"Well, Aunt Nelda, I guess that saying is true 'Once you learn to ride, you never forget'."

"Yes, but it doesn't say you won't be rusty," came back Nelda's reply. She now addressed the group loudly. "I'm not going to ride with anyone down this mountain, because I'm taking my time. I want to enjoy the scenery and stop to snap pictures along the way."

"Do you think you'll be okay, Aunt Nelda?"

"Of course I will. You and Jake can have a downhill race."

Jake made a face, but didn't try to talk Nelda into coming with them. They waved good-bye and soon were hidden from Nelda by a bend in the mountain road.

Nelda put on her crash helmet, waited until everyone was out of the parking lot, then started down. She anticipated company before she reached the bottom of the mountain. Excitement caused her heart to race, because she was almost sure she had figured out who the murderer was. Nelda hadn't gone far when a panoramic view of the mountains came into view. Carefully she stopped her bike, got out her camera, and stepped to the edge of the road to take a picture. As she lifted the camera, she sensed the presence of someone behind her. Her mouth turned dry, her heart pounded, and she thought herself a fool. Why did she expose herself to the killer this way? She blew sharply on her whistle, and turned to see

-SHEF

Dennis and Marcie racing toward her on their bicycles. Quickly, she moved to the middle of the road as they screeched to a stop. Marcie spoke with a worried note in her voice.

"No need to use that whistle for us, Nelda. I just wanted to tell you I've been dishonest with you and the sheriff."

"How's that?" replied Nelda, wondering if Jake had heard the whistle, and how she was going to escape from them if he didn't.

"I stayed at Sardy House with Albert and didn't tell the sheriff. It was painful for me to talk about my relationship with him. Now that I have Dennis, I just wanted to forget the past."

Nelda breathed a little easier after she saw Jake pedaling toward her. She still watched Dennis out of the corner of her eye.

"What about Hotel Jerome?" Nelda asked.

"No, I wasn't with Albert then. Someone else came into his life three years ago. He started acting cold toward me, even trying to get me to leave. Our love affair was over and I was bitter, but never vindictive. I grieved for him when he died."

Dennis came over and put his arm around Marcie. She lifted her face to his with tears in her eyes. Nelda knew these suspects could be crossed off her list and she was glad. Marcie deserved some happiness in her life even though the misery she'd suffered was self-imposed.

Nelda gave Jake the okay signal before answering Marcie. He quickly disappeared in a grove of spruce trees.

"I believe you, Marcie. I hope you and Dennis can put all this behind you and have a good life."

She watched them pedal out of sight before she remounted her bicycle. As she cycled through the green shade of an aspen grove, Nelda had a premonition of danger yet to come. Up ahead she could see a spot of red on a bicycle and knew instantly who it was. Suddenly, the person turned, started pedaling toward her while maneuvering her bike with great dexterity, and looking as much at home on the bicycle as a participant in a mountain-bike race. Nelda was mentally prepared for an encounter this time. She stopped her bike, dismounted, and stood by it. Violet skidded to a halt, swung off her bike, and approached her with a sardonic grin.

"This is perfect, Nelda."

"What do you mean?" Nelda responded.

"We can ride down this mountain together."

Nelda reached in her shirt for the whistle, but Violet yanked it from her neck and stuffed it in her pocket.

"*Dies infaustus,*" Violet said with a guttural laugh.

"Unlucky day" is right said Nelda interrupting the phrase silently. She looked into Violet's wild eyes and knew she had to keep her talking until she came up with a plan to save herself. Violet was stronger and could certainly overtake her on her bicycle, but what choice did she have? She had a better chance on her bike then running. A rush of adrenaline, caused by fear, helped Nelda to keep focused.

"I know you're the killer, Violet."

"How?"

"You wrote the Latin phrase and put it on the handle of my suitcase."

"You have no proof."

"I saw red lipstick on your hand in the airport. When I spilled coffee on you, you cleaned it off on my handkerchief. It had to come from the note writing, because you were wearing pink lipstick."

"How clever, you nosy old bitch. You can enjoy your success while sailing down the mountain."

"Why did you kill Coldsby?"

It all started four years ago when I was working summers in Aspen waiting tables. In walks this big tipping doctor, and I was taken in by his sweet words that hid his black heart. He promised me a job and marriage."

"But once he moved you to Stearn, Coldsby told you he wasn't going to divorce his wife."

"That's when I found out about Marcie wasting her life on him. I made up my mind not to waste mine. Latching on to Walter would be my salvation, but "Doctor Evil" wasn't giving up. He started blackmailing me by threatening to tell Walter about our affair if I didn't give in to his sexual demands."

"And then Walter with his high ideals wouldn't have you," said Nelda. "But why kill his wife, Joan?"

"I heard her talking to you at the antique show. She knew about my affair with Coldsby and was going to tell you. Walter was sure to find out from you or the sheriff. I had to shut her up."

"You caused Sally and me to have a wreck, and left all those clues written in Latin didn't you?"

She laughed wildly, pulling off her helmet, and running her fingers through her long blonde hair. "Yes! yes! I did it all. I knew you'd never give up trying to solve the murders. The Latin phrases gave me great pleasure. They let you know I was one step ahead. Yes! a dead language for a soon to be dead old sleuth," she shouted.

"Did you kill Carol?" asked Nelda.

"No, I put a Chanel lipstick in her medicine cabinet, so you and the sheriff might think she killed Coldsby, but society killed Carol."

"Don't you realize the killings must stop?" Nelda said quietly.

"Not yet, I've waited too long to get rid of you, and don't think I've been blind to that hussy, Sue. She wants Walter, but it'll never happen. I almost killed her on the fishing boat and I'll succeed next time. No one will take my dream away from me. No one!" she screamed.

Nelda knew her best chance of getting away was now. Frantically she mounted her bike and pedaled down the center of the road. Violet threw her helmet down, ran back to her bicycle and started cycling toward Nelda. Even though Nelda was pumping with all her might, Violet soon pulled along the left side of Nelda's bike, and started forcing her toward the edge of the road. Violet slowed, let Nelda get a little ahead, then came back again to nudge her to the right. Desperately, Nelda reached out and grabbed Violet's long, blonde hair and yanked hard. In retaliation, the murderess clawed Nelda's hand, causing her to momentarily lose control of her bicycle. The two bikes almost collided. Nelda trembled in fright knowing that one or two more encounters with Violet would certainly send her over the edge. Even now, she could see with clarity the meandering stream several hundred feet below. Up ahead there was a sharp bend in the road to the left; she was sure Violet intended to push her over the mountain at this point. Nelda gradually put on her brakes and prepared to jump from her bike, but couldn't make herself do it. What if the fall caused her to be an invalid for life? She knew there was only one way to stop Violet from running her off the mountain, an accident had to happen. Nelda closed her eyes and leaned sharply to the left, pulling the bike with her. She fell directly into Violet's path.

Jake, coming back up the mountain to check on Nelda, heard the sickening crunch of metal as Violet bounced nosily over the prostrate rider and her bike. He saw Violet struggling to right her bike as it skidded in the loose gravel on the side of the road. Frantically, Violet worked to gain control of the bike only to face the sharp turn in front of her. She squeezed the hand brake hard, stopping the bicycle on the brink of the mountain road. The sudden deceleration caused her to lunge forward over the handle bars upsetting the bike's precarious balance on the edge of the mountain. In a split second, bicycle and rider disappeared from view. Her screams echoed in the valley below as her body tumbled down the side of the mountain, coming to rest near a grove of spruce trees.

Lying on the ground in pain, Nelda looked up at Jake and added a Latin phrase of her own, *pax vobiscum,* "peace be with you."

* * *

Nelda looked out over the mountains from her hospital room window. She was pensive about the events that had taken place in the last few weeks. Images of Joan, Will, Carol, and Shelby paraded before her eyes. From now on, she decided, she'd try not to be so judgmental about her friends' shortcomings. Life was too sweet and fragile to bother about the little things.

Then, there was a tap on the door, and in marched Jake and what was left of the clinic personnel. She wanted to smile, but her face hurt.

"Well, Aunt Nelda, what do you think of the view from your hospital bed?" Sue asked.

"It's just beautiful, but when am I going to get out of here to really enjoy it?"

"Tomorrow," said Elizabeth, "you're lucky no bones were broken, but you sure are bruised. The stitches in your arm will come out later."

Walter spoke up. "I'm so thankful you're alive, Nelda. I didn't realize Violet was mentally ill. She always seemed so sane and in control around me. Her confession makes me realize how little I knew about her." Tears rolled down his cheeks.

Sue put her arm around Walter's waist and he pulled her close.

Marcie reached over and gently took Nelda's bruised hand. "What did Sheriff Moore have to say when you talked to him, Nelda?"

"I haven't heard him so excited since he worked with my husband, Jim," Nelda replied. "John was past ready for this case to be solved."

Jake edged his way toward the head of the bed. "I've got a message for you, Nelda. Richard called and wants you to stay an extra week at the lodge, and you're to invite that nice teacher friend, Sally Feddington, to stay with you after Sue leaves."

Nelda laid back grinning, ignoring her pain and asked Jake a question. "How do you feel about old brown Labs?"